11-1

X

WITHDRAWN

I've travelled the world twice over,
Met the famous: saints and sinners,
Poets and artists, kings and queens,
Old stars and hopeful beginners,
I've been where no-one's been before,
Learned secrets from writers and cooks
All with one library ticket
To the wonderful world of books.

RIBBONS IN HER HAIR

Laura Montgomery, said her family, was born with a silver spoon in her mouth and ribbons in her hair. Beautiful, aristocratic, and with all the charm and resourcefulness of her Irish ancestors, Laura had no trouble finding admirers in the raw new cities of Western Australia. But her heart was still in Ireland, and the man she truly wanted was the heir of the Irish Montgomerys, her cousin Danny, and he was beyond her reach.

LUCY WALKER

RIBBONS IN HER HAIR

"A pity beyond all telling
Is hid in the heart of love . . ."
W. B. Yeats

Complete and Unabridged

ULVERSCROFT
Leicester

First published
(as by Dorothy Lucie Sanders)
1957

First Large Print Edition
published March 1981
by arrangement with
Collins, London & Glasgow

© Lucy Walker 1972

British Library CIP Data

Walker, Lucy
Ribbons in her hair.—Large print ed.
(Ulverscroft large print series: romance)
I. Title
823'.9'1F   PR6073.A412R/

ISBN 0-7089-0594-3

Published by
F. A. Thorpe (Publishing) Ltd.
Anstey, Leicestershire

Printed in Great Britain by T. J. Press (Padstow) Ltd.
Padstow, Cornwall

With love
To those who stay
And those who turn back

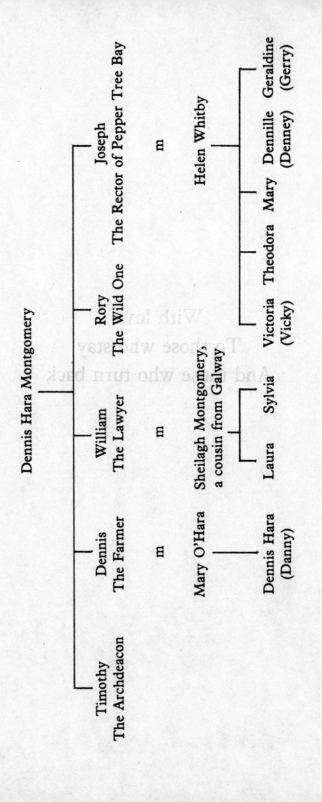

Dennis Hara Montgomery

- Timothy
  The Archdeacon
- Dennis
  The Farmer
  m
  Mary O'Hara
  → Dennis Hara (Danny)
- William
  The Lawyer
  m
  Sheilagh Montgomery, a cousin from Galway
  → Laura, Sylvia
- Rory
  The Wild One
- Joseph
  The Rector of Pepper Tree Bay
  m
  Helen Whitby
  → Victoria (Vicky), Theodora, Mary Dennille (Denney), Geraldine (Gerry)

Love is
a time of enchantment:
in it all days are fair and all fields
green. Youth is blest by it,
old age made benign: the eyes of love see
roses blooming in December,
and sunshine through rain. Verily
is the time of true-love
a time of enchantment—and
Oh! how eager is woman
to be bewitched!

1

DUE to luxury-loving and spendthrift habits, Magillicuddy, the ancient home of the Montgomeries, had become dilapidated and sorely in need of better husbandry. It was the worst possible thing that at such a time there should be born five sons to Dennis Hara Montgomery, our grandfather. These five sons, soon motherless, were brought up by their father, stewards and friends, to foster, not their assets, but their social and luxury-loving habits. There were three things all of them could do well. They could ride a horse, talk themselves through the eye of a needle and drink large quantities of Irish whiskey.

All? Well, not all! There was Timothy the eldest, for instance. He could do all of these things moderately because he was a moderate man. The only moderate man yet born to the Montgomeries in three hundred years. Moreover he was a good man and a kind man, much concerned with the welfare, physical

1

and spiritual, of troubled people anywhere in the world.

All the five Montgomeries were tall, very handsome and were endowed with liberal quantities of the renowned Irish charm. This fine appearance, together with the charm, made them something of leaders in whatever they did. So long as they stayed in Ireland, and Magillicuddy could support their extravagant habits, all was well for them.

It was when they left their native land—and in due course they all did, save Dennis the second eldest—that charm did not prove to be the substantial support that the acres of Magillicuddy had been formerly.

Timothy went first.

While at Trinity College he had become imbued with the need to lead the Church in the colonies and antipodes. He was not the first clergyman in the Montgomery family by any means; there had been several through the generations. In fact those Montgomeries who had not farmed their land had gone into the Church, Law or the Navy, in that order. But never, you understand, into trade.

Offshoots of the family might dabble in school-teaching and one or two had even sat on advisory boards governing enterprise. But

2

no Montgomery ever went into trade. That was an axiom of life that came before the Ten Commandments.

How or why any Montgomery ever came to enter the Navy, an English institution, is unexplained, though Laura told me that one of the aunts on her mother's side once told her there had been a Montgomery who had run away to sea by boarding a fishing-vessel off Galway. This began a tradition that it was right and proper for a Montgomery to have an interest in the sea. The fishing-vessel became, by right of legend, an auxiliary vessel of Her Majesty's Government. That put a stop to the nonsensical talk in the family that a Montgomery had had anything to do with the buying or selling of fish. That would have been *trade*.

Timothy went to South Africa, where he built with his own hands the first Church in some remote and quite unpronounceable place in the veldt.

Meanwhile his father, our grandfather, died and the remaining four sons were running wild. Timothy returned to Meath, put the affairs of his family in order and arranged the finances of Magillicuddy so that Dennis and William would continue to farm it while

Joseph the youngest would be put to school and University and use his qualities of leadership, hitherto exercised in the leading of the poachers against his own pheasants, in the service of the Church.

Rory, the fourth son, Timothy could do nothing about at all. Rory was a wild one. Whenever, in the next generation, anyone asked, "And what happened to Rory?" the reply would always be, "Oh, Rory was a wild one. No one could ever do anything about Rory." And the subject would be dropped.

If Timothy, my dear and loved Uncle Timothy, could do nothing about Rory, then Rory must have been very wild indeed.

The years passed and Joseph the youngest, my father, completed his degree at Trinity College and followed his elder brother into the Church and subsequently out to the antipodes.

This time the brothers, one very much older than the other, made the gold-fields of Western Australia their frontier for the Church.

They had heard of the wicked and godless life of the miners on the diggings, and with true Montgomery conviction in their own ability to put other people right, they set out to save the souls of some three thousand miners dry-blowing on the Hannan's gold-field four hundred miles into the desert from the West Australian coast.

They arrived in Western Australia in the year 1900, in time to start reading the funeral services of the poor souls who were more preoccupied with dying of bubonic plague and typhoid than with wringing the gold from the earth.

Four years later my father married my mother and three years later than that I was born, the second of what were to be five daughters. The only thing important about this event, that of my birth, is that I was born with a caul on my face.

Two months earlier William Montgomery, in Ireland, who had married a second cousin, had sired a daughter, Laura. She also was born with a caul on her face.

And this is where the story of Laura begins.

Her name was another example of Mont-gomery arrogance. In those days nobody called anybody "Laura" unless she was a servant or a favourite cow in the cow-house. Laura, as a name, was an outrage in polite circles. But the Montgomeries, on Aunt Sheilagh's side, produced a Laura in nearly every generation.

5

It was because, way back, a member of her family had married a beautiful and rich woman from Italy. In Italy Laura is *not* a name fit only for servants.

Since it was the Italian lady's wealth that had more or less set up the Galway branch of the Montgomery family, then they honoured her in posterity. There was always a *Laura*, call what you may the creatures in the shed and the kitchen. And it was pronounced "Lowra", not "Lora".

Thus, within two months of one another, in the year 1907 there were born to the Montgomery family two babes with cauls on their faces. One child was born in County Meath, Ireland, and the other in the middle of a desert more than thirteen thousand miles away. But that didn't matter. They were both Montgomeries . . . and they had cauls on their faces! It was better than being born with silver spoons in their mouths and ribbons in their hair. Though some said Laura had all three.

For days my uncle Timothy, the Venerable Archdeacon of the Gold-fields, walked about Kalgoorlie buttonholing his friends and acquaintances and saying, "Have you heard

6

the news? A second niece! and *both* with cauls on their faces."

My mother, more prosaic and not knowing anything about cauls until her babe was born, said to the nurse, "Burn the thing," meaning the caul, not the baby.

Fortunately for the caul the nurse was Irish, and Mother never forgot the shriek of horror with which the nurse greeted this command.

My father, outraged, took the frail web, wound it round a piece of cardboard, put it in an envelope marked "Theodora's Caul" and put it away where it could never be tampered with and where it would be forever safe. He put it away so carefully he could never remember afterwards where he had put it.

Laura's caul, in Ireland, was saved. It was dried, put in a parchment envelope and consigned to the bank. Where it probably is to this day.

It has always been considered by the family that Laura has greater wit, brains and beauty than I have because the whereabouts of her caul are *known*.

In the latter half of this same year my father took charge of the parish of Pepper Tree Bay, the exclusive reserve of those pastoralists from the far north or the deep south who had made enough money by their courage, intrepid enterprise and endurance, to retire seasonally to the calmer reaches of a lovely river flowing placidly into the Indian Ocean some twelve miles south of the capital. Half way between Perth and the river's mouth the river took a reef in its serene progress to the sea and formed the lovely bay called after the trees planted around its shores by its first proprietors, the graziers of the north and south.

Here we lived quietly and happily in a somewhat exalted but static society, the replica of that English society from which the former generation of pastoralists had stemmed. Everything was done in Pepper Tree Bay exactly as grandparents had done it in England. Nothing was different except the accent and the climate. Time had stood still in this corner of the antipodes for fifty years.

In Ireland, Laura prospered, but her parents, alas! not so well.

William, the second of the Montgomery brothers, had gone into Law first and then back to Magillicuddy to show Dennis, his elder, how to manage things. Dennis did not agree with William on any single issue. And neither of them could handle Rory. Between them all they spent more and more money and Magillicuddy got more and more shabby.

Hearing from Timothy and Joseph in Australia that fortunes were being made in gold-finds in the middle of the West Australian desert, William decided to sally forth and likewise make a fortune.

In 1911 he came to Australia with his lovely wife, our Aunt Sheilagh, the four-year-old Laura and a tiny little pink-and-white fairy of a child, with one leaky valve to her heart, our cousin Sylvia.

Thus the family was divided. There were two brothers Montgomery remaining in Ireland, and three in Australia.

There was one son, Dennis's, in Ireland. And in Australia, in due course, there were to be seven girls. The five daughters of the Rev. Dr. Joseph Montgomery, and the two daughters of William Montgomery.

Of them all Laura, who had inherited all the beauty and most of the brains, was the one destined to suffer most from the division of the family.

Laura and I both loved our Uncle Tim passionately. This could possibly be because Uncle Tim loved us. He loved us better than the others in the families because we were born with cauls on our faces.

I remember one day we were all at the Rectory in Pepper Tree Bay. Laura and I were six or seven years old.

The three Montgomery brothers were standing talking to one another in the hall. Lovely, lovely Aunt Sheilagh was standing in the doorway of the drawing-room and Mama was standing near the three men. They were saying amusing things because I can see now the look of derisive laughter on Aunt Sheilagh's peaches-and-cream face, and the look of earnest wonder on Mama's.

Mama was pretty too. She had lovely blue eyes. She always looked at the Montgomeries with an expression of wonder. She was not Irish and she was very hard working, and earnest, which none of the Irish we knew were. She loved them, she was moved and excited by them. But she didn't understand them.

Laura, a child whose extraordinary blue eyes dominated her whole face, came through the front door just as I emerged from between the velvet curtains leading into the passage and the dining-room and schoolroom.

We stood and looked at the men just the

way Mama was looking at them . . . in silent wonder.

They were so tall and handsome and their voices were rich and sweet, full of the tender sounds of the Irish countryside. They were all six feet. My father and Uncle Tim wore clerical black. My father was young and handsome with jet-black hair and my Uncle Tim's hair was snow white. He wore gaiters. Uncle William, Laura's father, was somewhere half way between Joseph and Tim in age, but his hair was all black, like my father's, and his face was a little bit wicked where the faces of Uncle Tim and my father were charming and kind. Not that Uncle William wasn't kind. He was. But he liked to be a little bit wicked so that Tim and Joe would not get too above themselves because of their "cloth".

We were very young but we knew these three men were different from all other men. Father and Uncle William saw to that. Uncle Tim couldn't help being different, just in the nature of things. His face was always full of loving kindness and his blue eyes twinkled.

Just now he saw Laura and me at the same time. He held out both his hands, his right hand to Laura and his left hand to me. It was a gesture that seemed to say to our childish hearts, "Come to me!"

When I think back on that day I add the words, ". . . and I will give you rest." Because that is exactly what Uncle Tim did for both Laura and me.

He drew his hands in until we were pressed against his sides.

He looked down, first at one and then the other. His eyes twinkled as merrily as a schoolboy's.

"Put your hands in my pockets," he said.

We did, and we each drew out a bag of chocolates.

We were not surprised because this always happened. When he came to the Rectory he had five bags of chocolates in five different pockets of his clerical clothes. The bags in his side pockets were always for Laura and me. Denney was a baby and Gerry not yet born, else there would have been seven bags.

Then he said, "Come and eat them outside because otherwise you'll put sticky fingers on Mama's curtains. Then what will become of Uncle Tim?"

We went outside with him and he said, "Exercise before you eat, otherwise you'll get fat and never grow into beautiful Irish ladies."

We put the bags of chocolates on the edge of the verandah and raced to the boundary fence. The only thing that was different about this little game was that today Laura fell on the gravel path and scraped her knee. It bled.

She started at once to cry. Uncle Tim picked her up, but remembering me and holding out his spare hand to me, took us towards the big gum tree that stood in the middle of the lawn. He pointed to a great scar in the bark of the tree.

"Look," he said. "Once it happened to the gum tree. When it was young it fell down. Then someone straightened it up and all that's left is the scar."

Laura was still of a doubtful mind about her crying. She gave another gulping sob.

"It doesn't hurt the tree any more," Uncle Tim said, shaking his head as if in wonder. "The scar is there to show that once a great and terrible adventure befell the tree. But it doesn't hurt any more. *Time* healed it. Dear old Father *Time*. He heals everything." Then his eyes twinkled at Laura. "Even Laura's knee," he added.

"Will I have a scar?" said Laura a little sceptically.

"Well, let's hope so," said Uncle Tim. "It's always pleasant to prove that once we met with disaster."

His eyes were laughing and we had to laugh with him.

"*Time* always heals," he said. "Don't ever forget that, will you, chickabiddies?"

Uncle Tim always said things like that. That's why we knew he would always be able to look after us. We depended on Uncle Tim to look after us. We didn't know that "disaster", as Uncle Tim would have called it, had other ends in view.

Laura was eight when she had her first love affair. Love affairs were to be the milestones of Laura's life, but there was never anyone for her but our cousin Danny, Dennis's son. But Danny comes later.

It was in the fourteen-eighteen war, when my father went overseas with the troops and we were all sent to a boarding school near the capital. That is, Vicky, who was older than me; myself; Mary, who was younger, and Laura. Sylvia, Laura's sister, was too delicate to go to school.

14

Uncle William and his family were rich by our standards. They'd made quite a lot of money in gold by this time. They had a big house in Kalgoorlie, overlooking the mines, and another big town house in Pepper Tree Bay, overlooking the river. They had a sort of swinging life between Pepper Tree Bay and the gold-fields. In both places Aunt Sheilagh was definitely "society". Wherever there was "society" there was Aunt Sheilagh because that was her life. Because she came from Ireland she wasn't regarded as a *t'other-sider* by the older wealthier pioneering families of Western Australia, and that meant that she was not only acceptable in "society" but because she was beautiful and witty and gay was allowed to be something of a leader. A *t'other-sider* never had any chance of being anything but barely tolerated. And so it is to this day.

"*T'other-siders*" came from the eastern seaboard, two thousand miles away.

When people in Western Australia wanted to go abroad for a holiday, or on business, they went to England or Scotland or Ireland. It didn't cost any more and if they went to the Eastern States they only met *t'other-siders*. Whereas, by going to Britain, although there was always the slight danger of meeting the stock from whom the earliest convicts came, it was better than hob-nobbing with *t'other-siders*.

A family such as the Montgomeries was readily accepted because it was an example to the *t'other-siders* of what they could not be and why they could not be accepted.

In early childhood, we only saw Laura for short intervals. Sometimes she was in Pepper Tree Bay and sometimes on the gold-fields. The only time we spent a long family period together in those years was when we were sent to the same boarding-school.

The boarding-school to which we were sent was really a small dame school and there was one boy in it. Goodness only knows why he was there except that his sister was there and they were very rich people. If you are rich you can always get into places most people would think unheard of, except the drawing-rooms of Pepper Tree Bay.

We were very young. There was nobody in the school older than twelve years of age. The pupils all came from pastoralists' families or those with gold-mining interests so they were all very well off. Except ourselves. I mean

16

Vicky and Mary and myself. But then we were Montgomeries. It helped to be the daughters of clergymen.

Laura, of course, was both well off and a Montgomery. That more than got her by but I don't think it had anything to do with the fact that the one boy in the school, Basil Forsyte, fell in love with her.

When a boy of eight falls in love with a girl of eight he woos her this way.

He waits for her as she goes along the corridor to the bathroom past his own little cubicle and darts out and puts acid drops in her long tangly hair. When he passes her bed in the dormitory verandah on his way to his own lonely cot around the corner he apple-pies her bed. When she runs across the grass lawn that is the playground he puts out his foot and trips her up. When he passes her desk in the schoolroom he upsets a bottle of ink on her exercise.

The significant part of this conduct is that he doesn't do it to anybody else. Laura means something to him, and everyone in the school recognizes that this is an overt way of making love and accepts it as Laura's right.

Laura found it all highly satisfactory. Laura, in spite of her worldly possessions, her long red-black hair and her beautiful mobile mouth, and her three Montgomery cousins, was a lonely person. Deep inside there were wells of emotional disturbance that were not understandable to anyone, except perhaps myself.

Somehow, though Laura did not love Basil Forsyte in return, it was deeply satisfying to be loved by a member of the opposite sex. It made Laura happier than anything else except the fact that Uncle Tim loved her.

This was destined to be the pattern of all Laura's love affairs. Except the one with Danny. And the dreadful affair with Peter Stevenson.

Laura exulted in her conquests. They made her happy. They gave a sparkle to her eyes and colour to her cheeks. They caused her to walk proudly and confidently but they never deeply touched her. All except that with Danny. And to Danny she gave her heart.

Laura was very happy at boarding-school.

Then Uncle Tim died.

Mama came to school to fetch us in the middle of school work one afternoon.

She had been talking to the headmistress before we were brought into the room and as soon as we came in we saw that Mama had been crying. There were still tears on her cheeks. There was a heartbroken look on her face.

I think that Mama loved Uncle Tim better than anyone else in the world.

She told us very gently. She didn't have to try to tell us in well-chosen words because her own grief spoke for her.

"Darlings," she said. "Uncle Tim has gone . . . has . . . has died. He was so good . . . and I think God must have taken him because He . . . well, because He needed him too."

She was thinking out aloud and somehow it was the best way to tell us.

Laura and I said nothing but Vicky began to cry. Mary said, "Where has he gone?"

"To God . . ." Mama repeated, looking down at her hands in her lap.

Then the matron came in to say our clothes were ready and we could go home with Mama.

We went all the way to Pepper Tree Bay in a cab, six miles round the river, and it seemed to take hours. Nobody talked at all.

At the Rectory my father was shut in the study with Uncle William, and Aunt Sheilagh was sitting in the drawing-room

19

looking suddenly pinched and very white as she talked to one or two visitors who had called when they heard the news.

Mama told us to change our clothes and go out and play.

Uncle Tim had had a heart attack while giving his sermon in his Church in Kalgoorlie. He had been carried out and had died the following day.

People grieved in Pepper Tree Bay as much as they did in Kalgoorlie for whenever Uncle Tim had come down to the coast he had preached in father's Church and people had loved to come and listen to him as much as they loved to listen to my father.

Looking back now I sometimes think the people came to the Church in Pepper Tree Bay, and packed it out, as much to see and listen to these two Irishmen as to worship God. Specially the women.

In the days that followed Laura said nothing. Neither did I. Uncle Tim had gone away from us. It was something not to be accepted and believed. One day soon we would wake up and find it had all been a terrible and pointless dream. One that shook the very foundations of life.

One day, a week or two later, Laura and I

were both in the dining-room in the Rectory. On the big mahogany table were some papers and a black leather writing-case. My father had been working there a little while earlier. Laura and I were both looking for books in the bookcase that lined the whole of one wall. We didn't have a library room in the Rectory in Pepper Tree Bay and the books that overflowed from the study were housed in the dining-room.

After a while Laura went over to the table and her fingers rested on the writing-case.

On it was printed in gold letters,

T. McM.

"Uncle Tim's . . ." said Laura.

Suddenly her face puckered up and a dreadful sob racked her whole body. Then she ran out of the room.

At tea-time nobody could find Laura. Mama sent over to Aunt Sheilagh's house to find if Laura was there and Aunt Sheilagh sent over to our house to know if Laura was with us.

It was nine o'clock at night before they found her. She had put herself to bed and pulled the bed-covers up over her head. She was asleep when they found her and the pillow was wet with the tears she had shed.

2

ONE of the joys of the return of the William Montgomeries to the coast from the gold-fields each summer was that they brought Brian Borhu with them. He was a big wicked tan-coloured Irish terrier. He had brown eyes that pleaded but a snarl that could terrify.

He didn't terrify any of the Montgomeries or any of the boys from my father's school. Half the joy of Sunday afternoon tea-parties on the school lawns was the mischief Brian Borhu would provoke amongst the boys.

There were always a select number of boys invited to these sedate afternoon teas where even we children were taught to eat our sandwiches with our gloves on and where the Curate did indeed pass around the "curate's delight".

My father once had an Irish curate. His name was the Reverend William Finnegan and he was both fat and lazy. He hated carrying the "curate's delight" amongst the ladies, not because it pointed to his status or was

23

undignified but because it was too much trouble.

When he first came from Ireland my father insisted my mother take him into the Rectory as a house guest until he was able to find other accommodation. It soon became clear he did not intend to go to the trouble to look for other accommodation.

My father, who could never see ill in anyone who came from Ireland, would do nothing about him and Mama did not like to appear inhospitable to a stranger to the country and she didn't want to have a row with my father over William Finnegan. They had to have rows over things like the boys breaking the chairs over at the school and the necessity of getting a new matron. It was Father who founded and ran the school but it was Mama who did the worrying and much of the work.

One day, at a Sunday afternoon tea-party on the school lawns, the Reverend William Finnegan gave Brian Borhu a kick and called him a vile animal. He didn't hurt the dog but he did something to Laura's feelings. Thereafter she haunted the activities of the curate and reported to her own father and mother on his lazy habits.

One Saturday when Laura returned to her own home from a visit to the Rectory Aunt Sheilagh asked her, just for the sake of conversation, what the family at the Rectory was doing this fine sunny day.

"I suppose Uncle Joe is over at the school," she said.

"No he's not," said Laura. "He's making them all work in the vegetable garden. As soon as I came in the gate he gave me a hoe and told me I had to do the onions. He's got five hundred onions planted so I had to *work*."

She said this with considerable indignation. She never knew when she set out for the Rectory whether life was going to be exceedingly tough or exceedingly pleasant. My father's moods were always unpredictable.

Aunt Sheilagh laughed. When she laughed it was the loveliest sound in the world. She had a small red mouth and a row of small shining teeth that were like pearls. Her eyes closed right up when she laughed.

"You wouldn't laugh," said Laura, "if you had to spend a whole Saturday afternoon hoeing onion-beds. And Brian Borhu got into trouble. He messed up the new radishes chasing the cat."

25

"Well now . . . I can't see Uncle Joe doing anything about Brian Borhu."

"Not when it's somebody else's garden. But when it is *his* radishes . . . !"

"What did he do?"

"He threw a rake at him and then shut him outside the gate. The one nearest the back door. So Brian sat and whined all the afternoon and Mr. Finnegan who was sitting on the back stairs and reading his papers and smoking threw things at him."

Aunt Sheilagh stopped laughing.

"What was Mr. Finnegan doing sitting on the back steps smoking and reading while everyone else was working?"

"He always does. Aunt Helen said the only time he moved was when the maid was chopping the wood. Then he went inside because he couldn't bear to see a woman cutting wood."

Aunt Sheilagh frowned and looked sideways at Uncle William.

"I don't know why Helen doesn't get rid of the loafer," she said. "William, can't you do something about it?"

Uncle William said it was worth more than his life to interfere with Joe when he had his mind set on a thing.

So Aunt Sheilagh went around the parish and found a widow who was willing to take in the Reverend William Finnegan. She then went and told the Reverend William herself and he complained bitterly that he was "haunted by the William Montgomery dislike."

"He shouldn't have kicked Brian Borhu, or thrown stones at him," Laura said darkly when she was telling us all the story.

It was an unwise thing to endanger oneself in Laura's affections. Feelings, with Laura, stayed put a long time.

Vicky was the next offender.

The William Montgomery family stayed the whole year in their Pepper Tree Bay house after Uncle Tim's death. This had nothing to do with Uncle Tim's death but to do with the Stock Market as I knew many years later. At the time I dated everything from and because of Uncle Tim's death.

Sometimes, at the conclusion of the Sunday afternoon tea-parties on the school lawns, several of the boys were invited to go with us back to the Rectory for supper. We were bidden to play on the croquet lawn, but not to play croquet. We were not allowed to play organized games on a Sunday.

Instead we played hide-and-seek, chasings and a daylight version of Postman's Knock, games much more arduous and very much more doubtful than croquet. But such was the wisdom of our elders.

The Postman's Knock was a game in which one of the boys went through a hole in the fence where a picket was missing into the fig orchard. The girls, Vicky, Mary, Laura and myself, then each took a number one to four. Sylvia could never join in. She was delicate and had to sit like a sweet little pink-and-white doll on the banks of the lawn and watch.

The boy in the orchard would call out a number and the girl who owned it had to go through the hole in the fence and stay with him while everyone else counted fifty. Then it was the next boy's turn.

The fifty had to be counted out aloud as tangible evidence that everyone else was a long way away from the picket fence and no one was peeping through the cracks.

When the orchard occupants emerged through the hole their faces were always red whether they had kissed or not. The only time their faces were not red was when Laura emerged with Lowell Thompson. He looked a little white and Laura looked composed and haughty. One knew at once that this was another love affair of Laura's. She was probably ten at the time.

Laura was really fond of Lowell Thompson and when he fell ill with meningitis Laura haunted the Rectory for news of his progress. This was the first time a boy at Father's school had ever been seriously ill and the whole parish took a solemn and preoccupied interest in the boy's welfare. Parishioners rang up the Rectory or the School every day and one Thursday night my father held a special service in the Church to pray for him. The Church was quite full, only God himself being absent, for early the next morning Lowell Thompson died.

This seemed a frightening thing for somehow we had associated death with the old, or the very good, like Uncle Tim. Lowell Thompson wasn't good because he had several times kissed Laura behind the picket fence in the orchard. We feared for Lowell's immortal soul and we all wept profusely. That is, except Laura. Laura didn't come to the Rectory for the rest of that week.

On Sundays when the William Montgomeries were in Pepper Tree Bay we sat in
the same pew at eleven o'clock Matins. On
the Sunday after Lowell died we were all
there as usual, except Mama, who had to stay
home to cook the vast dinner the combined
family ate on Sundays. Even Uncle William
looked white-faced, for somehow we knew,
dreaded, and anticipated that some time in
the service my father would make a reference
to Lowell's death. All the boys sat in the
School pews with a tiny black ribbon in their
button-holes. Uncle William and Aunt
Sheilagh sat with Sylvia between them and
Uncle William held Sylvia's hand all through
the service. He was feeling that Sylvia was
delicate and some day she too might go from
them.

It was at the beginning of the sermon, from
the pulpit, that my father spoke of Lowell
Thompson and an awful wracking sound like
a snort came from Laura, who was sitting between me and Vicky. Then when my father
bade us bow our heads and say a special
prayer for the dead boy the tears dropped
down on to Laura's gloved hands. She was
too ashamed of herself to use her handkerchief and for the rest of the service little

badly hidden sniffs kept coming from her.

Vicky kept a diary and against that Sunday she wrote in pencil . . . *Laura cried in Church over Lowell Thompson.*

Weeks after when we were playing in the schoolroom Laura saw Vicky's diary and opened it and read the pencilled words. She rubbed them out surreptitiously and went home and wouldn't come back for evening supper.

When Vicky discovered what Laura had done she re-wrote the words in ink.

I suppose the diary had a fascination for Laura, for when she came to the Rectory again she found the diary and saw the inked-in words. She screamed and tore out several pages and threw them in the fire.

She didn't speak to Vicky for years.

3

SHORTLY afterwards Laura and her parents went back to the gold-fields.

One of the delights of life in the Rectory was Aunt Sheilagh's weekly letter to Mama. Aunt Sheilagh's letters were just like herself and Mama said that when she read them she could see Aunt Sheilagh and hear her lovely soft voice.

The letters were about parties and musicales and who was seen at whose house. They ended by saying that Laura was well but just as difficult as ever. And that Sylvia looked more like and nearer the angels than ever. Aunt Sheilagh often said that Laura was difficult. "Those funny moods, you know!"

At the end of the year they came back to their Pepper Tree Bay house for the long summer months.

The return to the sea-coast of the William Montgomeries was, of course, the gala event of the year. First of all it meant Mama running backwards and forwards between it and the Rectory getting the house ready.

Then it meant stocking it with fruits and pro-visions, always the lovely things we could so rarely afford ourselves but which we knew in due course we would be invited to share.

Besides Laura and Sylvia we adored our uncle and aunt and we looked forward to those long grown-ups' sessions to which we, in those two open Irish houses, were privy. Uncle William and my father would sit or stand about and talk, and talk, and talk. It was always in those charming mellifluous but emphatic voices. The things they said to one another, and talked about, had fascinations as strong as fairy-tales and adventure stories. Sometimes it was about Ireland or Australia, but mostly it was about people. They would tell strange and wonderful anecdotes about people so that when in the ordinary passage of life one has come across some of these people it has been like meeting characters in a story. We had actually been living the long serial of their lives for them.

Sometimes one wondered why this par-ticular man didn't look quite as wicked as we really knew him to be, or why that one whom our father and our imagination had invested with such magic seemed just an ordinary human being after all.

My Aunt Sheilagh talked about people too and her lovely laugh would tinkle out like bells. The only time Aunt Sheilagh wasn't smiling was when she was considering an invitation list to one of her dinner-parties, or, even more important, whether she would or would not call on a certain new-comer to the district. The new-comer's antecedents would have to be gone into as well as her suitability to fit in with the social group of mining directors' wives and the wives of the big station owners who also arrived like a summer invasion in their town houses around Pepper Tree Bay.

The members of the ordinary normal social hierarchy of Pepper Tree Bay, that is, those who lived there all the year round, were very busy calling and returning calls on river-side houses but their magic dominance was now willingly delivered up to the land and mining owners for the season. They stood back and waited to see who, or if anyone, was going to call on a new-comer.

As we grew older we began to see very clearly the sharp line of demarcation between some of the ladies of whom, in parish affairs, we had stood in considerable awe throughout the winter, and the station owners and people like Aunt Sheilagh. The royal families of Pepper Tree Bay weren't those who lived there habitually, after all. They were those who came and went with the summer breezes.

Laura was perhaps the earliest to perceive these things, and in a way they were things which she subscribed to all her life, yet which she never ceased to ridicule.

Laura was a strange person. She despised the elevation of Mrs. So-and-So because her husband ran a pastoral property of half a million acres, but at the same time she tolerated only the Mrs. So-and-Sos because she could not abide the bourgeois qualities of those who did not have money and land. All her life she despised people who locked up their houses, windows and all, when they went out; and checked the contents of their pantries and their purses. She would say, "It's the sort of stock they come from." No Montgomery house or car was ever locked. Mama said ours wasn't locked because the Rectory, like the Church, must always be open to those in need but really it was because it was an Irish house and it would drive my father into a rage to see a key being turned.

"For the love of God," he would say. "What is there in a poor clergyman's house that anyone would want to steal?"

Aunt Sheilagh just never thought about it at all. She never locked anything up.

Once Laura and Vicky and I went to play with a child of a well-known Church worker and when in the afternoon a cab was sent for us, and our hostess said she would go up the town to do a little shopping and began closing and latching all the windows and finally locking the back, the side and the front doors, Laura stood and watched her.

"Why do you do that?" Laura asked.

"So that nobody will get in and take anything."

"But who would want to take anything?"

"Well, you never can tell. It's best to be careful."

When we were left alone in the cab Laura was thoughtful.

"Who'd want to steal her stuff?" she burst out at last. "Nobody in Pepper Tree Bay steals at all. And if they did why would they go to that house?"

"I suppose she likes her things," Vicky said.

"She couldn't," Laura said flatly. Then

after a little silence, "It's where she came from. There were thieves where she came from, so she goes on locking things up in Pepper Tree Bay."

She gave a snort of contempt and tossed her head.

"You're just a snob," I said to Laura, feeling that as a daughter of a clergyman I ought to have better manners towards our late hostess than Laura entertained.

Laura looked at me with derision.

"Even if it was worth something I wouldn't lock it up," she said.

This was sheer arrogance on Laura's part but I was too young to think of the right word to apply to her then. Besides, I was a little frightened of Laura's contempt of other people. I had to go to Church three times every Sunday and I knew a lot of the lessons by heart. I knew that Christ was humble and that it was a sin to look down on other people. I also knew I was dreadfully sinful myself and I was fearful of adding yet another sin, that of false pride, to the already overwhelming catalogue. The recording angel was always just around the corner and it wouldn't be long before God was acquainted of any further misdemeanours.

Yet somehow I loved the careless arrogance of Aunt Sheilagh and Laura. It had a great appeal. Perhaps secretly I wished that like Laura I wasn't brought up in the shadow of the Church and could have acted and spoken with the same abandon as she did.

Uncle William was seeing my father when we got back to the Rectory, and just as we were coming in the door he was coming out of the study. He took out his gold watch and looked at it.

"Hell and damnation," he said. "I'm late." Then looking up at us he gave us an edge of his wicked smile.

"You brats are always under a man's feet when he wants to swear," he said.

The cab that had brought us home was just turning round in front of the Rectory drive and he hailed it and got into it with Laura. As they drove away at a spanking pace I looked after them wistfully.

I knew it was a frightful thing for Uncle William to swear, but oh, how I envied him the power and the right and the manner to do so. It seemed to me the most wonderful thing in the world to be able to say "Damn!" with that kind of reckless abandon.

We were twelve when Danny came to Pepper Tree Bay, and Laura's real love life began.

Uncle William had gone home to Ireland to see about family affairs. There had been disturbing drifts of conversation coming through the study doors of the Rectory, or on the front verandah of Uncle William's house by the river and it seemed that all was not well at Magillicuddy, the home in Ireland.

This was serious trouble because though my father talked openly in front of us about Uncle Dennis, the head of the house, and his addiction to race-horses and Irish whiskey, when they mentioned Uncle Rory they dropped their voices and sent us all out of the room, or off the verandah, according to which house it was in which the discussions were taking place. Shame didn't seem to be a thing much associated with the Montgomeries, so evidently Uncle Rory had done something really awful.

Uncle William, from the deep chair on the verandah, said a lot about having to keep the whole family together and Aunt Sheilagh said nearly as much about the gold-mines of Australia doing it.

So Uncle William went back to Ireland and six months later came back to Pepper Tree

Bay. Nothing more was said about Rory or Dennis Montgomery or else nobody listened, for all our hearts and minds were taken up with Danny.

Danny, aged fourteen, coming down the gangway of the ocean liner that brought him to Australia, was an astonishing figure. He wore a black cut-away suit and a top hat. Nobody in Pepper Tree Bay had ever seen anyone dressed like that before.

Both families were on the wharf, partly to welcome Uncle William and Danny, and partly because it was a day's outing, and quite a treat to see an ocean liner come in at Fremantle. Mama and Aunt Sheilagh had had quite a time keeping us together, our dresses and gloves spotless and our behaviour reasonably decorous. They had no further trouble after we all saw Danny. We were spellbound, and stayed like that all the way back to Pepper Tree Bay. It wasn't only Danny's clothes. It was the way he looked and the way he said, "Oh really!"

Nobody in Australia ever said "Oh really!" and if they had said it it wouldn't have been said that way. Nobody but an Englishman or an Irishman, can say "Oh really!" properly, which is probably the reason that no one else ever says it. The inflexion in the voice gives the phrase a curious questing quality, and yet it is not an invitation to continue. It is the most devastating expression in the world when used in conversation with people from other countries. It silences them. Mama when she got upset in her later years about the British Empire said, "If they'd only stopped saying 'Oh really!' ten years before they did they would never have lost the Empire." Mama didn't consider the British Commonwealth the same thing as the Empire at all.

Danny was so different from us all he silenced us for quite a long time. This is a considerable feat and Danny didn't even know he'd done it, nor probably cared that he had done it. There was a polite air of indifference about him. One didn't know whether it was a façade or not. After all he was only fourteen.

Apart from all these things—his cut-away suit and top hat, his beautiful but devastating accent, his polite and polished aloofness—he had the kind of handsome pale face that made Pope Gregory say, "Non Angli, sed Angeli." It didn't matter what Danny was as a person, you loved him. He never had to do anything

41

about it all his life. People just loved him with a poignant and proud love.

Laura had known Danny in Ireland as a very little girl, but it was when he came to Australia she first loved him.

She stood on the wharf quite silent while he shook hands with us all and kissed Mama and Aunt Sheilagh on the cheek. She was the only one who said nothing. She stood and scowled and after a few minutes walked away and stood in the shadow of the Customs shed. That was after Mama said to Uncle William,

"Why on earth didn't you take him out of that suit before you landed?"

"What for?" said Uncle William down his long aquiline nose. "If they don't damn' well know how to dress in this country why in damnation should a Montgomery change his ways?"

Aunt Sheilagh sighed. It was quite clear Uncle William was going to be very difficult about Australia all over again. It always took him six months and a lot of big dividends from the gold-fields to take life this side of the world benignly. However, Aunt Sheilagh's loveliness softened Uncle William for he stood looking at her proudly while we stood in a solemn-eyed row and looked at Danny.

"How is Sylvia?" Uncle William asked when he had kissed Aunt Sheilagh twice.

"We didn't bring her. The heat, and the standing, might have been too much for her. But she's waiting on the verandah at home."

My father was having a glorious time with the Customs. He wore his clerical suit and his clerical collar and a big brown topee on his head. He also did a lot of waving about with his walking-stick. His Irish voice, his autocratic air and his clerical collar did all that was necessary with the Customs officials, for within a very short while we were all packed in three cars and heading towards Pepper Tree Bay.

Danny sat in the back of one car between Vicky and me. Laura sat in front beside the chauffeur and she never once turned her head or spoke to any of us. That's how I knew she loved Danny. Ordinarily she would have been bossing us all around.

Now and again we would try to tell Danny something, or point out to him some wonder of the river, and he would say,

"Oh really!"

It was so polite, yet so silencing. In the end we gave up and just spent the rest of the time looking at him. He was very beautiful.

We all went, of course, to the William Montgomery house for morning tea. Through the trees the river shone in its deepest indigo blue. The wide verandahs round the large house were cool and inviting. Sitting upright in one of the deep cane chairs, and looking like a frail tinselled fairy, was Sylvia.

Danny got out of the car and went towards her. He took off his shiny top hat and held out his hand. They shook hands with one another and said "How-do-you-do?" like two marionettes on a shadowed stage with a backdrop of dazzling river. They looked at one another and then very slowly they both smiled.

That was the beginning of tragedy in Laura's life. That very moment her life took a turn and it never again came back to a really straight line.

She never loved anyone else but Danny, but she had to give him up to Sylvia, for Sylvia was frail, and soon might die.

The only thing that was really natural about Danny, by our standards, was his capacity for cream cake and fruit salad. Something happened to him when the tea was brought out by the maids, and the traymobiles loaded with rich and varied food were wheeled on to the verandah. Also, considering his hat was such an astonishing and probably expensive thing, it was funny how he cart-wheeled it on to the floor some distance from where we were all sitting. It made us all laugh with delight.

He stopped smiling at Sylvia when he saw the cake and he didn't sit down to eat it. He just took large helpings, walked to the edge of the verandah and ate it in huge bites. He also wiped his hands, first on a beautiful white linen handkerchief, and afterwards on the seat of his black tailored pants. This, one felt, was out of character, and only Laura thought there was nothing odd about it.

Laura had adopted a faintly belligerent attitude. One imagined that if we were going to be critical of Danny then it would have to be over Laura's dead body. Oddly enough nobody felt that way about him at all. But we were frightened *for* him. We didn't know how the boys of Pepper Tree Bay would treat him in that suit and that hat. Possibly we even feared for his life. We thought Danny would be a prize joke. Yet we didn't think he was a joke ourselves. We were passionately proud of him, not because of the cut-away suit and the top hat but because of his way of carrying his head, of unexpectedly smiling and above all, his polished indifference.

The next day my father took him to the Grammar School—that was my father's own school that stood on the corner of the Highway and was the finest thing in all Pepper Tree Bay. Moreover, in spite of Mama's protestations, he took him in the suit and top hat.

All day we wondered what would happen to Danny. When he came across to the Rectory after school, nothing seemed to have happened. His long fair wavy hair was still in place. His face still kept its serene beauty. There were a few more grease-marks on the seat of his pants where he had wiped his fingers a few more times during the day, but otherwise he seemed just the same.

"Danny, how did you like school?" Mama asked, cutting him the biggest piece of cake I'd ever seen her cut anybody.

"Very well, thank you."

That was all. The cake was much more interesting than a discussion about school.

"The children had better take you down and show you the vegetable garden when you've finished," Mama said. "The apricots are over, but there's plenty of figs and grapes."

Danny said, "Splendid!" and we all blinked our eyes. We hoped that Oliver, that wretched caretaker's boy, wouldn't be hanging, with his bare legs and ragged pants, over the back fence. Oddly enough we were more concerned about what Oliver would think of Danny than what Danny would think of Oliver.

Of course Oliver was there. His urchin face and brown smouldering eyes were transfixed between two pickets of the fence. Danny didn't have his top hat on then, but he had the suit, and his fair hair was dangling over one eye in a manner which is simply not allowed in Australia.

Oliver said, "Cripes!" and shifted his weight from one foot to another.

"You go away," I said. "You're not wanted."

"You make me," said Oliver.

I shrugged and looked at Danny.

"Don't take any notice of him," I said to Danny.

"Why not?" Danny seemed surprised. "Is there anything wrong with him?"

"He quarrels."

Danny looked at Oliver in surprise.

"Oh really!" he said.

I expected Oliver to do something about that. He did.

"Come up here on the fence, you," he said rudely. "You can get better figs this side than that. If yer game to try."

"Oh splendid!" said Danny. Then he went up on the top of the fence, coat tails and all.

"Cripes!" said Oliver. "You can't climb in them things."

"Don't believe I can," said Danny, and he tucked the tails of his coat up under his waistcoat.

"Take the flaming thing orf," said Oliver. "It's too flamin' hot anyway."

"I believe I will," said Danny, and he pulled his coat off so that the sleeves were inside out showing the lining, black-and-white striped like the ticking of a mattress, and threw it back into our lettuce patch. Then he and Oliver disappeared.

We waited quite a long time but neither Danny nor Oliver reappeared. We ate a lot of figs and grapes ourselves and then decided to report the loss of Danny to Mama.

This put Mama in a fix. She had

ambivalent feelings about Oliver. I think she really liked him, but he had such execrable manners. Moreover he over-used the words "damn" and "bloody". Why "damn" should be unforgivable coming from Oliver and cause him social banishment and yet be tolerated in silence from Uncle William was past my understanding. Evidently it had something to do with the accent in which it was said.

It was Laura, coming down Queen Victoria Drive from her own house, who found Danny. He was poking gum with a long stick out of the wounds of a big old gum tree that stood in the vacant lot where now stands a garage opposite the school.

Laura and Oliver hated one another and they demonstrated it in the usual way. Laura tossed her head and Oliver spat on the ground.

While Laura commanded Danny to "come home because tea's ready", Oliver stood and grinned wickedly at her and flicked little pebbles in her direction so that every now and again one hit and stung her ankle. Laura was too proud to take any notice of Oliver. She merely repeated her command that "tea was ready".

The nicest thing about Danny was that he was obliging. He said, "Oh splendid! I'll come at once."

"See you some more," said Oliver, his brown eyes watching Danny curiously.

"Oh rather!" Danny said. "Do you know where I left my bloody coat?"

"In there," said Oliver, jerking backwards with his thumb. "You don't have to eat with yer coat on, do you?"

"Well, what do you think?" Danny inquired of Laura politely.

"You'll have to get your coat. You can't walk up the street like that. And for goodness' sake look what you've done to your pants. You've got a tear in them."

"So I have," said Danny indifferently. "Well I suppose I'd better get my coat." He turned to Oliver. "I'll see you again," he said.

"It's just bloody possible," said Oliver coarsely.

"You're probably bloody right," said Danny equably.

Laura never said what effect this colourful conversation had on her but when it was repeated en famille Uncle William threw back his head and laughed. Aunt Sheilagh's

50

lovely blue eyes had a tearful kind of smile in them. Mama looked worried and my father said he'd take his stick to young Oliver Harding. I never heard my father use a swear word in all his life, and I never knew him to thrash Oliver Harding either . . . though once he boxed a choir-boy's ears in the middle of a service in Church. But he was always going to thrash him. Oliver kept out of my father's way.

The interesting thing about Oliver's relation-ship with Danny, fragmentary and short though it was, is that Danny ought, in the climate of Australian boys' attitudes, to have been the subject of scorn or even ridicule. He was everything that Oliver, and his kind, portentously despised. Yet by some magic alchemy of personality, Oliver accepted Danny. Moreover, if there was a jest in the situation at all it was at Laura's expense. Possibly ours too. We had been afraid for Danny. Mentally Laura stood at the ringside with clenched fists waiting for someone to offend. Behind Oliver's sardonic eyes there was a knowledge of this, and it amused him.

Nothing, of course, ever had, did or would intimidate Oliver.

By the following morning a tweed short coat and knicker-bockers had appeared to relieve Danny of his tails. The top hat was only seen again at Church on Sunday mornings. In Church everyone looked but nobody ridiculed. I do not know whether it was Danny's unconscious but subversive charm or whether it was his physical beauty, but everyone looked, nodded, smiled gently, and got on with his prayers.

Aunt Sheilagh, of course, took the whole situation as natural and in the proper perspective of things as she knew them to be in her own life.

I do not know whether Aunt Sheilagh's attitude to Australia was that of the temporary visitant, or whether at any time she thought she might remain here for ever. She carried on her life as she had carried it on in Ireland, bowing only to such changes as climate demanded.

Being Aunt Sheilagh she could do this without any trouble at all. She gave the kind of dinner-parties to which everyone liked to be invited.

It was at one such dinner-party that we had our first inkling of Uncle Rory's offence.

We children were all invited to dine in the

schoolroom for, though the grown-ups had no inclination for our company at the dinner-party, they liked the aura of family life. Somehow children in the background was the kind of back-drop without which the Montgomeries could not do.

Of course we went through the preliminaries of washing and combing and presentations in the drawing-room.

We, that is to say, my father's children, had our usual derisive attitude to all this and though we loved the powdered and perfumed ladies and the rustle of silk, and the really grand jewels Aunt Sheilagh wore, not one of us would have admitted it.

We loved the men's gruff and hearty voices and were Australian enough to prefer the arrogant tones of Mr. Batson and Mr. Maynard-Arnold, pastoralists from the north-west, to the more cultured and softer voices of the men from overseas in the company. Of course no voices were comparable with those of my father and Uncle William. They were special, different and quite unique. They belonged to the Montgomeries which was the same thing as saying they belonged exclusively to the only people who were *right*.

After the presentations—I cannot call them

less—we were marshalled off in an orderly way to the schoolroom. The way my mother and Aunt Sheilagh did this has often caused me to look back over the years with envy. It was done with a gaiety and an assurance of all being well in the best of possible worlds that belied the fact that there was every possibility in this world of one or other of us doing something outrageous before the evening was out.

This anxiety must have been with them but it was never great enough for them to resist the temptation of retaining the charm of children in the background.

From the schoolroom we could hear the guests proceeding to the dining-room, hear their voices and the occasional tinkle of glass. We could see the two maids hurrying backwards and forwards down the long passage with silver serving dishes.

Round about dessert time the company inside was merry enough for one or other of the children to parade the passage without being noticed. The velvet curtains at the head of the passage made an ample screen for those who paused and listened.

It was thus we heard about Rory.

No one in our family had ever been in "trade". This was some unthinkable activity in the world that the Montgomeries admitted existed but that was all.

How this was reconciled to Uncle William's activities with the gold-mine is a mystery I have never been able to solve. He sat on directorates, he consulted with owners and the first thing he did every morning was read the Trade and Finance section of the newspaper, beginning at the first word on the top line and not finishing until he had read the last word on the bottom line. Also he made notes with a pencil and paper. Though this page was his bible and his barometer, still Uncle William had nothing to do with *trade*. Trade was something quite different, according to the Montgomeries, from the buying and selling of stock and mine management.

When we children knew that Uncle Rory in Ireland was in disgrace, we assumed the very worst had happened. Uncle Rory must have gone into trade. We were too ashamed to mention it even amongst ourselves.

We were at our listening posts when we heard our parents talk about Rory. Some of the guests present had known him and several tales were told of Rory and his wild scrapes.

"Well, he's come to the end now," my father said. "It's a wonder to me and the whole Irish nation he had such a notion in his head to take up the way of life, it is."

"He'll get a bit of discipline there," said Uncle William. "Nothing disciplines a man like a tightening of the purse, and there won't be much over for a kettle of broth by the time Rory draws his weekly pittance."

"Och!" my father said. "What a sorry business it is!"

The word "business" was synonymous with "trade" to us listeners and with these words of my father we bowed our heads. Our fears had been well grounded. Uncle Rory must be in trade.

We knew that Montgomeries always talked about one another openly, and ordinarily we would have felt no shame in a little malicious airing of the weaknesses of other members of the family. But to let our fellow Australians know about Rory and trade . . . That was carrying things too far! If our parents had no shame at least they might have considered the damage they were doing to the future prestige of their children.

It was when Mama and Aunt Sheilagh

came to the schoolroom to see how we were faring that we let them know the frightful position they had placed us in in relation to our friends and neighbours.

"Why did you tell them about Uncle Rory?" I almost shouted in shame and rage.

"Oh tut!" Aunt Sheilagh said. "Everyone knows about Rory. He's a scandal from one end of Ireland to the other."

"But in *trade*?" I wailed.

"In trade?" Aunt Sheilagh's pretty arched eyebrows went up and the laughter trilled from her. Even in that moment of humiliation I could mark its lovely sound. "My *darlings*, Uncle Rory has done dreadful things, and this time a shocking one . . . But in *trade*? Even Uncle Rory wouldn't go into trade."

"Then what has he done?" Laura demanded. "Has he gone to gaol?"

Aunt Sheilagh looked at Mama out of the corners of her eyes and brushed Laura's hair back from her face.

"Ask Uncle Joe," she said with a laugh. "It's not as bad as trade, but it's much worse than gaol."

By this time Uncle William had come, with one of the guests, to look in the schoolroom

57

door, and Aunt Sheilagh told him of our worries.

Uncle William had a little gold knife that hung from his gold watch-chain and with this he snipped off the end of his cigar.

"He's joined the Royal Irish Constabulary, my dear children," he said.

"What's wrong with that?" I asked. "Does it mean he's just a policeman?"

"No . . . it means he's a traitor. Or sooner or later will be one."

All the same Uncle William was smiling as he twisted the newly snipped cigar round and round in his mouth.

"The end will all be the same," he added indulgently. "If he don't get someone from behind a hedge first, then bedamn someone will get him from out of a drain instead."

Everyone laughed except Mama and somehow we knew this had something to do with the troubles of Ireland. These were things we could never straighten out, for when my father and his friends had been talking for hours about the troubles of Ireland they would always end up by saying "They should shoot 'em all." I often wondered why they should argue so much about who was right and who was wrong if in the end they thought they *all* should be shot.

Theoretically my father and my uncle thought the Royal Irish Constabulary was a good thing and that its members were a fine brave lot. But with the same logic that did not admit Uncle William's activities had anything to do with trade they now decided Uncle Rory had done a terrible thing.

"They'll hang him," said my father, who had now joined the others in the schoolroom. "Sure as my right hand is my right they'll hang him."

One felt that my father would get a lot of satisfaction when he met Uncle Rory in the after life in saying "I told you so."

As the grown-ups had further obligations to their guests they now left us to our own discussions of the problem. Only Laura and Danny were silent, and each was thinking on quite a different line.

Sylvia said in her frail childish voice, "I think it is a terrible disgrace."

Laura tossed her head.

"I don't," she said. "I'd sooner be a policeman and shoot men from behind a hedge than be a horrid old whiskey sponge like Uncle Dennis and shoot harmless things like foxes

59

and birds." She said this with an air of challenge and her blue eyes fixed on Danny, almost as if what she had said had been designed to hurt him, or prod him from his aloofness. It was very insulting because Uncle Dennis was Danny's father.

Danny was leaning against the window and looking at us as if he was hardly following her conversation. He did not even glance at Laura but somehow his eyes lighted on Sylvia's face. His smile was very sweet but just a little lop-sided.

"I'd rather go into trade than be any of them," he said. "At least one could make enough money to fix the stables at Magillicuddy."

This shocked the entire family into silence.

Sylvia looked puzzled and Laura stood still, her bottom jaw very firm and her blue eyes quite navy blue with sombre thought.

In those few minutes Laura must have made up her mind that Danny would have to be watched and guarded all his life. And that this was her vocation.

Intervening, of course, was the hazard of Sylvia.

4

WHEN Laura was born and the foundations of her personality and temperament laid down first by heredity and then by the rest of us it was meant she should proceed from the womb to the grave with great singleness of purpose. It was meant she should not go round obstacles but through them or over them.

It was not given to her to adapt herself.

Relatives intervening, however, had first placed her so that she had to spend the first twenty-five years of her life with one foot in the northern hemisphere and the other in the southern hemisphere. As far as the climate of culture was concerned she was neither of this world nor that, but something of both. Psychologically she journeyed perpetually between heaven and hell. Whichever country she was in the other was the heaven that awaited her return.

In love she was meant to see and take. Perhaps in love more than anything else she was contrived to be ruthless. The entire population of the world could not have stopped her from this course . . . except Sylvia.

And the one person Laura loved, loved Sylvia first.

Sylvia had something wrong with one of the valves of her heart and she was destined, for as long as she lived, to be an invalid. She was born of a family, and in an age, when this fact was accepted almost philosophically. In the first decade of the twentieth century child mortality was still high and the religious dogmas had plenty of biblical clichés to cover the situation.

Sylvia was doomed. The family accepted this. They did not, however, provoke doom but rather sought to push it further and further off into the future. Sylvia was nurtured and protected, idolized and generally mourned over from the first few weeks when her ailment was discovered to be congenital and incurable.

We, her cousins, took this a little sceptically. But not so Laura. Laura did not so much love Sylvia as she perceived in some mysterious way the inconsolable grief associated with one who might die young. Laura was so alive and vital. The thought of death was not to be tolerated, and yet daily she had to sit down with death as her breakfast companion.

I don't think anyone ever knew what went on in Sylvia's head about her future. Sylvia was a lovely picture, a cardboard character in the fiction of the Montgomery life.

She was fair, blue-eyed and frail looking. The frail appearance was largely due to the fact that she rarely went out into the sun and so kept her lovely Irish complexion. Her slightness was due to the fact she was kept on a diet as any tendency to weight put too great a load on her heart.

In temperament she was gentle and docile. She was an onlooker of life and seemed to find no grievance in that.

Sometimes she went on minor excursions with us but only on those occasions when we were first objured to take care of her and then sworn to walk slowly, and only on flat country.

These occasions were sometimes tedious, for Sylvia was a brake on us. When we, my father's children, frequently resisted the brake, Laura, who was meant by God in the making of her to be selfish, restless and adventurous, never hurried or walked too far. She kept the pace at Sylvia's capacity.

She did it silently and sometimes sullenly. But she did it.

Two or three weeks after Danny came to Australia we set out one day to walk towards the swamp. We would have liked to have gone duck-shooting but as this had recently been banned by the local law we had to be content with the prospect of wild-flower picking.

Whether it was Danny's presence, or the distant shadowing of the dreadful Oliver, our thoughts were not, as they should have been, on Sylvia. We argued as we walked. We stopped to show Danny things. Every now and again we would try to lie in ambush for Oliver, who like the stalking Indians of American fiction was never seen or heard, but quite constantly *felt*. Every now and again a gum nut would descend into the road appreciably near someone. Or a pebble would skid along the dusty road just a shade too near our legs for comfort and the desire to ignore him.

Whatever were the causes, we drifted off our course and turned sou'-sou'-west and were gradually, a milling vociferous gang of boys and girls, climbing the gradual slope of

Swanbourne Hill without even noticing we were doing it.

Perhaps the tang of the sea air coming in wafts over the sand dunes lured us on, for on we went.

If one was now and again uneasy about the distance we were taking Sylvia, one soothed one's conscience by the knowledge that after all we were walking very slowly and every time we paused to plant an ambush for Oliver Sylvia sat down by the wayside.

We were having a good time and we didn't want it spoiled by Sylvia's presence. Perhaps we thought too much fuss was made of her altogether. Perhaps we never really quite believed that Sylvia's heart was as weak as it was. I don't remember what we thought, I only remember we took Sylvia too far, and we took her to the top of the hill.

We reached the last rise of the hill and Danny had decided to distract the enemy in the rear by drawing arrows in the road directing the follower in the opposite direction from which we intended to take. Moreover I was occupied in scrawling in the dust such legends as: *Gone down to the sea by the rifle range* or *You're not wanted go home or else.*

Vaguely one knew that Sylvia had sat down

in the bush at the side of the road but no one took any notice. She always did this when we paused to get on with some more static type of nefarious activity.

Oliver, the true bushman, was approaching silently from the flank and it was he who found Sylvia.

She was lying, propped back against a bush. Her face was blue and she was struggling for breath.

Oliver probably had, in modern parlance, an Intelligence Quotient of 150, for he certainly had no education and no former experience of first aid to the sick, but he did the right thing.

He did not wait to spoil our fun in the roadway but got on with the business of reviving Sylvia. When Laura first looked round Oliver was holding Sylvia up in a sitting position and massaging Sylvia's back over the region of the heart and commanding, "Breathe deeply . . . breathe deeply. Breathe slowly . . ."

In a horrified and frightened group we gathered round and no one interfered with what Oliver was doing. We watched him in the kind of awed silence one watches the expert perform miracles.

Gradually the blue receded from Sylvia's face, leaving it quite white except round the lips. Gradually her breathing obeyed Oliver's measured commands. You could see her eyes watching his as mesmerized and see her breathe in as and when he did, breathe out as he did.

Soon she appeared back to normal though she still lay exhausted against the bushes.

It might have only been minutes but it seemed a long time and for the whole of it Danny stood, his hands in his pockets, his face whiter than Sylvia's. The chief difference between Danny's face and Sylvia's was that Sylvia had a blue shadow round her lips and Danny did not.

"What shall we do?" Vicky said, looking from face to face.

"Get a cab," Mary said.

"It's a mile to walk and find one," I said.

"We'll carry her," said Danny.

"You can't," Laura said. "She's too heavy for you."

She said it as if all her feelings were concentrated on despising Danny because Sylvia's weight would be too great for him.

"Cross hands?" Oliver said, looking at

Danny as one general might look at another on the eve of battle.

Danny's hands came out of his pockets and his right grasped the wrist of his left. Oliver did the same and each's spare hand grasped the wrist of the other. They thus made a seat.

Oliver's belligerent eyes looked from one to the other of us.

"*You*," he said to Mary, thus singling her out, and probably quite accurately, as the sanest of the bunch. "Help her sit up. Then wait."

We were much too frightened to interfere with Oliver's orders. Mary got behind Sylvia and levered her into the sitting position in which Oliver had been holding her when we first discovered what had happened.

"Now," said Oliver, walking crabwise with Danny attached to his hands like a Siamese twin and jockeying them both into a position behind Sylvia. They stooped so their hands were on the ground.

"Go on," commanded Oliver, probably knowing that Mary's Intelligence Quotient was near his own and she didn't have to be told how to lift Sylvia on to his hands.

Mary stood in front of Sylvia and pulled on her arms and as Sylvia came an inch or two off the ground Oliver and Danny slid their hands under her.

Sylvia put one arm round Danny's neck. Their eyes met and some message passed between them that was far beyond their years of knowledge. Laura put Sylvia's left arm round Oliver's neck and the two boys began thus to carry Sylvia down the hill.

At home we wept and excused ourselves when confronted with our parents and Aunt Sheilagh and Uncle William. Only Laura remained silent.

She sat in an armchair too big for her. She lay back, her arm along the arms of the chair, her eyes dark blue and uncommunicative. She looked only at Danny.

Danny leaned against the wall, one lock of hair over his eyes but so far away from us all we felt he had never been with us. Oliver had gone home.

No one ever thanked Oliver for what he had done, though thirty-four years later, when Oliver came back into our lives not only in the guise of Pan but with all Pan's mysteries and power, Mama, who then fought him with all the weapons of the matriarchal tiger, remembered. In the very climax of her wrath she suddenly sat still and silent in her chair. She leaned back and after a few minutes very quietly said, "Once he saved Sylvia's life."

After that day we treated Sylvia with awe. Our hearts were troubled. We knew she had nearly died. We knew fear. I also knew that Laura suffered deeply, and it was not all on account of Sylvia's nearness to death.

Three months after that Danny went back to Ireland.

When he boarded the ship at Fremantle it was not in the tails and top hat but in a tweed coat and a pair of long-'uns Mama had insisted on being bought for him in Australia.

Uncle William pooh-poohed this.

"At Bombay the ship turns into an English ferry," he said loftily. "In India the English don't adapt their ways to the Indians, but vice versa."

"I know," said Mama firmly. "But from Fremantle to Bombay he's with Australians."

"Well, Danny my boy," said Uncle William, "consider your company when you change your clothes at Bombay."

"It will be in the tropics," Laura put in defensively.

"There's always the English Channel," said Uncle William.

One got the impression he didn't care very much what Danny wore, or looked like, so long as he perpetrated some kind of a joke against somebody, preferably the Australians and the Indians. Also he had that adult attitude that suggests a boy of fourteen or fifteen can look after himself, especially if he has been brought up in the adult atmosphere of the old country. Australians, Uncle William was frequently heard to say, never grew up.

It was approaching summer when Danny went away and Uncle William's family was going to continue at the river-side house until March, so that we were all still together, and I was able to sense the loss that Danny was to Laura and Sylvia.

Laura had changed. She was restless and often moody. She despised our company and spent most of her time going to dancing lessons and a riding-school. Already there was a marked difference in the preparation for life between Laura and our side of the family. Laura did not seem to do the things like riding and dancing out of joy or pleasure but almost fiercely as if she were laying out a field ready for a campaign.

At this point she shed the leggy young girl look and showed signs of blossoming into a beautiful adolescent. I am quite sure that when Laura and I were side by side she looked at least two years older than I. It was something to do with poise as well as expensive clothes.

Sylvia sat on the wide verandah of the house and dreamed over the river. She also took to reading and surreptitiously writing poetry.

She kept a diary and sent long excerpts from it to Danny. Also Danny wrote to Sylvia, but no one else in either family had a line from him. Not even at Christmas time.

It was in this summer holiday, immediately after Danny's departure, that life on the river took on a new vitality for us. Hitherto we had gone swimming, fishing and prawning in the river. Occasionally we had sailed in a yacht or even a small launch. But this was the year of high note in finance for the pastoralists. They bought themselves bigger and better town houses along the river frontage and bigger and more luxurious launches.

Socially it was much more "ton" to give a launch party than a garden-party.

Again my relatives preferred their social life against the background of children. This is one of the most delightful features of river life. Even the elderly owners of launches never dreamed of putting out without at least half their passengers being young people. Whether they really loved young people or whether it has something to do with the picturesqueness of the scene, I do not know. Certainly a pretty girl or two, a bronzed youth or two, added something to the spread of sails or the trill of laughter in the saloon of a big launch.

Younger children, provided they were not too young, were a further asset. They provided the suitable awe and curiosity about marine engines or the rigging of sails to satisfy the most egotistical of the boat-owners.

It was sometime in January that it was rumoured round the drawing-rooms of Pepper Tree Bay that Mr. Maynard-Arnold was to organize a launch picnic in which all the big launches of the Freshwater Bay Club could take part. This was to be no single family affair but a combined social event that would go down in the annals of history.

Everyone knew about it weeks in advance and everyone hoped for an invitation to one or other launch. To be left out would be a social stigma from which one's prestige would never recover.

It was the first and most exciting topic of conversation in anyone's drawing-room, and Uncle William contemplated buying a launch for the occasion.

I do not think he or Aunt Sheilagh had any fears of being amongst the uninvited for their prestige was too high and their own dinner-parties too prized for the whole of Pepper Tree Bay to be indifferent to what might happen if no one invited the William Montgomeries. But being a launch-owner was suddenly an exciting thing to be, and besides Uncle William had plenty of money. Moreover it was important to demonstrate to his mining colleagues just how much money he did have. He did not indulge in trade himself (he said) but he expected other people to indulge in the kind of trade which would look to him for finance.

Uncle William took Laura and Mary and Vicky and me on expeditions around the boat-yards of the river, viewing launches for sale. I think that memories of his own boyhood stirred him to this for he anticipated the wild joy it was to us to look over possible purchases. While he was preoccupied with engines and sea-worthiness we were preoccupied with saloon drawing-rooms, cabins below deck and concealed lockers. A luxury launch has infinitely more mystery and variety than a modern caravan. Nautical names to things add to this.

In the long run, and greatly to our disappointment, Uncle William did not buy a launch. The only reason was that he could not find one big enough and in good enough condition to compete with those of his friends, in so short a time.

"Don't snivel about it", he said when he saw our fallen faces. "You've had all the fun of looking, and you won't miss the picnic. We're all going on Baston's *Valhill*."

We had been quite certain we would be invited to go on the *Valhill* anyway so this wasn't as much recompense as Uncle William would have us think. The Bastons, like my own parents and relatives, loved a back-drop of children, fortunately for us. They never did anything exciting without asking one or all of us. They adored my father first and

Vicky next which was probably the reason, but we, the rest of us, came in for the fun. So we did not mind who or which of the Montgomeries it was that engaged their affections.

The night was made exactly right for the great occasion. It had been a hot day and the slight southerly breeze that had come in at sundown had dropped leaving a still, stifling atmosphere on the land and a sky dark as velvet littered with stars for lamps. On the river one would be able to wear cotton dresses without a jacket, and the air over the water would dispel the closeness from the atmosphere.

It was almost impossible to describe the excitement of the preliminary of going to the Freshwater Bay Club in a caravan of cabs and cars.

First of all there had to be the usual skiting amongst our friends. Oliver was told over the back fence where we were going and how. We then left him to commiserate with himself as a socially untouchable. Oliver, of course, knew just exactly how to deal with this situation. He got himself a job as engine-boy on the biggest, most luxurious launch and once aboard smartly lost himself amongst the seventy-odd passengers. He had the time of his life.

Mama had trouble with finding us the right clothes that didn't look like Laura's or Sylvia's cast-offs . . . but somehow with needle, thread and machine she managed.

Uncle William and the Bastons were taking us as a family between them to the Club and we set off in three cars, hoping all our neighbours were looking and knew where we were going.

My father disapproved of cars.

"New-fangled notions," he said.

"Oh come Joe," said Uncle William. "A cab may set off a personality such as yours . . . but for the rest of us, one has to sell luxury as an advertisement to success, y'know."

This was puzzling because Uncle William had nothing to do with buying or selling. So all the Montgomeries said.

Laura was too astute not to notice this paradoxical situation but she was still too young to understand the ramifications of dealing in the Stock Market. One felt there was a query at the back of her mind just as when Uncle William spoke disparagingly of the Australians and Australia.

He would read the pronouncements of politicians in the daily papers and throw down the sheets in exasperation.

"Fools and rapscallions!" he would cry. "Now if they'd only consulted me! I could tell them where their foolishness is leading them."

And of the country he would say, "A terrible place. A God-forsaken hole!"

And occasionally when in a most sentimental mood his eyes would mist over and he would say, "Ah, poor Tim! To think he came to such an end! To be buried here in these wastes, away from civilisation and decent men and women."

It seemed to them, our elders, the greatest sorrow of Uncle Tim's death lay in the fact he was buried in Australia and not Ireland.

Not, however, to Laura and me. We both knew, though we never confided it to one another, that Uncle Tim would have straightened out all the perplexities for us. He would have explained the paradox of our situation.

The Freshwater Bay Club was festooned with gaily coloured lights leading in streamers along the jetties where we were to embark.

The launches were alive with pretty women in gay dresses and bronzed men with their yachtsmen's peaked caps lending them the right touch of glamour. To the uninitiated the ramifications of getting a launch out from the jetty, turning it about and making for midstream was a mystery of the most sublime.

We were allowed to press our noses against the glass window of the wheel-house and watch the skipper at work.

Ours was a big launch and the skippers from those fore and aft came along the jetty to organize the casting off so their own craft didn't get a scratch on the new paint-work.

While we headed quietly into the middle of the river, the gentlemen and ladies on the aft deck, or in the saloon, were drinking from tall frosted glasses and nibbling at olives, prawns and prunes wrapped in bacon.

The other launches followed us in order of the line and it was like a lovely coloured necklace of light weaving behind us.

Sylvia sat in a little cane-chair on the foredeck and gazed silently out over the dark river, the darker bank and the illimitable wastes of star-studded sky.

But Laura had already captivated the fancy

of a young man. He was about Danny's age and since he was a relative of the skipper and a junior member of the club he too wore a yachtsman's cap.

There was considerable distinction in being singled out by him. Laura liked it. Under the deck-light she tossed her head so we would all notice her success and for quite a time she exerted herself to be gay and attractive.

"Go away and don't be tiresome," she said when I sought to take a seat by her. "Don't you see we're *talking*?"

The young man looked as if he was in agreement with these sentiments. This was hurtful so I too tossed my head and said,

"Who wants to sit beside you, anyway."

I went across to Vicky who was still standing with her nose pressed against the glass of the wheel-house.

"Look at Laura," I said. "She's being *common*."

To be common was the worst offence any well-bred person could commit. Seen sitting with or talking to boys too much was considered very common indeed.

Vicky was not interested. She was fascinated by the skipper who could drink something from a frosted glass with one hand, steer the launch with another and keep up a laughing conversation with two of his passengers at the same time.

The launch was very gay. Only Sylvia sat quiet. When great plates of walnut cake and pink sponges were brought around she scarcely nibbled at an offering.

When the launches reached Attadale Bay they came alongside one another and were made fast. Then everyone began scrambling over the railings backwards and forwards from one launch to another. The older people greeted one another as long-lost friends and the younger people explored the saloons, the wheelhouse and the more secret recesses of each and every launch. Throughout plates of laden food were passed, glasses tinkled and girls trilled with laughter.

Laura and her young man were as madcap as any.

"I've had a piece of cake and a sandwich on every launch," she said proudly. "I know where all the lavatories are, and who's got the best."

This, of course, was shocking and I looked at her companion to see just how embarrassed this would make him. But he too wore a mischievous expression as if the locating of the lavatories on the launches were of greater importance than the engine-room.

Yet for all her brashness Laura was only playing a part. The beauty and luxury of the scene excited her emotionally, the vanity of being immediately singled out for attention by a personable young man set her all adrift inside herself. It was all ephemeral and she didn't know why. She giggled a lot and talked too loudly until Aunt Sheilagh, coming on a voyage of exploration in the children's direction, heard her.

"Laura!" she said sharply. "Not so loudly. Do you have to draw attention to yourself as much as that?"

Even I felt for Laura. I adored Aunt Sheilagh. I loved her pretty smile and her lovely clothes and even admired the way she could carry her head and look disdainful when some undesirable person was under discussion, but I never could understand why she would find fault with Laura . . . *aloud* . . . and in public. Even when Laura was deserving of censure.

A black sullen cloud came over Laura's face. If she had been happy before she wasn't any more. Her giggling and conspicuousness had probably been due to the fact she was escaping into the occasion from something deeper and more troubling in her heart.

"I'm not talking loudly," she said sulkily.

"Of course you are. Now why can't you sit quietly, as Sylvia is, and enjoy the evening? I'm sure young Master Baston would prefer it that way."

She looked at the young man archly.

"Now wouldn't you?" she asked, giving him her most radiant smile.

Master Baston being only about fourteen could handle this situation only clumsily.

"Oh well, I don't know," he said. "Guess I'd better see what the Pater wants. Excuse me please," and he disappeared at top speed in the direction of the saloon.

Laura looked at her mother, her dark eyes sharp with bitterness. She had been made to look a fool and the irony of it was that Aunt Sheilagh would never know.

Laura flung away and found a new seat for herself along at the rails on the port side. She leaned her head on her arms as they lay along the rails and sat brooding out over the river.

She stayed thus all the way back to Pepper Tree Bay.

Vicky, Mary, young Master Baston and I

could get nothing out of either Laura or Sylvia. They sat on opposite sides of the deck, their backs to one another and, one thought, to the world. They dreamed out in silence over the river.

It was not of young Baston that Laura dreamed. He had been no more than an appendage, a walking-stick, a foil to her own liveliness. Who knows of what Sylvia dreamed, unless it was her diary and her letter-writing to Danny.

They were very young to be troubled by romance.

We were too tired and sleepy to have our attention much engaged by the business of return and tying up. We trundled off the launches, found our way through a maze of people to a maze of cabs and cars and so by the river road crept back to Pepper Tree Bay and our homes.

This was the hour when our parents did not feel the children were an asset. They would have liked to stay longer in the Club talking to their friends, and they would have liked *not* to deal with a handful of tired and disagreeable children. For we were disagreeable, chiefly on account of Laura who was alternately rude to her parents and then her cousins. Only Sylvia escaped her barbs when she was in this mood.

It was shortly after this that Laura went back to Ireland. Word came that Uncle Dennis, Danny's father, had died. Within a few months word came that Uncle Rory had died in Canada. Till then we had not known that Uncle Rory had gone to Canada. It now transpired he had left the Royal Irish Constabulary to join the Canadian Mounted Police. This would have sounded very glamorous to us—if we had only known.

It seems Uncle Rory had been lost in the frozen wastes and he was now abandoned as dead.

This made two of our family, Mama's brother and Uncle Rory, lost and presumed dead in the vast silences of a new country. For years afterwards we built beautiful fantasies of one or other unexpectedly returning from the silence. Loaded with gold, of course. Rory, we were sure, was in Klondyke, just as Mama's brother was nursing a private and immense nugget somewhere in the desert north of the Coolgardie gold-fields.

"That's one down to Ireland, one to Australia, and one to Canada," Uncle

William said. Three of the Montgomery brothers had died and there was none left in the homeland. There was a kind of bitter irony in Uncle William's words for somehow this distribution between countries of the bodies of Montgomeries was something inherent in the principle of disintegration that seemed to be operating in the family.

"We'd better all get out of it," my father said, meaning out of Australia, as if our presence there had something to do with family catastrophe. I did not understand the tears my father and Uncle William had in their eyes for they had never spoken well of Dennis or Rory. One had imagined they were plague spots on the family escutcheon.

"At least he came to an honourable end," my father said of Rory. Of Dennis they said, "And a fine mess we'll find Magillicuddy to be," and then the tears would shine behind their eyes again, and again my father would say, "We'd better all get out of it."

For some time there was talk of both families packing up and going back to Ireland. It was all idle talk, for Magillicuddy had gone by inheritance to Danny and though Uncle William had money we had not. Moreover there was Mama. There was no pull back to Ireland for Mama, and I think she knew when she looked at my father with that little worried frown between her brows and a sharp sad light in her eyes that it wouldn't be long before it would be "Two down to Australia". My father did not have the health to begin again in Ireland. He was a sick man these days and looked it.

So Uncle William went back, chiefly to see how things stood with Danny, who was now sixteen, and to see how much of his own money he might put back into Magillicuddy. He took Laura with him. It was regarded as quite the thing to take a young girl abroad for the sake of her education.

"And so that she can learn to speak properly," Uncle William added.

I think Mama would have liked her children to go abroad as part of education. Her feet, however, were more firmly planted on Australian soil than those of the Montgomeries.

She was alone in the world, without a relative, except her children. Her father, a structural engineer, had come to Australia at the invitation of C. Y. O'Connor to assist in the construction of Fremantle Harbour but he never put his foot on the land "down under".

He had an obscure kidney complaint that the sea voyage lit up. He died two days out from port and was buried at sea. Mama landed with her mother, a redhead with a glorious voice, a divine figure and a feather brain, her sister and her brother. The children were all less than sixteen years of age. Arthur the brother set out for the gold-fields and joined a gold-rush out of Coolgardie. He was never heard of again and doubtless, like so many others, had died of thirst in the desert. Mama's sister married very young and died in childbirth. Her mother, who had no stamina for this strange harsh land, developed galloping consumption and died after a few weeks' illness. Mama had been alone in a strange country and she had made her own way by means of the nursing profession. She understood the battle for life. Australia had been her enemy, and she had come to terms with it. In Australia one knew what one was fighting, and if one had the will to survive, one survived. In Ireland there was nothing to fight, except political troubles, yet somehow decline was insidious in a family like the Montgomeries. Mama could fight the tangibles but had no weapons for the intangibles.

Fundamentally she recognized her children

were Australians. Different from Laura and Sylvia, they were born in Australia. Though their father and uncle would never admit it, they belonged to this vast continent down under. They had taken from the land that sired them its tenacity and its way of life. They were a living contradiction to their father and their uncle.

Mama could not have formed any of this into an argument, or even into words. She behaved instinctively and resisted an uprooting and a return to Ireland.

It was decided that Aunt Sheilagh and Sylvia would remain in the Pepper Tree Bay house for the winter while Uncle William and Laura were abroad. They would wait on their return to make any final decisions.

None of us, however, had any doubt about it that Uncle William had gone home to Ireland to take over Magillicuddy and Danny and put them both in order against the return of the rest of his family.

He bargained, however, without Danny, without Mulligan the steward at Magillicuddy and above all without the Stock Exchanges of both London and Australia. But this is anticipating my story.

5

MRS. PRESTON lived in a small five-roomed cottage around the bend of the river from Pepper Tree Bay. She was a medium-sized woman of middle age, a little shabby, very plain, though generally known both amongst the young people and the older of Pepper Tree Bay as kind.

For some reason unknown, except she was remotely connected by marriage to one of the pioneering families, Mrs. Preston was quite an identity in Pepper Tree Bay. She had no wealth, indeed seemed poor in comparison with the pastoralists. She had no particular charm and certainly no looks. Yet throughout the year nearly everyone who was somebody in Pepper Tree Bay would perform the rite of putting on a calling dress and hat, a long pair of gloves and announce, "I'm going to call on Mrs. Preston." And a formal call would forthwith be made.

There was no social function at which Mrs. Preston was not present.

"Lady Denton is having an At Home," Aunt Sheilagh announced to Mama.

Mama nodded.

"Yes. I had a card last week. Shall we go together?"

"Of course. Do you suppose I might ask the cab to call for Mrs. Preston as we go round the river?"

Mama nodded again.

"I'm sure Susan Baston and her mother will call for Mrs. Preston, but we might inquire."

It was taken for granted that Mrs. Preston, who was no particular friend of Lady Denton's, would have received a card, and that someone would call for her.

Lady Denton's At Home would be something a little different from the usual functions of Pepper Tree Bay so there was even less reason for presupposing Mrs. Preston's presence.

Lady Denton was a *t'other-sider* and there had been considerable deliberations between the ladies of Pepper Tree Bay as to whether she should be called on at all, let alone admitted to their circles. Her antecedents had been gone into and a great deal of her personal history aired in a thorough-going way. The fact that Lady Denton had considerable position and prestige in New South Wales and was married to a distinguished lawyer and politician did not in any way influence things in her favour. She was a *t'other-sider* and had come to Western Australia on the exact terms of all *t'other-siders*. Sir Ronald Denton had seen the possibilities of the development of the State and had come west to see for himself, possibly to invest and even take up residence. In the meantime he and his wife had taken a house in Pepper Tree Bay for two years.

He had done the right thing by getting himself nominated for the Pastoralists' Club and buying a luxury launch. Lady Denton had done the right thing by appearing elegant, correct, and attending Matins at eleven o'clock on Sunday mornings.

But still the residents of Pepper Tree Bay deliberated. The permanent residents could do nothing until the pastoralists and members of the pioneering families had made a move. No matter how much money these former people had, they were humble fry compared with the pastoralists and they knew that Lady Denton would know the difference in status and *not* be flattered by an original move coming from them.

Aunt Sheilagh had sat in our drawing-room and discussed the matter with Mama.

"She really appears to be a charming woman," she said solicitously, as if being born or bred on the other side of Australia was a kind of leprosy that made charm add pity to the disease, much as anyone says of a cripple, "And such a pretty girl too!"

"Well, I shall call," said Mama firmly. If she thought everyone else's attitude was silly she didn't say so.

"That's all right for you, Helen. You're the Rector's wife. You can. In fact it's your duty to call on everyone."

"I shall ask her to the Rectory to meet other people."

Aunt Sheilagh's delicate eyebrows looked as if she would like to ask, "Mrs. Phillips of the Ladies' Auxiliary? Miss Tennant of the Girls' Friendly Society? Mrs. Sampson of the Mothers' Union?"

But she didn't ask those questions. In her heart she knew very well that if Mama asked Susan and Anne Baston to come to the Rectory to meet Lady Denton, they would come, chiefly on account of my father's charm and

93

Vicky's love for them. But they would come and that would be quite enough to establish Lady Denton.

So Aunt Sheilagh went away and said she would consult Mrs. Maynard-Arnold.

In the fullness of time everybody called, including funny, drab, insipid Mrs. Preston, taken along by the Bastons. Lady Denton then left cards in the proper quarters and now here she was, accepted and established, sending out cards for an At Home.

Laura, had she been here instead of in Ireland, would have seen the irony of this situation. Not about Mrs. Preston but about Aunt Sheilagh from all the way across the world deciding on the desirability or otherwise of someone coming from across Australia. The arrogance of the Montgomeries again!

Basically the reasons for this kind of closed society were not snobbish but sound. The members of it had one thing in common—the ownership of the land from which they extracted such wealth as maintained the State, and be they rich or poor they were together for the sake of one another's society and claim to kinship. And they did stick together, rich and poor. Hence Mrs. Preston.

The *t'other-siders* represented business and their society with one another was competitive. The poor amongst them were outcasts. From this group the landed gentry walled themselves off. To it they admitted the clergymen for the sake of their souls and people like Uncle William because they too, in their own country, came from the landed gentry.

To it Lady Denton was more or less admitted though it was never forgotten that she was not one of them. This might have been the case with Uncle William and Aunt Sheilagh too, but I was never likely to know it. I think her beauty and Uncle William's savage wit and charming Irish voice helped surmount all difficulties.

Lady Denton's At Home was the kind to which some exalted families might bring their eldest daughter. Since Vicky was in bed with bronchitis, Mama dressed me up in Vicky's best dress and I went instead.

I don't remember very much about the At Home. It was like most others, except that, in looking back, I remember that the sheep sat on one side of the elaborate drawing-room and the goats on the other. That is to say, the

95

Bastons and their relatives, the Maynard-Arnolds, the Lessiers and the Cooles were ranged together in a begloved and feather-waving group, some of them extremely dowdy, like Mrs. Preston, and on the other side were several very elegant ladies who wore imitation jewels and flowers on their hats because feathers had gone out of fashion.

Old Mrs. Stockman would raise her ear-trumpet and ask, "What is her name? What did you say her name was? Eh?" This of a lady she had met in other drawing-rooms quite a number of times. One knew that Mrs. Stockman would never remember the other lady's name. Not as long as they both lived. It was a matter of principle.

Mrs. Preston asked Aunt Sheilagh why she had not brought "dear little Sylvia", since Laura was in Ireland. Aunt Sheilagh said Sylvia was not really quite strong enough for so strenuous an occasion as an afternoon tea-party.

"Dear Sylvia," said Mrs. Preston. "She must come and have lunch with me one day next week."

"Sylvia would love that," said Aunt Sheilagh. "How good and kind you are, Mrs. Preston." Aunt Sheilagh then turned to those on her other side. "Sylvia is to have lunch with Mrs. Preston next week." This was said with an air of triumph much as she might well say on another occasion, "Of course one will have to buy a new hat for His Excellency's garden-party. The Governor is such a *dear*, isn't he?"

Sylvia when confronted with the invitation would say "Yes, of course. How kind of Mrs. Preston!" Just as any one of us would have said.

She would put on her second-best dress and her second-best gloves and ride around the bay in the gentle dignity of Williams's cab. At Mrs. Preston's house she would not notice the musky smell or that Mrs. Preston, while quite clean, still did not look as if she'd had a bath that morning. And there would be fly-spots on the paper flowers and some of breakfast's crumbs still on the table. Just as none of us would have noticed these things, not intentionally at any rate. Moreover for several days after Sylvia would say, just as any one of us would have said, "On Wednesday I went to lunch with Mrs. Preston." This would be received with a nod of approval by the listeners.

Laura, when she was older and back

amongst us, was the only one who could give an explanation of the mystery of Mrs. Preston's position with old and young.

"First of all, they" (by which she meant the pastoralist society) "are loyal to their own kind. She's one of them, though very insignificantly so. She is the outward and tangible demonstration of the fact that a family matters more than beauty or money. But mostly it's a kind of insurance against fate itself. Drought or flood might destroy their vast properties in the north but nothing can destroy their place in society. Mrs. Preston is a precedent to which any one of them, if the fates are unkind, might look."

When Laura said this I remembered another incident of that At Home of Lady Denton's. One of the more elegant ladies from the goats' side of the drawing-room, that is to say, those who occasionally were with the sheep but never of them, was in some gay and laughing moment of conversation with Susan and Anne Baston when Lady Denton decided it was time to play musical chairs with her guests and move them about amongst one another. She suggested this lady, a Mrs. Smythson, might like to come and chat to Mrs. Strickland, Lady Denton had already seen to it a chair had become vacant beside Mrs. Stockman.

Mrs. Smythson turned on parting from Anne and Susan.

"You must come to see me. I am having some ladies in to tea on Friday week. May I send you an invitation?"

"How very kind of you," said Susan, then looked at Anne with a wrinkled forehead.

"That is the day Mrs. Preston is coming to show us her preserving recipes," said Anne.

"Perhaps I could come another day," Mrs. Preston, who was sitting quite near, said in her kind voice.

"Not at all," said Susan. "We had arranged that day. It cannot be altered. Perhaps Anne and I might call on Mrs. Smythson some other time."

And that was that. Mrs. Smythson was not snubbed. On the contrary Susan said "some other time" quite eagerly. But a date with Mrs. Preston was as inviolable as a scientific law. If Mrs. Smythson knew Pepper Tree Bay she knew that. A date for exchanging recipes with Mrs. Preston was as unalterable as a garden-party at Government House.

Aunt Sheilagh was meticulous about arranging the day for Sylvia's lunch with

Mrs. Preston and also about a later day when she herself might call, though it was less than three weeks since Aunt Sheilagh had last called on Mrs. Preston, and less than ten days since Mrs. Preston had returned the call.

Was it possible that Aunt Sheilagh in some mystic way could dip into the future and see herself a second Mrs. Preston, never plain or uninteresting, of course, but nevertheless in society because of herself and not because of her big house and fine clothes?

Returning home to the Rectory in the cab—Aunt Sheilagh was dropping us off—Mama said, "I really must find time to call on Mrs. Preston. It's such a time since I was there. It's the Girls' Friendly Society and Mothers' Union that takes up so much of my time."

Aunt Sheilagh inclined her very elegant head with its equally picturesque hat.

"I've arranged myself to call on the twentieth," she said. Then added with an air of firm approval, "*Dear* Mrs. Preston."

Mama agreed. There was no one in the world, not even we children, who would have dreamed of thinking, let alone saying, "But she's such a dull dowdy woman."

It was Mrs. Preston, however, who unwittingly sounded the first note of alarm in the Montgomery households of Pepper Tree Bay.

When Sylvia returned, again in Williams's cab, from her lunch with Mrs. Preston she said, "Mama, what is a buyer's or a seller's market?"

"Something to do with Papa's business," Aunt Sheilagh said. "It has to do with goldmines . . . though what I really never asked."

"Mrs. Preston said that Mr. Preston said that the market had turned and was now a seller's market and he was surprised that Papa had chosen such a time to go abroad."

"Whatever could Mr. Preston have meant?" Aunt Sheilagh inquired of Mama.

Mama's forehead puckered. Before she had married our father she had nursed on the gold-fields and she knew that gold shares rocketed or fell away to nothing according to manipulation and the Stock Exchanges quite as much as they did according to how much gold there was in any one mine.

"You should write and tell William what he said," Mama said. "Rumours are important things in the gold market . . . and Mr. Preston does work in a stockbroker's office."

"The great part of William's fortune is in Coolgardie Mines," said Aunt Sheilagh confidently. "They're full of gold."

And in her great confidence she neglected to write and tell Uncle William of Mr. Preston's remarks.

6

IT was six months before Uncle William came back to Pepper Tree Bay. He had left Laura behind.

There were many family conferences in the study at the Rectory and this time we children were not privy to them all. We only overheard when habit was too much for my father and Uncle William, and they forgot to shut the door. Or when my father's feelings were too great for him and words burst from him at the table in our big book-filled dining-room.

My father looked much older, and often sick these days, though Mama said it had nothing to do with Montgomery affairs. It had everything to do with himself . . . and his heart.

"Has he got a bad heart, Mama?" I asked, remembering that beloved Uncle Tim had had a heart attack and died just when we, his family of nieces, most needed him.

"Not a bad heart . . . just heartache," Mama said.

I knew it had something to do with the fact that he had overworked when establishing the Grammar School on the corner and the fact the Church had a policy of what my father called "unwieldy obstructionism". It also had to do with the fact he was an Irishman in exile and though he railed continuously against his own country he never really liked Australia.

Spiritually he was homeless. Uncle Tim should not have died. We all needed Uncle Tim, and he had gone from us. Moreover we children had all developed most of the Australian characteristics that were least liked and loved by the men from the old country. Uncle William didn't help by saying on the day he arrived back from Ireland, "Thank God I left Laura behind. Those children's voices, Joe! You'll have to do something about them. And they run wild!"

He had forgotten that in Ireland they also had run wild, which was quite acceptable as an Irish characteristic in that country, though unforgivable in a new country.

Uncle William was worried about things other than his nieces' manner of speech.

"We'll have to sell the town house," I heard him say to my father. "Sheilagh will just have to alter her way of living for a few months. I need the capital. Next year the market will turn again. There's plenty of gold in Coolgardie."

The house in Pepper Tree Bay was sold and the William Montgomery family returned to the gold-fields. We did not see them again for many a long day.

Then my father died.

Up there in Kalgoorlie one imagined Uncle William saying, "Two down to Australia!" and the pain of Father's death would chiefly be expressed in horror that another Montgomery was to be buried in these barbaric wastes.

If ever Uncle William got very rich again one imagined him having all the dead Montgomeries disinterred and taken home to Ireland.

In the meantime he came down from the gold-fields to bury my father but he could do nothing about helping us as a family. He had lost all his money.

"You'll manage, Helen," he said to my mother. "You've got what no Montgomery ever had, *Stamina*. You're a fighter. All I can give you is my blessing."

Aunt Sheilagh, one understood, was resorting to selling her jewellery.

"Not the pearls . . . and the emerald necklace . . . " Mama cried in dismay.

"If the market doesn't turn, they'll go next."

"But what about all the gold in those mines?"

"It's there. It costs too much to take it out and the price of gold is still dropping."

He was weary and tired. His face was lined and his eyes had the pale blue misted look that all the Montgomeries wore when there were tears behind them.

"And Magillicuddy?"

"They didn't want my money when they could have had it for the asking. That Mulligan, and those Dublin lawyers! Ha! Fools and rapscallions! Afraid I'd stake a claim on Magillicuddy and wrest it from Danny! Now if they'd consulted me about Danny's education, and the stables at Magillicuddy, I'd have helped them. I had money then. But no! Not at all! Wrapped up in their own importance and never a good word to say for anyone who had left the old country!"

Thus spoke Uncle William, bitterly.

"And Laura?" Mama asked.

"She'll have to come out. Can't keep her there eating her head off when there's barely enough to put oatmeal on the table in Australia."

Uncle William went back to the gold-fields and Mama took us all, five of us by this time, round the bay from Pepper Tree Bay nearer the city where she could earn a living for us partly by nursing and partly by letting off rooms in the ramshackle house that became the family home.

Once or twice Aunt Sheilagh came down from the gold-fields but we were too busy with our own affairs and our own troubles to do much for Aunt Sheilagh. She still had her emeralds, and her pearls she still wore in bed at night "to keep their lustre".

Laura came back from Ireland and for one year both she and I were in the same class at school. Laura was a boarder and I was a day girl and it was my solemn duty to keep Laura fed with any tit-bits that fell from our table. There weren't many tit-bits in those days for any of us, and Laura never quite believed I didn't have the apples and cakes to bring her. Laura's ideas of being poor were the ideas of

107

her own side of the family. They only had one house now, and no car. Aunt Sheilagh didn't buy new dresses for them all every change of season. But she wore her pearls, locked up her emeralds, and the table was always full of good food. They simply didn't understand that ours was not. And Mama, in all her life, was never to own pearls or emeralds.

Laura, now sixteen, had come back from Ireland not only taller and older, but much more beautiful. The cold northern climate had restored her complexion, and her features, her high square forehead and aquiline nose, were moulded in their pattern for all time.

Her associates in Ireland had planed away the rough edges of an Australian accent. She did not have what is called an "Irish brogue" but she had a lovely speaking voice, a little deeper than ours with a mellifluous round of her sentences. It was as much a striking part of her personality as her dark hair with the bronze shining through it when it was washed or when she stood in the sun. She had an oval face with a firm jaw and a generous mobile mouth. Her eyes were too solemn for beauty when she was not smiling. But when she did smile or laugh her whole face transformed itself and the muscles round her mouth and at the corners of her eyes worked so hard one was never sure whether Laura was going to laugh or cry. It was then that her eyes, due to their colour, were truly brilliant.

She could not bear to hear anything sad, or a sad poem or story read. She always wanted to cry, but was ashamed to show it.

Once she was called upon to read aloud in class, and the passage chosen was from *Scott's Last Expedition to the South Pole*. When Laura came to the passage where Captain Oates walks out into the snow she stopped.

"Go on," the mistress said. "Why have you stopped, Laura? This is the most heroic part of the whole story."

Laura opened her mouth, and then closed it.

"Is something the matter, Laura?"

"I have a cold. My throat aches."

"My poor child. You should have said so before. Take the book and continue, Pauline Dulvertin. Laura, you may go outside and get a drink of water."

I knew that Laura couldn't go on and read where Oates walked out into the snow because she would have cried. A shameful thing for a sixteen-year-old girl to do in a classroom.

In the playing-fields Laura had moderate success but she was never very popular with the other girls. She was too aggressive and often impatient of other people's mistakes. She was very good at hockey though not fast enough for the position she played on the wing but she was quite intolerant of other girls' tardiness. In tennis a different side of her character appeared. She played in partnership with another girl who was selfish and childish. This girl, Bena Turner, would not use her backhand. She would not play on the left-hand side of the court for this reason. Laura, oddly docile in the face of real selfishness, always played the left-hand side, though she much preferred the right-hand, and she often ran behind her partner to take the other's back-hand strokes for her. She never complained of her partner's short temper. In fact her role was always to mollify and even sympathize when others knew that Bena Turner really needed a good slapping. Even when Laura climbed two places on the bumping board and should have played with the number one girl in the first pair she remained in the second pair as Bena's partner because, as the sports mistress said, "No one else could possibly play with Bena."

There was no possible accounting for Laura's role in this odd partnership for she and Bena were not particular friends and once off the tennis-court saw little of one another.

Somehow one associated this with Laura's offering to, or a placating of, the gods—her gods were many in Ireland—and the Literature mistress in the school.

Nobody confused Laura's attachment to the Literature mistress with one of those unhealthy passions the young sometimes have for those older and in authority.

She did not go about dreamy-eyed, or writing poetry. She merely said, "Miss Lawson is my favourite mistress," and continued to say it flatly all the year. She took Miss Lawson's snapshot more often than was necessary and she liked to walk with her to the studio for morning prayers. Yet one felt that a good deal of it was play-acting. Miss Carson, the mathematics mistress, was generally set up to be the class idol, and Laura, incapable of falling in with the mob, set up one of her own.

"How you could possibly have a 'pash' on

Miss Lawson!" one girl said sarcastically. "Why, she has big feet. I bet she takes size six in shoes."

Laura hadn't noticed Miss Lawson's feet but she took particular note of them now. True the feet were rather long but on the other hand they were very narrow and beautifully shod. Moreover Miss Lawson had finely moulded ankles. Laura pointed this out and being an authority on horses—Magillicuddy bred horses from their own stud—she insisted Miss Lawson's feet were a criterion of good breeding.

When Laura was at loggerheads with her class companions she would advance towards Miss Lawson at the end of a lesson and ask politely, "Please Miss Lawson would you mind my taking your photograph in the quad?" This in spite of the fact a photograph had been taken only a week or two before.

Miss Lawson always walked and talked and looked like a perfect lady. She would incline her head with just a hint of graciousness but also a touch of amusement in her eyes, and comply.

I felt quite sure the whole performance was a gesture of defiance to the class on Laura's part.

She did indeed tell me long after that while she never entertained the commonplace "pash" for Miss Lawson she did in time learn really to love her.

"She was such a perfect lady," Laura said wistfully. "I could have been making an ass of her, though I never intended that either, but somehow silliness turned to real admiration. Most girls are ashamed of their schoolgirl crazes but I'm never ashamed of my craze for taking Miss Lawson's photograph. If I had to behave like a fool over someone I'm proud I had such good taste in the 'someone'."

When Laura expressed these sentiments I did not ask her about the occasion when Laura presented Miss Lawson with a bouquet on the wrong birthday.

Laura, of course, had an autograph book and a birthday book just as everyone else in the school had one. Miss Lawson's signature was in both. Sometime during the week before Miss Lawson's birthday Laura must have looked at her book but confused the day. On the Tuesday she was determined Miss Lawson should have a bouquet of flowers from the class. She collected the money from the girls, ordered the flowers and arranged for herself to make the presentation.

On the great morning she had the flowers hidden under her desk until Miss Lawson had completed her lesson and was making for the door in order to give way to the next teacher coming in.

There was something unhappy about Laura and I think she had already discovered her error, that the birthday was not this day but next Tuesday. She could not possibly tell the girls, the ridicule would have crucified her. She must have been hoping that out of the kindness of her heart Miss Lawson would accept today as her birthday, without saying a word, and that no other girl had looked at a birthday book that might contain Miss Lawson's signature.

Laura's face was a flaming scarlet as she left her place and carried the bouquet to the desk.

"Happy Birthday from the class, Miss Lawson," she said, and the words were so thick and confused they gurgled out.

The other girls must have mistaken Laura's performance for the evidences of the real and heroic type of "pash", a disease that smote a few despised girls occasionally.

Miss Lawson inclined her head, smiled happily at the girls and said, "Thank you, girls. I think now I'm going to have a very happy birthday. And thank you, Laura, for bringing the flowers to me."

I am quite sure Laura's eyes met Miss Lawson's in an agonizing plea and that the merry smile Miss Lawson gave meant there would be a conspiracy of silence between them. Laura did not mind that the girls said, "Gosh, Laura, you're getting really quite goofy about the Lawson. Look out or you'll turn into one of those saddos who want to throw themselves out of dormitory windows under somebody's feet."

Laura shrugged. The next teacher came in and the incident was over. I knew it was the wrong day because this day was my birthday and I knew I had never before shared my birthday with Miss Lawson. But I never gave Laura away. And I never forgot her scarlet face.

The real reason why Laura was not entirely popular amongst her school companions was because she was different from them. She was a newcomer to the school, she had had a much wider and more cultured and liberal education than they had had and her voice set her apart. The Australian adolescent schoolgirl is a gregarious animal. She hunts in a pack and does her utmost to disguise herself as part of the pack rather than emerge as an individual. Laura was essentially individual, and her voice was the kind that other girls imitated behind her back with a touch of malice. It was what they called a "put-on" voice. Laura, on one occasion challenged with this accusation, remarked haughtily, "It is not I who have occasion to 'put-on' a voice, but you Australians. In Europe a bison is a thing men hunt. In Australia it's a thing they wash their hands in."

Of course as no Australian could hear herself say "bison" instead of "baison" they just didn't believe this. The statement was further evidence of Laura's airs.

As Laura could not bear to be looked down upon by anyone she determined to do the one thing that would exalt her in her own eyes if not in the eyes of the other girls. She would pass all her examinations with flying colours.

Against the wishes and will of her mistresses she took two years' work in one, passed her matriculation examination with ease, distinguishing herself in mathematics, and passed from the school into adulthood while the rest of us had to work at textbooks for another year.

Laura was not basically unhappy at school. I think she sought to please and the very endeavour robbed her of that sense of humour that is essential to real popularity. Quite recently she told me that for years after she left school she used to dream she was back there. She would dream she was talking in the quad, or climbing a staircase or knocking at the prefects' door. Each time she awoke from her dream she had a sense of desolation and loss. She was out in the world and could never go back again. Someone once told her these dreams belonged to the "return to the womb" and "the flight from life" theory of inadequacy. Laura pooh-poohed the idea scornfully. But I have sometimes wondered.

Laura had all the weapons for battling with life successfully. She was predestined to battle and succeed, to withstand all onslaughts except that of the heart. Whenever she failed she was betrayed by her heart.

For the next six years she was to succeed in all that she touched except in the matter of her love for Danny. In this she could not even fight, for Sylvia, by her frailty, took the weapons from her hand.

Laura never wavered in her love for Danny. She never admitted it to anyone. But it was there, with her, day and night. His beautiful angelic face, his air of never being quite with one, his very essence which was of Ireland, enslaved her. It enmeshed her in an alchemy of desire, and utter frustration.

She was not particularly tidy with her possessions and her writing-case was the kind that bulged at the seams. If she was looking for some postcard or old piece of correspondence then she scattered the contents of her writing-case all over her bed, and sometimes over the floor. That is how I knew she had hundreds of snaps of Danny.

Danny standing on the lawn in the front of Magillicuddy. Danny at the stables. Danny in a tweed coat with his gun. Danny dressed up in his high cut coat with a hard white collar with Mulligan, on his way to see the Dublin lawyers. Danny sitting down, standing up, lolling on the tennis court.

Miss Lawson had not been the only recipient of Laura's photographing attentions.

Sylvia likewise had snaps of Danny. Two of them, in miniature silver frames on her dressing-table. It was taken for granted in the Montgomery households that Danny was Sylvia's possession. A letter addressed from Magillicuddy either from Danny or Mulligan was always addressed to Sylvia. Sylvia read them aloud then filed them away neatly in a writing-case that did not bulge and probably held no other material. If Danny and Laura corresponded no one knew of it. And I doubt it.

When Laura first left school she enrolled at the University and stayed with us at "Forty-Five". Neither of these arrangements lasted long. As far as the University was concerned Laura could not bear to be bored and the lectures bored her to the point of illness.

"They go on and on and on," she cried in irritation and despair. "It's all in the books, if they'd only give us time to go and read them. They speak through closed lips and gaze at us blankly as if we were not there. I'm not good at listening. My thoughts wander and wander and then I have to go and learn it all up again somewhere else."

"That doesn't do you any harm," Mama said, feeling it was her business to keep Laura's feet on the earth. "And you seem to have passed your examinations well enough."

"But the hours of sitting still! I tell you, Aunt Helen, I can't stand it. The hands of the clock won't even crawl around."

Of life at "Forty-Five" she was equally frustrated and eloquent.

"It's so crowded, and everyone's so untidy. My God! The *noise*!"

Mama also thought "Forty-Five" was no place for Laura. She was of different stuff from her cousins and though Uncle William had lost his money Mama didn't see why Laura should go through the same kind of abyss of poverty into which we had suddenly plunged.

The William Montgomeries up there in the gold-fields probably had less income than we did, and we only had income from Mama's efforts, but they refused to suffer the indignities of the really poor. They simply accumulated debts, locked away the emeralds and various other pieces of jewellery, and awaited the day when the market would turn.

Mama never had a debt in her life and if there wasn't enough money to pay for butter on the weekly order then butter was omitted from it. This was bourgeois to Laura and not to be suffered. We didn't see why she should suffer it either when Sylvia and Aunt Sheilagh, four hundred miles away, ordered their butter up from Perth by the case.

So Laura abandoned the University and

went into the same stockbroker's office in which Mr. Preston was employed, and took a room with a balcony in an apartment house in Adelaide Terrace.

She bought herself a typewriter, taught herself typewriting from Pitman's Manual with a piece of cardboard over the keys so that she could learn "blind".

This reopened social connections with Mrs. Preston. Mama, probably feeling that as she was no longer doing for Laura what she ought to do for her by having her under her own roof, sought to consolidate Laura's position with the stockbroking firm by officially calling on Mrs. Preston. That Mr. Preston was little more in the firm than a kind of senior clerk was beside the point. Being who he was, Mama was sure that he would be of great future consequence to Laura. The idea sent Laura into hoots of derision.

"Why, he's just a frusty old man with an eye-shade on his head. He doesn't even *comb* his hair."

Mama ignored this. Laura couldn't possibly judge who was who at this stage of inexperience. It was beyond Mama's powers of comprehension that anyone so closely connected with the powerful pastoralists of the north-west and Pepper Tree Bay could be of "no consequence".

"You don't know what you're talking about, Laura," Mama said. "Mr. Preston is Mrs. Preston's husband."

There was no contradicting this, of course, and Mama drew on her gloves, kept Vicky home from the course for business girls that Vicky was taking, dressed her up in her best blue silk dress and proceeded in the direction of Pepper Tree Bay and Mrs. Preston's house.

She was able to write Aunt Sheilagh that night,

"Vicky and I called on Mrs. Preston today. Susan Baston was there and also two of the Miss Stockmans. We had tea and Mrs. Preston's usual cakes. She really is a *kind* woman. Mamie Strickland is entertaining us all to tea at the Swan Club next week. At least I won't look as shabby as Mrs. Preston . . . if I can manage to get there at all. But that is unkind of me. She is a dear good woman."

Aunt Sheilagh came to Perth to make sure that Laura was suitably settled in her "room and balcony". She stayed amidst the rabble in "Forty-Five" but unlike Laura she revelled in the family chaos.

"Oh darlings," she said. "It's just like *home* again. If only Joe . . . or dear Tim . . . were here to see how bravely you're all getting on."

She ate large quantities of fresh brown bread and butter, which Mama got in specially for her, and sat around and read novelettes. She took an inordinate interest in the "lodgers" and soon found they took an inordinate interest in her. Aunt Sheilagh passing through the main hall of "Forty-Five" was a sight for the gods to see. She wore her prettiest clothes, did her hair exquisitely, had a manner of drawing on her gloves and wearing her hat at an angle which said, "I'm just going to pay my call on the Governor" even if she was only going into town to do a little shopping. Besides, we all knew she had called on the Governor in her first twenty-four hours. When Gerry asked what did the Governor say to her we were all nonplussed and bitterly disappointed to learn that such a call merely meant entering the Visitors' Lodge and signing the Visitors' Book.

"What did you put on your best dress for, Aunty?" Denney asked.

"My darling, you always put on your best dress when you call on the Governor."

"But if he doesn't see you, does it matter?"

"Of course it matters. It's all a question of courtesy. It is *etiquette*. Just as much as it is a discourtesy *not* to call on the Governor when you're visiting the capital."

"But would he know you're visiting the capital, Aunty?"

"He would think it extremely discourteous if he did know and I hadn't called."

The expression in Laura's eyes as she listened to this conversation showed she was already in the ambivalent state of mind when she knew certain customs of society were fundamentally good and right but doubted their sense. She sensed the comedy in Aunt Sheilagh locking away her emeralds, selling the Pepper Tree Bay house, but continuing to make formal calls on the Governor.

"I don't suppose he even remembers her," said Denney in an undertone to me. Mama overheard it.

"I suppose he's forgotten us all," said Mama. "But that's not the *point*. It's a matter of courtesy and loyalty."

124

Evidently he had not forgotten us, after all. Or else his aide, or the man who reads the Visitors' Book, hadn't, for while Aunt Sheilagh was still in Perth, she and Laura, Mama and Vicky were invited to a garden-party at Government House.

This produced consternation not only in our *ménage* but in all the *ménages* of Pepper Tree Bay. Not the fact that *we* were invited but that there was a new Government in power and it was quite apparent to everyone that the new Members of Parliament would not wear top hats and morning suits. They would go in dusty grey melange lounge suits with the inevitable felt hats wedged down on their brows.

"I don't suppose they'll even take their hats off when they're speaking to His Excellency," said Mary Maynard-Arnold. "How ashamed we're going to be of those dreadful suits and those dreadful hats."

"Why do they get invited at all if they're so dreadful?" I asked.

"Because they run the country," Mama said.

"Ruin it," said Aunt Sheilagh, and this sentiment consolidated Aunt Sheilagh's position in Pepper Tree Bay.

"I don't altogether disapprove," Mama said thoughtfully. "After all they do represent the people, or some of the people. I suppose the Governor's here for them too."

This jeopardized Mama's position in Pepper Tree Bay for some years to come. Pepper Tree Bay thought that if Mama had to work she should keep quiet about it in the first place and even so she should keep herself in the position of the impoverished maiden aunt of Victorian days. She was not in a position to have ideas.

Throughout the discussions and preparation for the garden-party Laura remained truculent and hard to please. First she wanted an elaborate dress that would vie with the smartest imported by the richest. When it looked as if Uncle William would find money from somewhere to comply with this ("Can't have my daughter going round looking poverty-stricken. Anyone would think she was bog-Irish in having to argue about a dress") Laura suddenly changed her mind.

"Lots of people in the city are going," she announced. "The two partners in our firm are going, and they're not wearing top hats and morning suits."

"Nonsense," said Aunt Sheilagh, startled.

126

"They're both very well-known men. They can't possibly go unless they're properly dressed. They can't let Mr. Preston go better dressed than they are."

This caused Laura's latest expression to mutilate the contours of her face. It was one of extreme exasperation.

"Better dressed than Mr. Preston! His clothes belonged to his father, and they don't even fit him. What's more, they're never pressed or brushed; they just hang up in that dreadful wooden wardrobe on their back verandah waiting from year to year for the next Viceregal garden-party."

"A lot of people are like that," Mama said. "Nobody can buy those sort of clothes here nowadays, and they have to go looking like caricatures if they put on the things they've inherited."

"They should import them from England," Aunt Sheilagh said, still shocked.

"Some do," Laura said tartly. "But they always look as if they're showing off. The senior partner in the firm said it's a lot of bally nonsense for this climate anyway."

Aunt Sheilagh's face ought to have been photographed . . . the expression of astonishment and dismay was quite ludicrous.

"Whatever has got into you, Laura?"

"I'm not going over-dressed," Laura said shortly. "That's bad taste in this country."

"I don't know what William will say . . ."

"That I'm one more vulgarian and barbarian," said Laura. "That I've turned into an Australian and it all goes to show the leopard can change his spots after all."

This was what Mama called "Laura's Australian phase". I personally thought it was her "indecisive phase". She saw so much good in both worlds and so much that was regrettable, even ludicrous, in both worlds, and she couldn't make up her mind to which she wished to belong. She could understand that the manners and habits of another country and another climate would still be inviolate to first generation Australians. Indeed some she held inviolate herself. But she saw and agreed with the laughter that was in the faces of second and third generation Australians who just wanted to be Australians their own way.

None of these ideas could she formulate into thoughts any more than we, her cousins, could. She merely did one thing one minute and another thing the next. And believed violently and emotionally in what she did.

128

She got her own way about the dress, however, and wore one that was of a simple though striking pattern. Not realizing she was being inconsistent, she had it made by Miss Wilson.

Now Miss Wilson made all the dresses for the ladies of Pepper Tree Bay. She was expensive, finished off her work beautifully, but had one basic pattern. No one could mistake a Miss Wilson dress. There was something about the neckline and the way a belt was finished off that were hall-marks. In a sense one could have placarded all the ladies who were north-west ladies, or south-west ladies—meaning they were wives of the landed gentry—as they walked down the Terrace in the city or in and out of the portals of the Swan Club. Whether it be a morning dress or an afternoon dress, it had the unmistakable Miss Wilson cut. The ladies wore narrow long vamp shoes and real pearls. In time one began to feel this was the aristocratic look, just as in an older country drooping eyelids, a bent nose and slightly prominent teeth can often suggest noble birth.

There was no question about it, Laura looked very aristocratic as she stood in the hall of "Forty-Five" drawing on her long gloves and standing easily but exactly correctly in her lovely narrow long vamp shoes. And so, of course, did Aunt Sheilagh. Mama had broadened in the bust and hip-line and she couldn't afford Miss Wilson so she went as herself. Which to us was very nice. We didn't think the Miss Wilson touch would suit Mama and she could never have got her feet into narrow shoes. Besides she was never likely to own real pearls and we children couldn't see the difference between her imitation ones and Aunt Sheilagh's real ones. Mama had her lovely friendly face . . . which always made her look beautiful to us. Vicky looked just what she was too, a pretty china ornament off the drawing-room mantelpiece. When I once said this, Aunt Sheilagh said, "Don't ever call it a *mantelpiece*. That's a bourgeois word."

For the same reasons Aunt Sheilagh called a *waistcoat* a *westcot*. And she tried to teach us to say "tame" instead of "toime". In Pepper Tree Bay one said either "tame" or "toime" but never "time". I've often wondered how it is really said.

We four remaining Montgomeries had to wait till they all came home to hear how the

Members of Parliament got on in their lounge suits and felt hats. We sat and played around at home and grieved for the loss of prestige that would be inflicted on the community by our MPs.

We burst in a wave on the returning party and would not wait for them to enter the house.

"Well, how did they look? Tell us about it! Were they very shocking?"

"Whatever are you talking about?" Mama demanded.

"Did who look shocking?" Aunt Sheilagh asked, her pretty eyebrows arching in a gay kind of curiosity. Clearly they had all had a good time because they were gay and smiling.

"The Members of Parliament, of course."

"Oh them. I didn't see them, did you, Helen?"

Mama was pulling off her gloves and biting her tongue between her teeth in the effort.

"I don't know any."

"They were those men walking round the flower-beds with His Excellency," said Laura in her exasperated voice. "They didn't look any more dreadful than all the rest of the men. There were hardly any top hats at all."

131

"I thought you didn't agree with top hats, Laura?" I said accusingly.

"Neither I do. That doesn't say they needn't go to a good tailor occasionally."

"What about your own dress? You wouldn't have an imported one, and Uncle William *said* . . ."

"My dress was very good indeed," said Laura haughtily. "I'm glad I didn't look like Elizabeth Maynard-Arnold."

"Oh, what did *she* look like?" We goggled and got excited about this. Elizabeth Maynard-Arnold and her mother had been abroad—we'd read all about them in the papers, particularly about their trip to Paris. Elizabeth was quite a celebrated beauty and very soignée.

We were inside the house now. Mary was putting the kettle on for a cup of tea and Mama and Aunt Sheilagh were sitting back in the armchairs, their hats off and their shoes nearly off.

"We stood just behind her while we were waiting to be received," said Laura. "She had a black satin dress that was as tight as a glove and had a hundred buttons right down the back. I started to count them but she moved on when I'd just got to the waist-line. She had a little black satin pill-box hat . . ."

"She looked very smart," Aunt Sheilagh said.

"She did," said Laura airily. "Everyone looked at her all the afternoon."

"You could have looked just as smart, Laura. Your father . . ."

"I didn't want to look smart that way, Mama," Laura was beginning to get angry. Mama poured oil on troubled waters.

"Laura is much better looking than Elizabeth," she said. "She is not so affected and her complexion is *natural.*"

"Thank you, Aunt Helen," said Laura, still tossing her head a little. Mary came in with the tea.

"Thank goodness we can still pour tea out of a silver teapot," said Aunt Sheilagh with a sigh. "I don't know what Government House parties are coming to. Once they were small select drawing-room affairs and tea was poured from a silver tea service."

"Didn't they have one at Government House, Aunty?" Denney asked.

"My darling! How could they? All those hundreds of people!"

This subject of the top hats and teapots was debated in all the drawing-rooms and on all the front verandahs of Pepper Tree Bay.

Laura was in her exasperated mood.

"How could they serve all those hundreds of people out of silver teapots?" she asked as we all sat on the edge of the verandah at Innanup, the Bastons' house by the river. The grown-ups all sat in the armchairs and we were allowed to listen in to the conversation, occasionally to interrupt.

"They shouldn't invite hundreds," Mrs. Maynard-Arnold said with a touch of arrogance.

"Well...I...don't...know..." Mr. Maynard-Arnold drawled when he was thinking as he talked and he had curious views on changing customs. Unexpectedly some of the other pastoralists turned out to agree with him. "What's...it...all...about...anyway? Something...for you...ladies...to get dressed...up...about. And talk...about. Why shouldn't the...poor devils...go? It's ...a free...country."

"But they don't understand what it's all about." This with real righteousness.

"Who does?" Mr. Maynard-Smith was clipping the end of a new cigar. "Could any one..."

of the fools . . . ford a flood with . . . five . . . hundred . . . head of cattle. Could . . . they . . . fight the bloody drought . . . three . . . years . . . running?"

"You're damn' right, Bob," said old Mr. Baston, slapping his hand down on the arm of the chair. "Why don't they get out and open up the country the way we did? Sitting around polishing their top hats . . . .!"

One knew without the slightest shadow of doubt that Mr. Baston would never again wear a top hat.

We children now followed Laura's example and defected from the principle that all people worthy of an invitation to Government House should be rich and well-born. We smiled and wriggled our shoulders and were profoundly impressed with what our elders—on the male side—had said. Their words opened up visions of stampeding cattle, flood-devastated rivers and thousands of miles of country burnt to paper brown by the dreadful drought. Our idols ceased to be men of fashion and fine deportment and became the rugged north-westers who endured the privations of disaster for nine months a year as a prelude to coming to Pepper Tree Bay for the summer season and the launch picnics.

"You . . . know . . . Bob," said Mr. Baston, also beginning to drawl. "Remember the time we picked up Jim Connell . . . with a broken back . . . and carried him a hundred and thirty miles to Carnarvon?"

"By God . . . I do. What did we look like then, eh? The bloody niggers . . . had nothing . . . on us. How'd . . . it do . . . if . . . we turned up . . . at . . . Government House . . . like . . . that . . . eh?"

He roared with laughter. His laugh was a bellow that rang out over the garden and even down the street.

"How'd . . . you . . . ladies . . . like that . . . eh?" he shouted.

This irritated the ladies and they said so. Laura's face was a study. This was a different kind of arrogance and she wasn't sure it wasn't as snobbish as wearing a top hat. It was a flaunting of endurance.

So that when courtly, diffident and not very clever Mr. Preston turned in to the drive of Innanup Laura looked more kindly on him. She felt a sense of release as she watched him bowing, almost to the hips, over Mrs. Baston's hand, bowing in turn to all the ladies, and speaking in a quiet subdued tone about the weather and other correct and safe topics of conversation. Mr. Preston might be no more than a clerk in the firm of Beale and Beale, Stockbrokers, but he was a gentleman. So Laura was ranged again on the side of the upper classes that were *polished*.

She was quite sure that Mr. Preston would wear his top hat till it fell to pieces from decrepitude. And when it did fall to pieces, then he would absent himself from Government House altogether.

7

THAT notable week-end over, Aunt Sheilagh went back to the gold-fields, Laura went back to the stockbrokers and I went back to College where I was training to be a teacher.

We did not see a great deal of Laura for quite a while but from time to time one or other member of the family would report on her and occasionally she would turn up at "Forty-Five" to hide from Robert Doule.

Robert Doule was a minor clerk in Beale and Beale, Laura's firm.

He lived in a small middle-class suburb. He had a cap of black hair, a sallow but good-looking face and eyes so dark brown they were nearly black. He was thin, of medium height, his expression was sad and he was madly in love with Laura. He looked as if his skin might be clammy.

It began, of course, with Laura slewing her brilliant eyes around towards his desk too often in a morning's work.

Laura could not resist admiration nor could

she resist the temptation to have a young man in tow.

Robert began his attentions by hovering over her desk unnecessarily and bringing morning tea to her first instead of to the more senior people, an ageing spinster with untidy hair and Mr. Preston.

The fact that Mr. Preston would look across at her from under his eye-shade and shake his head soberly from side to side did not deter Laura from enjoying Robert's calf love. Mr. Preston was just a dull old dear and Laura had already forgotten he had ever epitomized the age of lost graces for her. Back in Beale and Beale he was just a frusty not very bright clerk. Robert, on the other hand, had youth. One might say, in that matter, like called to like.

Later Laura realized that her attraction for Robert held much more than that. She was the princess out of the pantomime come true. She was beautiful. Even in her extreme youthfulness she had a haughty air and she breathed an atmosphere that never penetrated the minor suburb of Carlton which occupied an undistinguished place on the north side of the main railway line.

That she should smile on Robert first astonished him, then disturbed him.

What's more she was clever. She understood the moves on the Stock Exchange better than several who had been years in the business. She sometimes said things to one or other of the partners about the Exchange that first caused them to laugh and then look at her, startled. She was a good stenographer and, like her father before her, read the Trade and Finance column of the daily paper from top line to the bottom full stop. She also kept a notebook with a lot of figures in it.

When Mr. Rushton Beale knew of it he laughed very heartily.

"They all do that to start off with," he said. "Think themselves financiers before they're twenty. Then they put a pound on a share or two, get their fingers burnt, and lay off for the term of their natural lives."

So far he wasn't right about Laura. She put no pound down on any shares. Nor showed any inclination to do so. She merely compiled statistics. She had never heard of that word and didn't know that was what she was doing. I thought at first it was a game with figures she liked playing until one day she told me she was "teaching herself".

"Teaching yourself what?"

"Why Da made money. And then lost it."

"Do you have to know?"

"Why not?"

Well, why not? I suppose that sort of thing had the same fascination for some people as nineteenth-century poetry had for me. Each to his own taste!

Laura's aptitude for figures enthralled Robert Doule, the junior clerk. As they were nothing but a tedious duty to him he found it a cause for wonder that anyone played about with them for fun. Especially when that "anyone" happened to be a female, young, beautiful and sophisticated—for that is how he saw Laura. For Robert Doule people like Laura were born sophisticated the same way as people of noble birth were born with blue blood.

The next thing that astonished Robert about Laura was that she was indeed aware of his interest in her, and was pleased by it. It was beyond his wildest dreams that Laura could think of him as anything but dirt beneath her feet. For a long time he was content to be just that. It pleased him to feel he held that honoured and sanctified position in her life. It exactly fitted his own opinion of himself at that time. He did not understand that it was only Laura's vanity that was pleased. For the rest it was merely her natural kindness to people that made her nice to him.

"Why do you eat your sandwiches stuffed under your table like that?" Laura asked one day, coming in early from luncheon. Robert had the last of a sandwich crammed in his mouth and at the sight of Laura tried to stuff away the crumby and crusty paper bag that had held his lunch into the paper-basket under his desk.

"Where else can you eat lunch?" he asked, trying hard not to sound as if his mouth was full.

"In the City Gardens. That's where I go."

"Full of people . . ." Robert stammered and swallowed violently.

"Doesn't matter. They're fun."

Robert's eyes goggled. That his princess should think the people littered about the seats and grounds of the gardens were "fun" was something that startled him. If she had lived up to the role in life that he had allocated her she would have disdained the wage-earning class, and the old men, the babies in cane carriages, the flappers showing too much knee, who prowled the by-paths of the City Gardens.

The next day, as she picked up her lunch-basket, she smiled across the room at Robert.

"Coming?" she said.

Laura, Laura! Why didn't that caul folded away on a piece of brown paper which once as an unborn baby you wore on your face give you the promised second sight that you might see the danger and not the generosity in your kindly invitation? Why didn't it tell you that here was a trap the powerful door of which you had this minute, with this simple invitation "Coming?" fashioned for yourself?

Who in that dingy office could have envisaged the depths of emotional potential lying still, and till this minute undisturbed, in the seemingly humble bosom of Robert Doule from Carlton on the north of the railway line?

"Why . . . why, yes!" he said eagerly.

He grabbed up his lunch-bag and if he was clumsy and his feet suddenly too big for him, Laura did not notice. She was walking to the door and thinking of the sunshine outside and the fact that Coolgardie Mines had fallen another penny-half-penny on the morning

'Change. Yet her father had said there was gold in those mines.

She waited at the door and then walked down the one flight of stairs to the ground floor with Robert by her side. He was saying, "Well . . . by gum . . . it's a bit of a change . . ."

But Laura was thinking the staircase in this old building was cedar and soon the steps would wear away but the balustrade would probably remain a thing of beauty. Pity no one thought fit to have it polished and kept clean.

They walked down the Terrace and Robert felt a bursting of pride. He hoped that other clerks in the city, some of whom he knew slightly, would see him walking with this striking girl. He too fell silent. He was imagining future conversations with these clerks.

"By jove, Rob, who was the flash girl you were with last Tuesday?"

"Flash girl? Oh, Laura? Oh, she's just one of my girls. Might think of taking her up some time. Got style. Not many around these days."

In his mind he had a number of conversations like this, each one showing envy on the part of the examiner and nonchalance in himself.

How do I know Robert thought this way?

Because Robert was that type. It was inevitable he should think this way, or something like it, because on that morning he was so silent. Laura told me that, and it was why she never guessed what she had done to him, and what she was about to do.

They found a square of lawn under a jacaranda tree and sat down. Laura hunched her knees up under her skirts and sat looking around.

"Look at that woman feeding meat pie to that baby." Her teeth flashed as her face creased up with laughter. "And that poor old man sleeping on that seat. He's there every day. On that seat, and always asleep. Do you suppose he sleeps forever and never moves off that seat?"

Robert, who ordinarily would never have noticed these people, now looked at them out of politeness to Laura's interest. He shrugged.

"We'll look and see tomorrow. I'll bet you he's there, just like that. Here are the dogs. Careful how you feed that black-and-white one, Robert. He snaps even while he's wagging his tail."

Laura loved these three half-friendly half-suspicious ranging mongrels always to be found at midday in the City Gardens. They were proud, she saw, and disdainful of mankind. They did not fawn or beg but took the scraps that came their way by the high right of being themselves, three dogs with whom the dog-cart had not yet caught up. They were three dogs who disdained dog-carts. They were sufficient unto themselves, and they were sublimely happy.

Robert wasn't interested in the dogs. He was only interested, and startled, in Laura's supposition that "they", meaning themselves, would be there tomorrow.

And so it was. On the next day when the hands of the big wall clock pointed the lunch hour Laura looked across at Robert.

"Coming?"

Last time that simple word was the fashioning of a door. This time it was a turning of a key. Robert and Laura went every day it was fine to have their lunch in the City Gardens.

Laura talked and laughed and showed her pretty teeth. Sometimes she held forth on

146

one of her theories and then she showed impatience and a touch of arrogance. This latter mood affected Robert more profoundly than her laughter or her beautiful eyes. It bewitched him and filled him with the kind of envy that we Montgomery children felt when we heard Uncle William say, "Damn and blast the thing to hell!"

The ability to say things like that that way was inherent in adulthood and position. Laura's dogmatic moods, her impatience and her arrogance were inherent in her superiority to Robert. He sensed this but Laura was completely ignorant of it.

"But Laura, why did you go with him every day?" I implored her when she told me the whole sorry tale much later.

"How did I know what he was thinking? Oh yes, I knew he was making calf's eyes at me. I didn't mind. I suppose I even liked it. What girl doesn't, even if it is only from the silly junior clerk? It amused me a bit, but I didn't flirt with him. I didn't encourage him. I just thought he ought to go out into the air. He's so pale, unhealthy looking. I suppose I was bored. No one else to talk to at lunch time. Oh *hell*! What do I know of what I thought? I just didn't think *anything*."

But Robert watched every word and every gesture. This one meant something, and that one meant something else. All these "somethings" meant she liked him today better, or not so well. Even the little sighing sounds she made when she sat down on the grass had to be thought about and milled over. Did they mean that today she was happy to be with him? Or that today his presence irritated her?

Laura sighed because she was relieved to be out of the office, relieved to be in the sun, and relieved that she could now get on with the never-flagging serial of the man who slept on the bench, the lovers who quarrelled and held hands every day, the child who essayed to climb the Morton Bay fig tree, and the pride of dogs sleeping or ranging in the sun.

This state of affairs went on for some weeks. Then one morning Laura noticed that Robert was in a state of mind. He hovered about her desk more often than usual. Each time she looked up and caught his eye he blushed to the roots of his hair. He half got up from his chair a dozen times and then sat awkwardly down again.

When they walked to the Gardens at lunch time he kept fingering his tie, coughing and occasionally kicking at a crack in the pavement with his toe.

She wondered if Robert was having troubles at home.

When they had finished their sandwiches and crumpled their lunch-bags Robert broke the news.

"I've got two tickets for the river trip on the *Timor* on Saturday night."

"Nice for you," Laura said. "I hope you enjoy yourself."

She had a vision of the overcrowded *Timor* with its hotch-potch of fat women, coatless men and screaming adolescents. She shuddered but was too well-mannered to let Robert see it.

There was a hint of smoulder in his dark eyes.

"They're for us," he said shortly. "You and me."

Laura was startled. She had never really looked into his eyes before. Something smote her. It was compunction, and deep in his eyes there was a hint of something more.

Laura was very young. For the first time she experienced some real emotion about Robert, other than amusement. She was sorry for him. He could never realize what a fantastic invitation it was. He could never know of the river picnics and luxury launch trips of people in Pepper Tree Bay. He could never realize that while Laura had a passionate objective interest in the fat woman who fed her baby on pies, and the man who slept on the bench, and the three dogs, she had no taste to be crowded up against them on a river-boat no matter how lovely the river might be by moonlight.

Laura was too soft-hearted to be anything but kind. So she smiled on Robert Doule as she said, "How lovely. Whatever made you think of *me*?"

The smoulder went out of his eyes and he nonchalantly tossed little tufts of moss in the air.

"Oh, I've been thinking of it for quite a time. I decided on a river trip. It's more romantic . . . eh?"

Laura was startled and touched. She wanted to laugh but knew it would be wrong. Her vanity was a little mollified but her kindness of heart acknowledged his attachment.

If she sighed as they rose to walk slowly back across the lawns and down the Terrace she did not let Robert hear it. She thought she was doing him a kindness by going on the river trip with him.

Throughout the afternoon she did not let her glance stray once in Robert's direction. He did not mind this. He read her conduct as a pact to secrecy. He thought they had arrived at the next stage in their intimacy, one in which the world was excluded by mutual consent.

If Laura was troubled about going on the river on Saturday night it was not so much on Robert's account. She was giving him pleasure . . . that would be his reward. But she hated being bored and knew she'd be.

Thus when Dirk Preston, Mr. Preston's eldest son, rang her up and asked her if she would like to go to his old school on Saturday afternoon to see the annual sports she nearly fell through the phone in her anxiety to accept.

Dirk was an equal mixture of his simple easy mother and his nice dull father. In addition, however, he had a great many good looks. He was tall, fair, and looked well-bred. Also he had very good manners. Going out on Saturday afternoon with Dirk would be a pleasure in view of the boredom she must endure on Saturday night.

This telephone conversation had gone on in the office and though Laura had kept her voice low—the staff was not supposed to accept personal calls during office hours—Robert from across the room knew that Laura had undertaken to go somewhere with someone, some day soon.

He made an excuse to bring some papers across to Laura's desk.

The little smoulder was in his eyes but Laura was too busy to notice it.

"Going somewhere? Who was your friend on the phone?" His tone was studiedly casual and Laura thought nothing of it.

"Mm. For an outing on Saturday afternoon. I'm going to Guildford. My cousins always go."

Robert knew about the five Montgomery cousins and that they were all girls. He was mollified. Laura did not lie in order to deceive Robert but to deceive Mr. Preston who was looking at them from under his eyeshade at his table nearby. Laura wasn't going to tell Mr. Preston his own son had broken the office rules. He could find that out for himself when he got home.

Laura had a new blue dress. It was crêpe-de-chine and the skirt hung in a thousand knife-pleats. Accordion pleating they called it in those days. It had a square neck and round her neck she wore pearls . . . real pearls. They were not Aunt Sheilagh's beauties but tiny little pearls of her own and they had a diamond clip. She wore a wide-brimmed biscuit-coloured straw hat and from under the brim her deep blue eyes swam in the reflected colour of the sun on the silk of her dress.

She had slim ankles and her feet were quite properly clad in the narrow vamp reminiscent of the ladies of Pepper Tree Bay.

Except for the pearls she wore no other ornament. And she was quite beautiful. The ladies looked at her more than the young men did . . . and that suffices.

Dirk Preston was fond of Laura without being in love with her and he was too used to well-dressed young ladies to feel any particular swimming in the head when with Laura. He was delighted to see his own friends and share her with them.

They stood, or sat, or walked about, a posse of young men scarcely twenty and one radiant girl. Laura was radiant because it was a fine day, she was the cynosure of all eyes, a lot of young men paid her attention, and she knew she was impressing the matrons sitting about under lacy sunshades and under the trees.

The young curate and two of the junior masters of the staff came to drink tea and spend a few laughing minutes with the group. The Headmaster shook hands with Laura and one young perspiring boy in white shorts and sand-shoes came to show her his trophy.

All the while, out of the corner of her eye, she watched the ladies nodding and smiling and looking in her direction. She felt quite sure they were all saying, "How beautiful Laura Montgomery has become! How she dazzles the young men! What a conquest she has made of the dear Headmaster and all those boys!"

She felt quite sure they would go home and say, "My dear, when Laura Montgomery moved away, half the male population of the field moved away too."

Who knows what the ladies really thought or said? The simple fact is that for the first time Laura realized her capacity to attract young men. She had no particular interest in any one man that day, but it exalted her to know they *all* enjoyed her company. She laughed and her blue eyes sparkled. She smiled and her strong even teeth flashed. She moved and the light played across the silk of her dress. Her white square brow was cloudless.

She held court, and from that day on that is what Laura expected to do whenever there were young men around.

In the evening she was agreeably tired and still elated from her afternoon's success. When she went to meet Robert Doule at the river jetty she had an air of calm beneficence, a look of replete happiness in the soft curves of her smile, a faint touch of wistful fatigue. It affected Robert Doule, who dared to hope he might himself be the occasion of it, so that he clumsily walked ahead of her through the barrier instead of standing aside to let her pass. He spoke sharply to the ticket collector at the gangway, which made the ticket collector reply in good offensive Australian. He jostled people in order to find a good seat for himself and Laura, so that people muttered such things as "Who do they think they are, anyway?"

Robert was too clumsy and quite suddenly two swelled-headed to notice. Laura, her tiredness from the afternoon's success folding her about like cotton wool, didn't think it was worth noticing or making a fuss about. She only thought about it all afterwards and somewhat shamefacedly regretted it all.

But she was nice to Robert and when he wedged his body close in beside hers on the narrow seat she did not mind, or draw away. There was not room to be fastidious anyway; one might as well relax.

If Robert was transported into another, violent world, Laura simply did not know. She leaned partly against him, partly against the rail. She dreamed out over the dark warm friendly river and thought of everything else in the world except where she was and who she was with. She was tired, and she was at rest. She faintly liked the violin and piano orchestra on the deck above. She didn't know the other people on the boat existed. She was just a little sleepy, and she leaned against Robert Doule and forgot he was there. She was neither happy nor unhappy. The great purple star-ridden sky yearned over her, filling her mildly with unnamed and unnameable desires. In the background of her thoughts there hovered the misty and mystic figure of Danny.

She was young. Life before her was an

unknown, thrilling and possibly perilous adventure in which love, hope and happiness were possibilities if not probabilities.

It may not have been so much Danny himself upon whom Laura's yearning thoughts rested but it was at least a figure, nebulous and imaginary, who bore the physical attributes of Danny, and the way he walked and talked was in the tradition of one of Danny's background.

8

LAURA'S urging towards a romantic ful-
filment took a sharp turn in another
direction after this quite memorable
Saturday. Though it was not a day, during
the passage of which, to strike Laura with its
importance, yet in retrospect she knew that
on that day she had grown up. She tasted the
sweets of success in the world of love and
society and she perceived also its pitfalls.
Thereafter, without conscious effort, she took
refuge in the world of affairs.

The day ended with poor Robert Doule's
clumsy efforts to kiss Laura good-night.

She had not expected this, probably from
inexperience. The situation affected her in
the manner of an electric shock and for no
other reason than that, though she could con-
ceivably kiss quite a number of young men,
including several of those with whom she had
held court that afternoon, she could *never* kiss
Robert Doule. From being the pimply companion of office days he suddenly became the
offensive sibling of a monster.

She had pushed him away with her hand and uttered the first words that came into her head, "Oh *no*. I'm not allowed to kiss people. I'm too young." A feeble excuse, for anyone who knew Laura knew she would have done exactly what she pleased had it pleased her to kiss Robert Doule. She took the line of least resistance in her excuse and fell back on parental authority.

Alas! Robert Doule believed her. Then had been the moment to repel him for ever. Instead she let him go away believing she was not only beautiful, one who lived on high social planes, but also of that purity and perfection with which every young man likes to invest his loved one. Though for a moment awkward, then embarrassed, he probably allowed his feelings to pass to exaltation and the belief that Laura would have *liked* to kiss him but her high standards and parental training kept her immaculate, a figure on a shelf to be adored from afar.

For Laura's part she went indoors rubbing ruefully the place where his hot hard hands had grasped her arms and his hot breath had fanned her cheek. Then she felt ashamed of herself. She was sorry she felt that way, but she could not help it.

Her behaviour during the next week or two was instinctive rather than thought out.

She could not, overnight as it were, snub the young man whose daily work was performed less than twenty yards away from her. Yet she could not exchange the kind of glances she now perceived he was directing at her. So she bent her head over her desk and worked.

As Robert Doule would know that in the nature of things she was not overwhelmed with work, she had to manufacture and acquire some. So she took her notebook of figures relating to the history of the shares her father held or had held in various companies and began to make a ledger of them.

She took the financial statements of other related companies from the office files and compiled statistics of them. She began to accumulate statistical histories of gold-mining companies. She made graphs in order to illustrate to Mr. Preston and Mr. Rushton Beale, people of inferior arithmetical calibre who could not or would not read a statistical table, the rise and fall, the cyclical nature of boom and recession in gold-mining.

Mr. Rushton Beale laughed uproariously at the activities of the junior stenographer but the elder partner, Mr. Paul Beale, pulled Laura's graphs towards him and spent a long time studying them. He took them home in his brief-case and brought them back again next morning. He continued to do this. There was a faint puzzle in the back of his businessman's eyes.

"Are you coming out to lunch today, Laura?" Robert stood hopeful yet fearful in front of her table.

"No. I'm going to do this graph all over again for Mr. Paul. See how it goes? Look, the upward curve is every twenty years . . ."

"Mr. Paul doesn't pay you for your lunch hour."

"Doesn't matter. I want to do it. Don't you see, Robert . . . one day I . . . you too . . . might get rich if we can understand when a curve will be at its lowest. It means *money*."

Robert was sceptical for two reasons. One because Laura was only an inexperienced girl, although a very clever one with figures; the other was he couldn't see, from out the depths of his own experience, the partners attaching any importance to what the junior staff did in their lunch hours.

He was right. Laura, however, had made an

unconscious discovery. There was a fascination in research that could be its own
reward. She liked working out problems in
arithmetic that involved figures in the
millions, and an hour's work in arithmetic, in
preference to discovering the answer by
algebra in a matter of minutes.

"I want to do it. I want to do it," she cried
impatiently. "One day we'll be rich. You
too . . ."

It was the only reason she thought he or
anyone else would understand. She did not
understand herself that the pursuit of a figure
or a curve in mathematics held the same fascination for her agile brain as the pursuit of a
figure or a curve clothed in skirts had for a
middle-aged roué as he sauntered down the
Terrace in search of eye-adventure as an hors
d'œuvre to lunch.

All this took more than a fortnight, of
course. It merely took about a fortnight to set
in train. She had started it as a manœuvre to
escape Robert and found herself in a field of
mental action that permitted no escape.

Everyone scoffed except the senior partner,
Mr. Paul Beale, who looked faintly perplexed
and sometimes surreptitiously interested.
Mr. Rushton Beale, the younger partner, said

162

Laura would become a "blue-stocking". This was a challenge to Laura's femininity so she took added pains with her dress and took to wearing make-up.

She also took to going out with young men at night time in order to assure herself that a genius for figures didn't mean she was lacking in the proper functions of womanhood. She deceived Robert Doule in this matter in so far as she always implied that she spent her evenings devizing a scheme by which they might both get rich quick.

Uncle William came down from the goldfields on an excursion into the realms of finance and the brothers Beale and Beale told him, not without some typically whimsical anecdote, of Laura's activities.

In the privacy of his hotel room Uncle William delivered himself of his opinion. He did not shout as my father would have done. Uncle William always understood that walls in Australia were only half as thick as those in Great Britain.

"At your age! Teaching your elders their business! Keep your fingers out of the money markets. They're meant for fools and charlatans, not children still in the kindergarten."

Laura understood that he himself was the exception to the class of adults employed in the business of passing the money round the world. It went without saying that since her father's affairs had more or less crashed in Australia it was the Australian firms and the Australian scene that was the cause of it all. "If they'd consulted me . . .! If they'd asked my advice . . .! What do they know about these things in this God-forsaken country? Rapscallions! Knaves!"

Aunt Sheilagh said to Laura, "Darling! You're so pretty. You've got such style. Marry someone rich, or at least good-looking and with good manners. Leave things like business to the men. Women never really understand about it." And then she turned to her husband. "Why did we ever come to this place? How full of excitement and, yes, merriment we were about the prospect before we came."

Then because she thought of Uncle Tim and my father Joe lying buried in the desolate wastes, her blue eyes misted over and her mouth puckered in sadly at the corners.

"It wasn't such a merry thing to do, after all," she said.

"It's cost us two members of the family

already," Uncle William said dramatically. "Who knows who'll be the next to go . . ."

Only Mama nodded her head in approval of Laura. Mama understood the battle for survival a woman can have in the world of men. Wasn't she already plotting a professional career for me and Mary?

"Splendid!" she said. "Where there's a will there's a way, Laura. Nobody ever succeeded who didn't first try."

This was a great battle-song of Mama's but to Laura it showed clearly even Mama didn't understand the fascination of pursuit and retreat for its own sake. Mama saw it as a personal affair between Laura and the manpower in her firm, as an ambition to recover fortune, as a challenge to the manhood in her family. She did not perceive that for Laura there was all this . . . and mystery too.

We were all very impressed with Laura. I remembered she had effortlessly topped the lists at school in mathematical subjects. We saw in her a steel and fire that none of us had except perhaps Mary, and certainly Mama. And Mama wasn't a Montgomery. We were elated that as time passed Laura's prowess in her own firm became somewhat known up and down the Terrace. It did not retract from her charm for the masculine population, either. Those who did not treat it as this year's pleasant little joke thought it was nice to know a girl at whom everyone looked twice and who had a few brains as well.

By a few brains they didn't mean, of course, enough to equal any one of their own. It just meant they thought she wasn't quite as innocent, ignorant and mentally incapacitated as most women, by virtue of their sex, necessarily were.

Robert Doule remained securely in a never-changing background. He was there. He watched over Laura. The future was full of great promise for him. He must wait until time and an added year or two had ripened Laura to that point when her parents would no longer disallow a kiss and when her purity would not be marred by his own tender ministrations.

Laura, except on the surface of things, forgot he existed.

In a flat adjacent to Laura's in Adelaide Terrace there lived a young business woman in her early thirties.

Each morning as Laura left her room and began the long walk under the shady trees towards the junction of Barrack Street where Adelaide Terrace inexplicably became St. George's Terrace, she saw her neighbour also walking in the direction of her unknown occupation. Laura took a vital interest in people she saw daily, whether she knew them or not. She no longer took her lunch into the City Gardens so she missed the fat women and the man who slept on the bench and she sadly missed the dogs.

In the meantime, however, she had a host of other eye-acquaintances. Who, for instance, was the very distinguished young man with the curly hair and well-cut clothes who walked so briskly, never looking to right or left, precisely on the same hour in the same direction every morning? Where did he go? And why did he carry brown leather gloves, a thing no man in Australia ever did? And was that an RAF badge he wore in his coat? He must be an Englishman! Laura wondered what his voice would be like. He never spoke to anyone, never smiled. He was almost intolerably good-looking.

Then there was the fat dumpy woman dressed in black whose hair was obviously dyed and whose make-up was a little too pronounced. She worked in one of the big stores. Laura had seen her there, even been sold a garment by her. Why did she live alone and who were her friends?

There were the two sisters, twins, who dressed alike and simpered alike. Quite a success with the young men perambulating the Terrace, they were.

And there was this young business woman in the early thirties who had a special attraction for Laura. She was exceedingly smart, had style, and an air of not being British. Laura couldn't put her finger on it.

She, this other, knew quite a lot of people. Often she walked along the Terrace with one or other of the people tumbling out of the flats and apartments at eight-thirty on a working day. Sometimes she stopped to speak to people and her manner was gay and friendly. She had a considerable amount of that intangible quality called spontaneous charm.

Her mouth was big and generous and she had a set of big strong white teeth. It was her mouth, and her tight curly hair, very fair, that made Laura think she was not British. Yet when she spoke, and there had been more than one occasion when Laura had overheard a few words in passing, the voice was the voice of an Englishwoman.

Laura's curiosity about the people in the Terrace was boundless but she itched more than anything to know who was the young man with the wings in his lapel and who was this charming sophisticated woman who looked as if she ought to be in the West End of London or the boulevards of Paris rather than in the sunny shadow-strewn cement walks of a terrace in Australia.

In talkative moments in the office she told Robert Doule about this woman, but instinct warned her never to mention the grave young man who must have been an aviator in the war.

Unexpectedly it was Robert Doule who finally revealed the lady's identity and brought about the friendship between the two.

Robert had his photograph taken. Like all people who do this for their twenty-first birthday he thought it an honour and a rare treat to bestow on friends expensive versions of this photograph.

Laura, who had forgotten it was his birthday and so did not have a present to offer, received one from him. His photograph.

"Good isn't it?" he said. "Done by Marion

Perrent. She's out of this world as a photo-grapher, don't you think?"

Laura knew all about Marion Perrent's photographs. They decorated walls outside her studio in Hay Street, and, more impor-tant, they decorated the mantelshelves of the homes in Pepper Tree Bay.

"Wonderful with children, isn't she?" A proud parent would display a group of brilliantly pretty and brilliantly dressed chil-dren looking selfconsciously into space.

Aunt Sheilagh had had her photograph done by Marion Perrent and had emerged above Mama's fireplace looking exactly like Aunt Sheilagh only a shade more proud, a shade more beautiful.

Aunt Sheilagh had wanted Laura and Sylvia to have their photographs done but Laura was much more realistic than Aunt Sheilagh. She knew the photograph would be another debt that would or should be an honour for any business woman to carry, "against the day when the market turned", and she would not succumb to the temptation.

Sylvia, in one of her short trips to the coast for a "breather" in summer, was photo-graphed instead. And Sylvia appeared on the mantelshelf looking so near the angels one knew the angels could never be far away.

Laura had to go into suitable raptures over Robert's photograph.

"I'm getting a couple of dozen postcard sizes for the parents," he said. "I'm picking them up at lunch time."

Laura looked at Robert with puzzled eyes. A postcard size for his parents? And this fourteen inch by ten for herself?

"Robert, give me the postcard size. Give this one to your mother."

"Wouldn't think of it." He waved his hand airily. "Only had it done for you."

Hell! Laura thought. But she was determined she wasn't going to have what his mother should have.

"Look here, Robert. I'd like the postcard size. I could carry it in my bag then. This size would have to stay at home. Besides I'd have to remember to hide it every time my father or mother, or cousins, came to my room. I'm not allowed to have young men. I'd forget, and get found out. Besides, a postcard size in my own bag goes everywhere with me. Doesn't it?"

Thus Laura once again out of cowardice,

and some kindheartedness, lying by implication.

Robert was torn between the logical soundness of her argument and disappointment in the reception of his truly magnificent present.

"Please, Robert," Laura pleaded. "I'd like to have one with me wherever I go. And I won't take two. That's flat."

"Very well. But you must come with me at lunch time while I get them. You haven't walked down the Terrace with me in weeks."

"Good," said Laura, relieved. "I'd love to do that."

And so small brick by small brick Laura was building a prison for herself. At the same time she met Marion Perrent, for the photographer of distinction, almost legend in Pepper Tree Bay, was none other than the mysterious lady of charm and interest who walked up the Terrace every morning at eight-thirty and of whom Laura had been so curious for so long.

Laura was quite excited when Miss Perrent came from between fabulously shiny velvet curtains to attend to Robert Doule's demands herself.

"Why," Laura said impetuously. "I know

who you are. I see you every day . . ."

Miss Perrent smiled. It was a gracious smile and she looked pleased.

"I've seen you too," she said. "You're the girl who lives in the apartments next door to my flat, and you walk so beautifully. I've often wished I could photograph people *walking*."

"I've admired you too," said Laura, and she actually flushed with pleasure.

"Well now we'll be able to talk as well as walk, won't we?" Miss Perrent asked in a friendly way.

Yes, her voice was English, Laura decided.

The photograph of Robert stuffed away in a back pocket of her bag, and forgotten, Laura looked eagerly forward to meeting Marion Perrent again.

For two successive mornings she missed her. On the first morning there was no sign of Miss Perrent. On the second morning Laura could see her too far ahead to be able to overtake without running and looking too eager. On the third morning Laura was an extra minute early and still there was no sign of her neighbour. At the first corner she looked back and saw Miss Perrent coming along fifty yards behind her. Laura waited. This, she

173

thought, would be a friendly thing to do, and not unduly eager.

Miss Perrent hurried her step a little and caught up with Laura. She had a curious swaying way of walking, her head a little on one side that added in some complex way to her attraction.

"Were you waiting for me?" she asked.

"Yes . . ." said Laura. "I . . . well I . . . I thought we might walk along together."

Miss Perrent touched her arm in an understanding manner. She carried her gloves and did not wear them. Her fingernails, very well polished and a little long made a scratch on Laura's arm. It startled her. Then she forgot it, for she was listening to Miss Perrent's voice.

She was talking about the weather, about the fact she adored walking along the Terrace in the early morning, and that she had a very complicated group to do this day.

"Mrs. Basil Everard and her two children," she said. "Mrs. Basil Everard is a beautiful woman and I want the photograph to be very very good."

There was the tiniest roll of her "r's" and Laura thought again that if Miss Perrent was English, she was something more as well.

Also, as Laura knew Mrs. Basil Everard, she was not impressed with the emphasis the other put on the forthcoming appointment. Mrs. Basil Everard was another *t'other-sider* and Laura had the usual Pepper Tree Bay superciliousness towards *t'other-siders* no matter how much money they had. She did not mind Miss Perrent being impressed by her client, however. Miss Perrent was not to know how Pepper Tree Bay-siders felt about this sort of thing.

In this Laura was profoundly mistaken. The other knew all about society in Western Australia—she dealt in business with its members both above and below the pioneering line—but she had not yet placed Laura amongst the Montgomeries of whom she was as knowledgeable as she was about anyone else. She had taken an interest in the girl because she was a striking girl. She would find out who she was, or rather if she was anybody, in due course.

"Strange how some of these Australian women can be quite beautiful," Miss Perrent said with a trace of condescension that was not just artistic. "I had one yesterday . . ." She said "one" as if it sounded like "wan" instead of the Australian "wun" and Laura knew for certain Miss Perrent was not indigenous. Besides, her remark spoken in the spirit of condescension roused the other side of Laura's ambivalent attitudes. Let anyone disparage the Australians and Laura would go down fighting their cause. So she told a taradiddle.

"I'm an Australian myself," she said. She felt pleased with that. Now Miss Perrent would not be able to be critical. It wouldn't be good manners.

Miss Perrent slewed her eyes round to Laura. She was laughing. Her fingernails brushed Laura's arm again. They scratched.

"You do not speak like one," she said.

"Then I wish I did," said Laura. This was more than a taradiddle, for of all things she was most afraid of it was losing her own intonation in speech and acquiring the Australian characteristics.

"Then your parents must have come from somewhere else." Miss Perrent was still laughing and Laura could not carry the lie any further.

"Yes," she conceded. "From Ireland."

"A Montgomery from Ireland. Could you be . . ."

Laura did not let her finish.

"My mother and sister had their photographs done by you."

If she felt vaguely shamefaced at the thought the photographs had never been paid for, she need not have done so. Miss Perrent was impressed. Aunt Sheilagh in her beautiful, elegant and pearl-and-emerald poverty came from a section of the people Miss Perrent knew only too well. Like her colleagues, the Savile Row tailors, she felt it was almost a privilege to have such people on her books. Aunt Sheilagh had the manner of a duchess, and not an impoverished one. She also had wit and charm and that was sufficient. Miss Perrent understood that perfectly.

She now looked at Laura with a freshened interest. The girl was very young but had an unmistakable air of distinction. What was she doing earning a living in a frusty Terrace office? The age had not yet arrived when these things were usual in this part of the world where society still lived in the manners and traditions of their grandparents, the first settlers. In 1926 the young girls of good families still led sheltered lives in a circuit of parish teas and drawing-room musicales.

"You live alone?"

"My parents live on the gold-fields. I have an aunt and some cousins; I go there when I'm bored or . . ." and truthfulness shone for a moment in Laura's blue eyes. She showed two elusive dimples. ". . . when I'm hungry," she added candidly.

Miss Perrent warmed more and more to the girl.

"You must come and eat with me sometime. I'm quite often alone."

"Oh thank you," said Laura. "I'd love to."

They parted at the corner, neither looking back at the other, but doubtless each bearing a mental vision, Laura of that slightly swaying cosmopolitan figure, Miss Perrent of the tall straight-backed girl whose whole bearing was just saved from arrogance by the lovely candour of her smile and the brilliant questing blue of her eyes.

9

THE friendship between Laura and Marion Perrent had a mixed reception from Laura's associates and friends. Aunt Sheilagh and Uncle William, away in the fastnesses of the desert, knew little about it and what they did know neither added to nor detracted from their feeling that Laura lived in a foreign world anyway, and strange people and strange things were likely to happen to her.

She had made her own bed and they couldn't even turn over the mattress for her.

"Such people as Laura knows!" Aunt Sheilagh said. "It's what comes of living in a strange place. One never knows . . ."

"She'll come running home for cover when she gets her fingers burnt," Uncle William said. To which cryptic remark he then added, "If she had asked my advice now, she would be here beside her mother and sister. Selfish. They're all selfish. The whole pack of them."

By this Uncle William meant everyone who

did not have the misfortune to live on the gold-fields.

Mama was disturbed.

"She's too old for you, Laura. Why, she must be over thirty."

"She's very nice and friendly, Aunty. What does it matter how old she is? She dresses beautifully, doesn't she? A sort of continental flair for cut, I would say."

When Uncle William heard of this remark he said, "Ha. These continental people! Neither flesh, fowl nor good red herring."

"What is she, Laura?" I asked. I had met her twice with Laura and had had precisely the same feeling of strangeness that Laura had experienced.

"She comes from Birmingham."

"Was she born there?"

"I don't know. I haven't asked her. She's partly Jewish."

This last she said defensively as if being *partly* something added substance to Uncle William's remark. It also showed that while Marion Perrent asked Laura exhaustive questions of herself Laura in turn did not probe the other. Perhaps it was a defensive mechanism, for Laura believed in liking people for themselves and did not wish to know things that would set the family talking.

Between us, Laura and me, we decided that Marion Perrent's "difference" lay in the fact she was an artist, and had travelled much. We called her cosmopolitan and let it rest at that.

Robert Doule, strangely enough, heartily approved the friendship. Perhaps he felt that if Laura was preoccupied with Marion Perrent she was not answering the admiring glances that came from the young men who passed her and wished her good-day in the Terrace. Robert Doule watched these latter advances jealously and though he sought to find occasions with which to stab himself he was never able to do so. He knew the expressions of Laura's face by heart and he knew that a minute after she had passed a personable young man who had raised his hat to her she had forgotten whom she had just passed. That a good deal of the time she had forgotten she was walking along with Robert Doule did not occur to him.

He allowed himself to think that the Terrace believed that Laura was exclusively his.

He thought that Laura's life was given up to her growing importance in the firm, to her preoccupation with figures, tables and graphs, and to Miss Perrent. And so it was, except that somewhere at the back of Laura's mind was a dream.

That dream was wrapped up in an instinctive knowledge that in spite of her youth, her inexperience, she knew there was a fundamental truth in the rhythm of figures. If only she could find or understand it. When and if she did, she would know more about the Stock Exchange business than the combined experiences of Messrs. Rushton and Paul Beale. She would have a *mind* that was better than that of a great many men. She was, in a world of affairs, discovering that a great many men were fools . . . and a great many women weren't.

Where or in what way this fundamental truth had anything to do with Danny and Ireland or with the fact that she was neither flesh, fowl nor good red herring herself, she did not know. She was neither Irish nor Australian but a little bit of both with something else—her mind—that was international.

Somewhere in this dream of success, mixed up with figures, was the nebulous figure of a young man. If it wasn't Danny, then it was his prototype.

Freud would have explained her friendship

with Marion Perrent, not in his usual con-
clusive way, but as the recognition of a *mind*
that was of the world but which was housed
in a body that was forced to own a passport.

She went to have tea quite often with
Marion Perrent and it was thus she learned
her friend was partly Jewish.

One night they were having tea—English
fillet which they both adored, fresh brown
bread rolls, butter and coffee—when Marion
had two callers.

They were two men. Tall, dark, unmistak-
ably Jewish.

They were introduced to Laura as Michael
Jacobs and Benny Joseph. That settled everything.

They were old friends of Marion's. They
sat about her flat in the manner of people
accustomed to it. They put on her records
without asking where they were kept or what
she would like. They talked to her about
unknown mutual acquaintances who all had
names like Rebecca and Stella and Izzy.
These friends were all in England and it was
quite clear these two young men had just
arrived from a trip to that country.

Laura was puzzled but entranced with the
company. She now heard conversation the

like of which she had only read about in books. The three of them, Marion too, were witty and polished. They talked music, pictures, the ballet, actors and actresses, as only knowledgeable people can talk of them well. They opened up whole vistas for Laura.

"We went round to the stage door afterwards and dragged out Ibanez, grease-paint and all. He'd given the performance of his life, and we all went to Sadie's. They were all there. Oh what a night we had! Benny Rosen played the Bach chorales as he never played them in the Wigmore Hall."

What was this conversation doing here on the edge of the West Australian desert between people who knew intimately someone who played Bach in the Wigmore Hall?

What were they doing here at all?

That soon became clear.

"Well, what have you brought this time? And do I get free tickets?" Marion asked.

"Ma Mi Rosette. Something to fill up the theatre and bring in-a da cash." Michael Jacobs had ceased to be the polished man of the world and became a caricature of his own race. He hunched his shoulders and spread out his hands.

"You wanta da tickets for free? You have

184

da tickets for only half free. Youse a goy . . . Ugh!"

Marion laughed. She had a beautiful laugh. It rang out free and musical and her teeth shone splendidly in the shielded lights in the corner. The jet beads round her neck sparkled. She looked enigmatic and beautiful sitting back in the armchair, her fair curly hair sitting in perfect groomed order around her oval face.

"Of course . . . she's Jewish," Laura thought. "But not wholly so, else why did Michael Jacobs call her a *goy*?"

The other man, Benny Joseph, not quite so tall but somehow more distinguished looking, was pausing before some photographs Marion had done.

"I like your lighting, Marry," he said. "You ought to come home and see the work of Baron and Beaton. They're just beginning but they've got art. They've got talent."

"One needs talent," Marion said.

"And you've got the 'know-how'," said Michael Jacobs. Then seeing a shadow of anger in Marion's face he added, "Sorry Marry." He lit a cigarette and looked at her through the rising smoke. "It's the truth," he said softly. "You'd never have come here if you'd had them both."

Marion's smile was fixed and hard.

"I came here to make money," she said.

"Don't we all?" It was Benny's turn to caricature his race. He hunched his shoulders and lifted cringing hands to Laura. "Mooney?" he whined. "Mooney for luv? You got mooney? You got luv?"

Laura looked into his eyes and smiled.

"If I did that to you—like that—you wouldn't like it, would you?"

He dropped his hands and returned her smile.

"Only a Jew can take off a Jew," he said. He sat down beside her and began to talk about books. Laura had to confess her ignorance.

"The only thing I know anything about is mathematics," she said. "And then it's only floundering around with statistics. Everyone else laughs."

"Laughs? Why should they laugh?"

"A woman is supposed to be too empty-headed for figures."

Both men were clearly and genuinely astonished at this. They began at once to quote many famous Jewish women who were

186

talented or clever in the business world.

"Why not you?" asked Benny Jacobs.

The absolute sincerity of his question struck Laura like a bracing blow. He took it for granted she could have a talent, and a future! He was astonished there was any doubt in her mind, or anyone else's mind!

When he saw the naïve wonder in Laura's eyes he turned to Michael and Marion.

"Why does she think she cannot have a talent?" he asked, puzzled. "Why does she think it is not possible to do something with this ability?" He turned back to Laura. "It is a great gift. It is like music. You have it, or you don't. Why should you doubt it?"

Marion placed a cigarette in a long ebony holder and lit it.

"It's the time and place she lives in," said Marion. "She's smothered by little gods . . ." She shrugged.

For once Laura did not defend her countrymen. She knew these people were speaking the truth. She knew that elsewhere she wouldn't be a pretentious oddity. Amongst the Jews she would be acknowledged and respected, if she had talent. There was another world somewhere else of which Messrs. Beale and Beale did not wot, undreamed of by her father and mother, Aunt Helen, and the five cousins.

This she must remember always. Whatever she did might be odd in this country, but not in the places Marion Perrent, Michael Jacobs and Benny Joseph came from.

She had talent. She would use it.

Her eyes glowed and a flush came to her cheeks. She talked about herself, the firm, her relatives. Floodgates were unlocked and to these three people, strangers in race and country, she told both consciously and unconsciously more of herself than she ever did to anyone else in all her life.

They listened. They smiled, they nodded. They appraised.

When the two men were ready to go they shook hands with her.

"Statistics are one thing," Benny Jacobs said. "But how to analyze them? Ah . . . that is the great art. Figures . . . that is talent. Insight . . . that is genius."

Laura never forgot the words.

It was hard to believe when she saw Marion Perrent the next day this was the same woman, the member of an international world of art and achievement. A woman who could talk with ease and on equal terms with men like Michael Jacobs and Benny Joseph, theatre entrepreneurs with a background of Bach thrown in for luck. True she was elegant, and charming as ever. But somehow Laura perceived that either the Australian or the business scene had touched her with hands that like vampires drew some of the splendour out from her.

Laura sat in her studio and waited for Marion to finish putting on her make-up before walking home with her.

"Why are you different today?" Laura asked.

"Different in what way?"

"Today you are a business woman, in the very place where you ought to be an artist."

"All Jews are like that. They live eternally in two worlds. One of the mind, and one of the flesh-pots."

"Why did Michael Jacobs call you a *goy*?"

"Because my father was not Jewish. Only my mother. I never went to the synagogue until I was eighteen, and I don't often go now. They don't really want me . . ."

Marion put the last touch of powder on her face, fitted on her head an enchanting feather toque and picked up her bag.

189

"Coming?" Her smile was on, full flash, and the subject was closed.

If Laura had the ill manners to wonder, who and what was her father? Who are her people? Where are they? she did not ask. Marion Perrent did not tell her, then or ever.

It was several days after this that Laura again saw the young preoccupied man who wore the aviator's badge in his lapel.

"Who do you suppose he is?" Laura asked Marion Perrent.

The latter shrugged.

"A commercial traveller probably, got up that way to look interesting. I should say he was a young man who was a nobody who has the flair for dressing and walking as if he was a somebody."

This shocked Laura. It disconcerted her to find this cynical streak in her friend.

"I think that's unkind," she said.

"A young man who is always alone is odd. When you know the world as well as I do you'll know when to pick the odd ones."

"Perhaps he's not interested in people."

"Oh yes he is, or he wouldn't dress himself in such a distinguished way. Your true recluse doesn't care a damn how he dresses.

All he wants to be is warm in winter and cool in summer, and not get run in if he's forgotten to put something on."

"If he's interested in people then why doesn't he speak to them or be spoken to?"

"That's part of the play-acting too."

The absolute hardness of these remarks disturbed Laura. What Marion had said was something outside Laura's understanding. Yet something stirred deep inside her. Marion had a knowledge of things ponderable only in the slimes of the human mind. Laura felt this without knowing it or framing it into thoughts or words. She felt an instinctive reluctance to pursue the subject.

For three days she did not see her friend. She didn't know why. She thought it was because it hurt her to find Marion hard towards strangers, and she didn't like hardness. Her mother and Aunt Helen were always filled with pity for the odd people of the earth. They did not condemn them.

Why should the young man be odd because he was well tailored and walked about briskly and alone?

For three days Laura went back to the City Gardens for her lunch. On the second day

191

Robert Doule discovered her intention and went too. The fat woman was there, and so was the baby, but not the old man who used to sleep on the bench. Laura wondered sadly if he had died. The dogs lay somnolent in the sun. She looked at all her friends around the lawns and on the benches. Robert Doule didn't seem so bad as a companion, after all.

"I wish I hadn't given up coming to the Gardens," Laura said wistfully. "I like it best here."

Robert Doule was pleased about this and read into it the fact that Laura, like a lovely opening bud, was slowly awakening to the possibilities of love. He knew the situation must be handled delicately.

I imagine he looked at the white skin of her neck and felt a little dizzy; that he looked at her profile and wondered why he felt faint.

One imagines he felt these things because long afterwards Laura remembered this day and the queer way Robert looked at her and that he had gone a little white. At the time she thought he didn't take enough vitamins in his food.

"Let's go back," she said, jumping up and shaking the crumbs from her skirt. She had jumped up just in time, but probably didn't know it.

On the next day she went to the Gardens again. Robert Doule was so far from her thoughts she forgot to ask him if he wanted to come too.

He saw her leaving the building and followed her. When he came to the place where they usually sat on the grass, he sat down beside her. He said nothing, but his hands as they turned over his parcel of lunch trembled.

"Hallo!" said Laura nonchalantly. "I forgot about you. So sorry!"

Robert looked at her, incredulous. It was impossible for her to have forgotten him. He watched over her by day and dreamed ceaselessly of her by night. His whole being was absorbed in the life both outer and inner which he led with her.

He went quite white and the rims of the pupils of his dark eyes were red with fire, but Laura did not notice.

"I saw the Black Maria come into the Supreme Court gate, over there," Laura said. "Do you suppose they're trying anyone very bad?"

Robert choked on his sandwich and Laura

forgave him, thinking he had taken too big a mouthful. It was not at all unusual and was one of the things that made her keep her face averted when he was eating.

"I'm not speaking to my friend Marion Perrent," she volunteered chattily, for the sake of saying something.

"Why not?"

Again she forgave the terseness of his tone. She thought he had some of the last sandwich in his mouth.

"She said unkind things about a man I like."

"What man?" His voice trembled.

Laura noticed it but didn't want to look at him and see why. She didn't like the sight of Robert eating.

"Somebody I've been seeing every day for ages. Just in the distance mostly. Never more than twenty feet near, anyway." Laura laughed suddenly. The whole thing seemed absurd now. "I thought he looked nice, and was nice, and I said so."

"What . . . what did Marion Perrent say?" Never more than twenty feet near her? That is what he, Robert Doule, had been for weeks . . . until yesterday and today. Could it . . . could it possibly be that . . . His

194

thoughts would carry him no further. "What . . . what . . . did she say?"

"That he was play-acting. You know, acting a part. That he was silent and remote to create an interest in himself. Do you know what? I just think he's a young man in love. What do you think, Robert? Do young men in love always look preoccupied . . . as if the rest of the world didn't matter?"

"The rest of the world doesn't matter," Robert said with passionate conviction. "There isn't any rest of the world. There's only . . . only . . ."

Why, he was almost crying!

Laura looked at him startled.

"Why, Robert!"

He was white and his eyes were black pools. He shook as if he had an ague.

With a flash of insight Laura saw Robert's feelings as if they were written in English across a sheet of notepaper. With an effort of control she did not shrink back nor let her face show what she suffered. A minute afterwards she felt only pity.

"Robert . . . don't ever feel like that about anybody." Her kind tone steadied his trembling. "Not yet . . . not while you're so young. You see . . . you would have to wait. Just as I would have to wait. We have to grow up . . ."

Her voice trailed to a silence. What was she saying? What sense, if any, did it make?

Just as pity had followed in the wake of repulsion so now irritation and a touch of the old arrogance brought up the rear.

She jumped up, brushed down her skirt.

"We can't do this again," she said sharply. "Let me go back alone, Robert. I want to work. I want to work and work and work. I don't want to fall in love . . . or be in love. I'm too young."

She hurried from the Gardens. She wanted to wash her face and hands as if they had something sticky on them. She wanted *not* to shudder. She wanted to be sorry for Robert but his pimpled sallow face with his hang-dog eyes would keep rising before her like a picture of reproach.

"What have *I* done?" she asked herself, bewildered. "Damn him. Now what sort of a life am I going to endure in the office?"

When Robert came in as the clock struck two Laura's head was buried over her desk. She worked until there was nothing left on her table and there was no more work to do. She went to the files and took out again the well-thumbed file on Coolgardie Mines. She compiled her statistics all over again. When Mr. Paul Beale sounded the buzzer on her desk she nearly cried with relief. She picked up her notebook and two pencils and went to the inner door without looking in Robert's direction.

Mr. Preston, from under his eye-shade, looked from one face to the other. He went on with his own work.

Perhaps Laura was the kind of person whose wits were sharpened by temper, for temper was what she now felt. She was angry with Robert and furious at not finding enough work to do. She took a perfect copy of Mr. Beale's letters and in record time. He glanced at her curiously and she looked up and caught his eyes on her.

"Mr. Beale, can't I be your secretary? Your private secretary in here? In that little cubbyhole through the other door?"

"My dear girl . . ."

"I'm not a girl. I'm a stenographer, and I know all about figures. My figures are more accurate than Mr. Preston's, or even Mr. Rushton Beale's. I could predict your Stock Exchange rates for you . . ."

Mr. Beale laughed heartily. He slapped his hand down on the desk.

"Dear Laura. If you could do that you would be a millionaire in a month and the Stock Exchanges of Australia would close down."

"I don't mean tomorrow's rates, or next week's, or the month after. I mean future rates and trends . . . yes, that's the word. *Trends* . . ." Laura stopped for a minute and fondled the word. She had been hunting for it for weeks. She had never heard of it in the context nor knew that it was written a thousand times in every book on economics.

Mr. Beale sat and looked at her curiously.

"I mean the *future*, Mr. Beale. Look at the fortunes that are won and lost in dealing in *futures* on the Liverpool wheat market! The same people are always on the right side of the bargain. *They* have people working for them . . . in figures . . . in trends . . . in market variations. Let me try. Please . . . please Mr. Paul . . . let me try . . . I could show you things . . ."

She was almost beside herself and jumped up and ran from the room. She returned immediately with her ledgers and her note-books.

She tried to show him tables but was too incoherent to be clear. She pulled out a sheaf of minutely squared paper on which she had made her graphs.

"Look, Mr. Beale . . . never mind wheat . . . take gold. When the price is high they all go up whether they've got gold or not. But the ones that have gold, but are too costly to mine, shoot to the sky when the price goes up. It goes up when the price of everything goes down because it's not goods that stabilize the balance of trade, it's money, and gold is money. Look . . . twenty years here . . . twenty years again . . . twenty years' time . . . that's about 1933. Six years hence. If there's no war or famine . . ."

She was going too fast for Mr. Beale and he wasn't looking at her graphs anyway. He'd seen some of them before. He was looking at her face.

"Laura," he said. "Sit down and stop talking—except when I ask for an answer."

Laura sat down.

Mr. Beale lit a cigarette slowly.

"Laura, in the business world it's dog eat dog. I don't have to tell you that?"

She shook her head.

"Sometimes a dog doesn't eat another dog.

He nurses him along, because presently that dog can do the fighting for him in another quarter. Understand?"

Again Laura nodded.

"Now I'm going to tell you something. Something I never intended to tell you, but you've stuck your neck out. You've come to me and set yourself up as an adviser to an experienced business man, that means you've got advanced ideas of yourself. If you believe in your ideas you can believe in the kind of punishment that can be handed out by one business man to another." He paused and drew on his cigarette. He looked at Laura steadily. "Your father owes me a lot of money. I've carried him. I am carrying him now."

Laura's face went pale but she said nothing. Mr. Beale watched her closely.

"The wages I pay you are debited against his account. Without his knowing it. When I took you here I took you in because I thought you were a bright girl and needed helping. Preston asked me to do this. I don't give charity so I decided that when William Montgomery settled his account, it would include your living which I have made available to you since you entered this firm."

200

He dropped his eyes from Laura's face, shook the ash from his cigarette neatly into an ash-tray, closed one eye to keep the thin spiral of smoke out of it and looked at Laura again. She was white but her eyes were dark. Her bottom lip was straight and firm, the line of her jaw had moved a fraction of an inch forward. He was looking at a face cold with anger, but she did not drop her eyes. The pencil in her hand did not move. Her hands were steady as rocks.

"You understand what I have said?"

"Yes."

"What are you going to do about it?"

"Nothing . . . yet. I've earned my living. I've been worth it."

"You're sure of that?"

"Very sure."

There was a long silence. Mr. Beale stubbed out his cigarette. His voice changed and his manner relaxed.

"You took that very well, Laura," he said. "That's the kind of reaction a business man has often got to show when he receives a shock. I couldn't think of a bigger test . . ."

Still Laura said nothing.

"You can get the cleaner to clear out that cubby-hole tonight. Install yourself tomorrow. I won't need you full time but when you're not doing my letters you can get on with those sums of yours."

"Thank you, Mr. Beale."

Laura closed her notebook and went to the door.

"And Laura . . ."

She turned slowly. He was still sitting at his desk.

"You are very young. You lack experience, but you've got the best brain of anyone I've ever employed in this firm. You've earned double your living."

"Thank you, Mr. Beale."

She went through the door and closed it behind her. She leaned back against it, her eyes closed. Her hand with the notebook and pencil hung down by her side.

Mr. Preston and the senior stenographer and Robert looked at her in amazement.

When she opened her eyes all three of them saw in them the strangest glitter, like a cat's eyes in the dark.

She neither saw, nor thought about, Robert Doule.

10

THE following year Danny came back to Australia.

Things weren't going well at Magillicuddy and the lawyers in Dublin, in connivance with Mulligan, the faithful steward, thought that Danny should try Australia again and see how luck stood in the manner of retrieving the family fortunes.

There were still sheep on those vast plains, cattle in the wilderness and gold in the desert.

Danny had been through a naval school, an English institution, and had acquitted himself as the finest horseman in the year. That is to say, when the officers of the wardroom were relaxing in the hunting field. This, Mulligan thought, was qualification suitable to sheep or cattle raising. He had read in a paper that horsemanship was the first and only requisite to a life outback. If a man had a good seat he would be equal to the best of jackeroos on the big stations.

So Danny came back.

The top hat, the high cut-away coat and the hard collar had gone, but the grace remained.

Danny coming down the gangway of the liner couldn't have been anyone else in the world but Dennis Hara Montgomery. He looked as if he had been in the habit of landing in Australia every two or three months of his life. He was quite casual about it. Australia was making no impact on Danny, whatever impact Danny was making on the Australians, particularly his cousins.

"Oh *Laura*," I said, quite overwhelmed. "Isn't he handsome!" I knew that sounded like a glamour magazine and somehow part of Danny's handsomeness was the love with which we invested him. And his detached air.

Some people achieve that air, and some are born with it. It is an enviable quality. He listened to people with a glorious politeness, his head just a shade on one side, his eyebrows lifted to a point that implied intelligent interest, his smile with just a suggestion of unconscious charm. He lifted his slender fine-boned hand and pushed the hair back from his forehead and said,

"Oh really!"

We felt like laying down our lives for him which all goes to show that it was not only his charm, but the fact that he belonged to us, and that we were proud of him, that so stirred our sense of family love.

I'm sure he had precisely the same reaction to us as he had to every other Australian. And I don't know what that was.

We bore him homewards.

"You've still got the damned heat with you," he said.

At "Forty-Five" there was order where there had been chaos. We had wondered if our come-down in the world would shock Danny and so we had cleaned and scrubbed and changed curtains and turned carpets. Moreover we had moved in with one another, making a large room available for Aunt Sheilagh and Uncle William. After much debate it had been decided that Sylvia should stay with us, instead of sharing Laura's room in the Terrace as first planned. This was specially on account of Danny. It was taken for granted that it would be Danny's wish, as it was Sylvia's, and everyone else's, that Danny and Sylvia should be as near one another as possible.

We were fantastically cramped together, so it was decided that after the first day Gerry and Denney should be sent to stay with friends in the country.

There was nothing for it but Danny had to have a small side room. There just wasn't a front room or a big room other than that for Aunt Sheilagh and Uncle William.

So we scrubbed and polished and repainted the small side room. We put up new curtains and changed the best pieces of furniture in our rooms for the shabby old ones that had belonged there before. We rehearsed an apology for the accommodation but Mama said,

"It's our best. Our very best. Danny will know that."

"My God! You should see Magillicuddy," said Laura. "It's a *barn*!"

When Danny came in he threw his hat on a chair and his valise on the bed and said, "Shades of the dead, Aunt Helen! Have you turned the place into a nursing home?"

"He means it's *clean*," Laura said.

"It's not a nursing home, it's an apartment house. The lodgers live upstairs and we live down," said Gerry, intending the family skeleton should be out and about as soon as possible.

"How do I tell a lodger from a member of the family?" Danny asked.

"The members of the family are all female," Mama explained. "You don't expect them to walk in their sleep, do you?"

"My way?" The fair eyebrows were raised. His eyes roved over us and his smile, sweet and suddenly seraphic, flickered from face to face. "Who knows?" he said. "So many, and so . . ." His smile grew faintly wicked, then faded away. But we had all caught his eyes, and laughed.

Dear Danny!

The only solemn moment was reserved for Sylvia. She was still fair, and very frail, gentle-eyed and enduring. She sat on the sofa in the lounge and waited for Danny to come to her.

Nobody knew whether we should all go in together or leave them for a private meeting.

"'Tisn't as if there's anything in it," Mary said crossly. "They haven't seen one another since they were children. Besides you can't tell me Danny hasn't had girls, lots of girls, in Ireland."

"He's written to her every Christmas, birthday and special day," Vicky said.

"Well, why not? She's his cousin, and she

was born at Magillicuddy. And she's sick. But Laura knows Danny best. Laura knows him best of all. She's *lived* at Magillicuddy."

Laura's eyes were dark, but she said nothing.

"Darlings, let Sylvia have Danny when he's in Australia anyway," Aunt Sheilagh said. "It doesn't matter what he does when he's somewhere else."

"I vote we let Danny decide for himself," I said.

I was sorry for Sylvia but I found this basic family idea that Danny should be paired off with Sylvia more tragic than absurd. Several times in the last three summers a heat-wave had nearly killed Sylvia. What possible future could she and Danny have together? The prospect of her loving Danny in anything but a cousinly way promised only tragedy for her. She should have been protected from it, not have it thrust on her. I thought Aunt Sheilagh was at her *silliest* when she talked this way. What Laura thought she divulged to no one.

As it happened, Denney and Gerry, who were always impulsive, escorted Danny to the lounge.

"Here he is, Sylvia. Here he is!"

Since Denney and Gerry were there, then we might all just as well be there. We crowded into the doorway.

I suppose when Sylvia was a very little girl she learned control. That is why she was more a figure on a frieze than a very live person. She merely sat very still and smiled at Danny.

"Sylvia! Oh now, it's grand to see you!" Danny walked across the room and stood looking down at her. Then he bent down and kissed her on the forehead. We stood and watched.

What an absurd scene we made! Danny and Sylvia were looking at one another, and the rest of us, posed in silence like statues in a miniature gallery, were doing the kind of arithmetic in our plaster heads that made five out of two and two.

Danny sat down beside the sofa and took Sylvia's hand in his. He counted her fingers, turning each up a little at the fingertips as he did so.

"Still got five on each hand," he said. "All of you is here, Sylvia."

Laura turned and went out of the room. When I went after her she was making the tea alone in the kitchen.

"I think he does love her," I said, perplexed.

"He does."

"How could he, Laura? He doesn't know her. She's lovely, I know, but so quiet, so still . . . Why should he love her all those miles away in Ireland?"

Laura poured boiling water on the tea-leaves.

"That's probably why he does love her. A portrait in a gilt frame. It would be spoilt if it came to life. Anyhow love is a funny thing. It doesn't ever make sense."

I guessed it was this way with Laura too.

We had the kind of lunch that families always have when they're netted together by a birth, a marriage, an arrival, or a death. All talked hard about themselves and their own affairs and in between trying to impress Danny with the wonders of our own country. This is always done by telling anecdotes of "characters" in the north-west or the deep south, of wrecks off the West Australian coast or floods that wipe out whole townships. They told anecdotes about themselves or one another for the benefit of the rest of the family.

Danny sat, his chair pushed back, his knees

crossed over one another and a cigarette in one hand, the left hand. Periodically he said, "Oh yes!" or "Oh really!" with an expression of polite interest that made one wonder if he heard much that was said at all.

Then unexpectedly he would catch someone's eyes, and smile. It was enough. No young man ever sat, the central figure in a situation, who was the recipient of so much love. He was the last of our line. The umbilical cord that tied us to our origins. It was enough.

Marion Perrent said, when she met him, "Good looking? Well, very attractive!" And she rolled the "r" of the "very" just a little more than usual.

"He has beautiful manners," she added. And she smiled when she said this.

For a pack of opinionated women we, for once, did the right thing about introducing Danny to the possibilities of sheep-rearing and cattle-raising. We left Uncle William to introduce him to the kings of Pepper Tree Bay.

This opened up again our old life for us. The Bastons, those never-failing friends, gave a garden party.

Sylvia was ensconced on the verandah in the biggest armchair and in the prettiest dress. Miss Wilson excelled herself and I never knew whether this was another account that was carried for the honour and advertisement of it or whether the firm of Messrs. Beale and Beale continued to carry Uncle William, even as far as portentous social occasions.

Enough that Aunt Sheilagh and Sylvia looked their part. They all, including Laura, wore real pearls, although Laura's were very tiny pearls, and perhaps Messrs. Beale and Beale recognized them for what they were worth and were easy in their mind.

Danny looked fine in his well-cut London suit. He bowed and said "How-do-you-do?" in a manner which made the guests think they were meeting nobility. One young girl, someone from the country who was staying at one of the houses in Pepper Tree Bay and who was thus included in a general house-party invitation, very nearly bobbed a curtsey. Danny inspired young unsophisticated girls that way.

He was led alternately by Susan and Anne Baston from one group to another and though there was a far-away look in his eyes when those he met spoke to him of their affairs or their adventures, each time he left the group the word "Charming!" floated after him.

"Laura," I whispered. "Ask him what Mrs. Preston and Lady Stenning have just said to him. I bet he doesn't know. I bet he wasn't even listening."

"I'll do nothing of the kind," Laura said sharply, which was her way of admitting I was right. "Anyhow he'd rather be round the back picking the figs and apricots than bowing to all the ladies of Pepper Tree Bay."

"In that suit? And in those manners?"

"Danny can't help his manners. He was born with them. And he doesn't care a damn about his suit when he wants to enjoy himself."

Laura, I reflected, knew another side of Danny. The one that hunted carefree over the meadows of Magillicuddy.

It was just then that Danny did the thing that won him to the hearts of everyone, including the anaemic heart of Mr. Maynard-Arnold and the iron-coated one of Papa Baston.

At the east end of the croquet lawn, upon which most of the guests were disporting themselves, were two almond trees. The gardener had swept up the litter of fallen nuts and their black withered coats, but thousands of orphan almonds hung brown and black on the straggly branches.

Danny had been standing listening to a group tell him of the wonders of Australia and his eye kept roaming up into the branches of the overhanging almond tree.

"Excuse me," he said suddenly and politely. He gave a little running jump over a flower-bed and pulled a long stake out from behind a bush. With a neat jump he was back on the lawn and was poking at the almonds causing them to rain down on those foolhardy enough to stand underneath. Quite a group gathered out of range of fire and stood watching and laughing as now and again an almond fell on his own head. Then he threw his stake, javelin fashion, back into the garden and stooped down and gathered up the almonds. He stuffed them in his pockets and began peeling others and as he ate them himself he offered them to those around. His conversation went on as from the last comma.

It was hard to know why you love a person for doing just what Danny had done. It was so spontaneous and carefree. He had behaved according to his temperament, with great ease. The whole atmosphere of the garden-party relaxed and people laughed and began to behave as themselves and not as fiction would have them behave.

Mr. Maynard-Arnold's laugh bellowed out over the lawns and with that they all knew they might now begin to enjoy themselves and it didn't matter a darn who ate their strawberries and cream with gloves on, and who cared so little for convention they took them off.

"Rescue me!" Danny said to Laura in an aside, in between spoonfuls of strawberries and cream.

Laura needed no second invitation.

"Excuse me, Mrs. Williams, I want to get Danny to speak to some people over here."

"Oh rather!" said Danny, looking vaguely in the direction of the side verandah. "Must meet everybody."

"Certainly, Laura," Mrs. Williams said graciously. "We mustn't monopolize the guest of honour."

Laura edged Danny towards the side veran-dah. When she'd got him ten feet away from the nearest group of people she said, "Take the route behind those rose-bushes. Keep going till you find the fig trees."

Danny did precisely what Laura suggested while she mounted the verandah, empty hand-painted plates in her hands, as if going to replenish them. Instead she disappeared through the side door and emerged at the other end of the house, under the fig trees.

She said later, "Danny had forgotten the garden-party. He was eating figs and throwing the skins over the neighbour's fence with the kind of reckless abandon that's not allowed in Australia."

When next I saw Laura she was walking through the garden with Danny. Her face was upturned to his and she was laughing. The far-away expression had gone from his face and he too was laughing. He was suddenly alive. He was talking, and his hands were moving through the air, more like a Frenchman than an Irishman. Laura's face was beautiful because it was radiant.

They continued right through the garden like this and finally emerged on to the path below the verandah.

Danny looked up and smiled at Sylvia. He put one foot up on the verandah and leapt up. He seemed to have forgotten Laura. He sat down beside Sylvia and began to talk to her. He leaned forward a little, which not only shielded her from other people but made his shoulder an impassable barrier. For all the world he had forgotten the garden-party a second time.

The radiant look on Laura's face ebbed quietly away. She blinked her eyes once. Then she turned away and began to collect cups and saucers from people who did not know what to do with them now they were empty.

After the garden-party Danny's mornings were taken up with formal calls, accompanied by Uncle William, or Mr. Baston and Mr. Maynard-Arnold. Further calls were paid on Mr. Coole and Mr. Lessier, pastoralists from the north-west who held their court and conducted their summer business on their front verandahs overlooking the lovely shining river.

It didn't take Danny a week to discover that a jackeroo on a sheep or cattle station was the kind of stockman, on a stockman's wage, who may sit down at the table with the owner; that to be an owner one needed to invest ten or twenty thousand pounds in a property and be prepared if drought or flood was the particular hazard of that season to lose the lot. Or

217

if a bumper season was handed out by the gods to the ants labouring on the earth's surface beneath, to double it. In any event, whether it was lost or doubled, one needed ten to twenty thousand with which to begin.

This neither Danny, nor any other Montgomery, had.

"Why don't you sell that place in Ireland?" Mr. Lessier asked. "You'd do better here with the capital."

Danny did not answer. Neither did Uncle William. Sell Magillicuddy? There had to be a depression, another world war and an inflation in death duties before people of Danny's ilk admitted that it was possible to sell one's inheritance!

So sheep or cattle raising was washed up as far as Danny was concerned.

The matter of gold had now to be gone into.

Aunt Sheilagh and Sylvia had gone back to Kalgoorlie since the overcrowding at "Forty-Five" was intolerable and even Aunt Sheilagh's extravagant tastes did not go as far as first-class hotel accommodation for an indefinite period. It goes without saying the whole family eschewed anything less than first-class accommodation.

Danny, in matters pertaining to gold, was left in the hands of Uncle William and Laura.

Even Laura was impressed with the reception her father and cousin received at the hands of Messrs. Beale and Beale.

How double-faced were her principals! Or weren't they? Was their every move and word an insurance against the future in the same way in which the ladies of Pepper Tree Bay elaborately called on Mrs. Preston as a kind of insurance against their own lot should fortune change?

Mr. Rushton and Mr. Paul Beale met Uncle William and Danny first at their club, where the partners gave them a first-class lunch, excellent Irish whiskey, and discussed weather, the state of affairs in Ireland, and the prospects of the Italians if they should go into Abyssinia.

The state of Uncle William's affairs was never mentioned. One would have thought he was an honoured and valued client. Uncle William knew, and possibly Danny guessed, that such could hardly be the case.

It was when they ascended the cedar staircase in the old building in the Terrace that Mr. Rushton Beale broached the state of affairs in the share market.

"Very dull . . ." he said. "Very dull . . ."

Danny said the only shares he was likely to be interested in were gold shares. Mr. Paul looked at him through one eye. The other eye was temporarily closed against a spiral of cigarette smoke.

"Gold?" he said. "We have an expert in the firm on the gold market. I'll hand you over to her. You've no objection to dealing with a woman?"

"Why should I?"

Laura knew of those words later, and they gladdened her heart. Only she and the Messrs. Beale had any idea of the battle she had with her principals' colleagues up and down the Terrace. After she had told them how they should have sucked eggs as children they listened to her with considerable respect, but up to that moment there was a lot of wear and tear on her nervous system.

Danny, like the two Jewish theatre entrepreneurs who had called on Marion Perrent, had a touch of the cosmopolitan in him. He may not have seen brilliant Irish women conducting business around and about Grafton Street, Dublin, but he had certainly known of them conducting it from the privacy of the boudoir or the publicity of the hunting-field.

He had the same kind of respect for the hand that rocks the cradle and shakes the double bed as a French politician has.

Danny and Uncle William were conducted, between the ranks of the bowing Mr. Preston, Robert Doule and Miss Smythson, to Mr. Paul Beale's private office.

Mr. Beale sounded the buzzer and when Laura came in, very smartly but simply dressed, he said, "May I introduce Miss Montgomery; we call her our Clerk-of-'Change for want of a better expression." He waved his hand in the direction of the chairs in which Uncle William and Danny were now sitting. "Mr. Montgomery and Mr. Dennis Hara Montgomery." He finished the introduction with a touch of irony in his manner.

He now closed both his eyes, almost to a slit, to prevent cigarette smoke annoying them.

Only Uncle William showed feeling. And he showed a considerable amount of it. He went a blustery red and said, "You're not going to set my own daughter to telling me my business. What's she doing in here anyway? If you'd asked my advice now, Paul, I'd have told you there's only trouble when you get families mixed up with business."

Laura stood quite still by the doorway and smiled at Danny. Danny winked at her.

"Bring in the market analysis for the last three months, Laura," Mr. Beale said. "And you might get Doule to look out the files on Coolgardie Mines, Southern Cross and the Great Boulder. You can leave Great Western out. There aren't likely to be any shares on the market."

Laura went out and Mr. Paul Beale tapped the edge of his desk with a gold pencil. He leaned back in his chair. His coat was unbuttoned and his tie had strayed to strange places across his shirt-front. Mr. Rushton Beale, more immaculate, studied his highly polished shoes.

Danny said he liked the stone façade on the building opposite and it was a good thing the windows let in a view as well as the air.

Uncle William got up and walked round the office and sat down again.

"I suppose you know your business, Paul," he said at length. "If you'd asked my advice now . . ."

Mr. Paul Beale leaned forward and stabbed the pencil through the air in the direction of Uncle William.

"I'm going to ask your advice in a minute, William. I'm going to ask you how much gold there is in certain of those mines. Where the water level is and how much the market has to go to the ounce to make the mining of them payable again. On that I regard you as an expert. On the prediction of market changes I regard you as no better than any other man on the Terrace. The only expert on that on the Terrace is in the other room getting out those files. Ah, here she is."

Laura came in and proceeded to spread the sheets of reports on the table.

"All right, Laura," Mr. Beale said. "I'm not going to waste your time sitting here while these gentlemen study these things. When they've had a good look at them you can bring in that work you've been doing on the statistics of probability."

Laura flashed her smile round the room and went out. It was half an hour before she returned to a chastened father and an interested Danny.

Within five minutes they forgot she was a relative as they joined with her in unravelling the mystery of cyclical trends.

The long and the short of it all was that Danny, from then on, spent many hours with

Laura; and Uncle William, discomfited, returned to Kalgoorlie. Danny shortly afterwards followed him thither, to look down into these same mines and see what gold looked like, and was away two months.

How much he looked into the mines and how much time he spent looking into Sylvia's eyes, if at all, no one ever recorded.

Laura must have spent that two months in the anguish of disintegration.

Someone once explained one of Picasso's pictures as man in his several parts, man in pieces. If Picasso had drawn Laura in this period he would have had her eye on the west end of the paper and her ear on the east end. There would have been the symbol of a fine dress, and the string of pearls, and no doubt somewhere tucked in the region of her pocket a set of figures reading two and two make four.

That she was elated, there was no doubt. The incident with her father and Danny in Mr. Beale's office had highlighted her success in her chosen career. It had fired again that burgeoning curiosity about figures. She was a master of statistics now but knew by this time they were instruments only. Their science lay in their interpretation. This was something she had to go somewhere and see if she could learn. She sought out a University lecturer and thereafter spent one evening a week with him.

Meantime she had become more closely attached to Marion Perrent. This woman was the only person of her own sex who understood intellect in a woman. She took it for granted as neither unusual nor psychologically indecent. This is what Laura craved—that she could use her brain professionally without being labelled as a freak.

Laura dressed well to off-set the "freak" or "blue-stocking" suspicions.

Marion Perrent weaned her away from Miss Wilson.

"All right for Pepper Tree Bay and Government House," she said laconically. "But not at all revealing to the opposite sex."

"Who wants to reveal oneself to the opposite sex? It's not the fashion anyway. Look at these frightful brassières—trying to flatten one out to the proportions of a Lesbian!"

"The personality, I mean. Not the body."

She led Laura to a French dressmaker, newly set up in Perth, who made Laura dresses not basically unlike Miss Wilson's yet with a subtle difference that highlighted Laura's youth yet added sophistication.

"Why for the opposite sex?" Laura asked. "Aren't I in the throes of despising it? You despise a man who hasn't got a better brain than you have."

"You mightn't be as good as all that," Marion said. "But we'll put it to the test. That's got nothing to do with *living* with the opposite sex, and a woman has got to live with a man, sometime or other. It's biological, my dear."

"You mean there'd be no future generations?"

"I mean there'd be no future for Laura, only a dried-out shell of a mathematician. I hate to say it, my dear, it's such a cliché, but a woman has to be *fulfilled*. It's something you can't escape, in the laws of nature. Just as your figures seem to obey the laws of balance."

Laura looked at her friend.

Marion Perrent was leaning back in a chair, her face in shadows because of the half-lights she always affected in her flat when she was not reading or working with her hands.

How very feminine Marion Perrent was!

226

What was the strange allure of this woman that brought her many friends, a great many of them men, yet somehow held up an intangible barrier that kept her single?

Sometimes Laura felt prickings of curiosity but good manners kept her silent. Good manners, and a wish to safeguard herself from knowledge. Without knowing of the primeval mire she instinctively avoided it.

Marion Perrent stretched her arms above her head and the big sixteen-diamond ring which she wore on the fourth finger of her *right* hand sparkled as it caught a ray of light.

"Get that god-like oaf, young Preston, to take you to the fiesta at Freshwater Bay next week. If you've got a personality you might as well show it off, only for God's sake don't fall in love with Preston."

"I couldn't fall in love with an 'oaf'. And I think you're being a bit hard on him."

"I'm not. He's charming and looks like a Nordic god. But he's got sawdust in his head."

"Poor Dirk. He's sweet, but terribly dull."

"A good walking-stick. The perfect foil. And you might meet someone interesting."

"I'd like to meet the airman who talks to no

one and who's got another new suit this week."

Marion sat up angrily. Her eyes were suddenly dark and alien.

"Don't get interested in rubbish," she said. "Where's that Irish cousin of yours?"

"In Kalgoorlie, with Sylvia. They're more or less in love with one another."

Marion studied Laura's face.

"You make me sick," she said violently. It was the first time she had ever spoken to Laura like that. Laura was astonished at the vehemence behind the statement.

"Get the Nordic oaf and don't come back till you've been to at least two dances. You'd better go now or you'll be late for your University professor, and figures."

Laura began to gather together her things and Marion walked restlessly to the window and stood looking out over the darkling street.

When Laura came back from the bedroom Marion was holding aside the lace curtain with one finger.

"Isn't that that Doule person who works in your office?" she asked as she peered down into the street.

Laura looked out of the window.

"Yes. What on earth's he doing down here?"

"What's he doing walking past this block three times?"

Laura looked at Marion with astonishment.

"He couldn't possibly be waiting for me. How would he know I was here?"

Marion looked at Laura speculatively.

"He's not waiting . . . he's watching. I'd keep clear of that young man. Go down the side staircase and round the next block of flats. Don't come round the corner till you make sure he's taking his walk down this end of the block."

She spoke peremptorily and pushed Laura in the direction of the door.

As Laura made her escape she thought unhappily of many things. What was Robert Doule doing? She remembered back to the time when he had last accompanied her to the City Gardens for lunch. It was eighteen months ago and they had been very, very young. He had had that funny black look in his eyes. Since then Laura had hardly noticed him. Sometimes she went out of her way to say good-morning or good-afternoon. Sometimes she shared a joke with him, or a snort of biting criticism of some rival on the Terrace.

Sometimes he'd brought her fruit when his home garden was bearing, and once she thought the flowers in her room had come from him.

Otherwise he'd ceased to exist for her.

That perambulating outside Marion's flat must surely be coincidence. It was an area of flats and apartments; there could be a dozen girls tucked away in its labyrinths who might be engaging Robert's fancy.

Yet in her heart Laura knew, or feared, this was not so.

Strange how Marion had known instantly, without any knowledgeable background, that Robert had had a stealthy purpose in the Terrace tonight.

How did Marion know these things? In what dark places had her own heart or mind dallied that she *knew* things about people? Things that were a little frightening. For the fact of Robert spying on Laura was a frightening thing.

Laura flung herself in the chair opposite her instructor when she reached his house and escaped from the human problem into the mental problems on the fleetest possible wings.

It was typical of Laura that when the

230

human problem troubled her beyond endurance she became the career enthusiast. In the battle between the mind and the body, the mind won by default.

If the love she felt for Danny troubled her it did not crucify her. There had been no exchange of endearments and so there was no food upon which her heart could feed. He, by being himself, did something to her that shut her heart away at that time from anyone else. Nobody came up to Danny's standards. For anyone to have taken Danny's place with her he would have had to look like Danny, behave like Danny . . . and, like Danny, been the other end of the umbilical cord.

It was sufficient for her to daydream in the matters of love and give expression to the urgency of youth and the young body by a physical and mental activity that exhausted all her relatives.

"Dirk! Take me to the fiesta. I want to go out and dance and sing and be very very stupid. Besides, I want to wear my new dress."

"Why Laura, sure! Sure! I'll round up a crowd."

"I'm paying my own way."

"By golly, you're not. You can stay home if you talk that way."

Laura tried her blandishments on Mr. Preston.

"I want Dirk to take me out, and I'm not going to have him spend his weekly pittance on me. Please, darling Mr. Preston, you finance him, and I'll finance you."

Mr. Preston raised a sorrowful gentleman's eyes to Laura.

"My dear. That would never do."

No, in Mr. Preston's day such a thing would have been unthinkable. He would have gone to the debtors' court before he would have allowed a lady to be her own escort, with a walking-stick tagging along.

So Laura approached Mr. Rushton Beale, the younger brother of the partnership. She rested her elbows on the table and fixed him with her brilliant blue eyes.

"What does a girl do when she wants to go out with the right young man and knows he can't afford it?"

"Ten years ago she stayed at home," Mr. Rushton said with a grin. "Today I understand she pays her own way. All the same it's not good for a young man."

Laura pouted.

"Why should I stay at home?"

"Don't tell me a young lady with your obvious charms can't find a cavalier."

Laura lifted her elbows from the table and ran her fingernail along the edge of a large ledger.

"I can find them all right. But never the right one."

"What about Danny? Have you taken him sight-seeing at night time yet?"

The tiniest quiver flitted across Laura's face like the ripple of a breeze across the shining surface of the river.

"He's in Kalgoorlie," she said. Then she looked up. "I thought I might go with Dirk. You know, Mr. Preston's son. He's my kind. He knows the people I know. He knows *how* to order a drink, but he can't pay for things. Not without going broke. I want to pay for myself."

"Well, there's Robert Doule in the outer office. He moons and glooms over you, Laura, to the point of everyone else's boredom. He's just had a rise, he could afford it. He never spends any money on himself."

Laura avoided Mr. Rushton's eyes.

"He's not my kind," she said. "He doesn't know people . . ."

"There speaks a helluva snob!" said Mr. Rushton frankly.

Laura's eyes flashed.

"I hate snobs," she said. "I hate them worse than I hate snakes."

"But you have to know a person who knows people?"

"I don't *have* to. I can't help it if a man's got to hold his knife the right way. I can't help it if he's got to pull out a chair for a lady. I can't help it if he's got to blow his nose in a way that doesn't tell the whole world he's got a head cold. It's the way my beastly parents brought me up. They gave me *tastes* in things and people and I can't get rid of them. The tastes, I mean. I wish I'd never been born in Ireland . . . or had Irish parents . . . or been taught you don't say 'gurl' for 'gel'. Look what it's done to me! Made me useless anywhere."

Mr. Rushton roared with laughter.

"Forget it, Laura," he said. "One sixth of the population of Australia is like that at any time. They've got one foot in this country and one foot in that. Be yourself, in any country of the world. I'll tell you what I'll do. I'll speak to Preston. He knows the kind of people who are our clients. I'll tell him a little social life amongst them is good for business. As a matter of fact, it's damn good for business. Freshwater Bay is the best stamping ground in the State for our kind of clients. Preston had better get out his ancient clothes and appear in the right circles. He can take you and Dirk along—for decoration—and the firm will pay the bill."

Laura looked doubtful.

"As a matter of fact, Laura, I happen to be making a good business proposition to you, in all seriousness. If you're shrewd you can sell the idea of Cornell Motors and City Omnibuses to a few people like Baston and Maynard-Arnold."

A sharp light flickered in the back of Laura's eyes. She knew these two new companies were about to be floated as West Australian concerns and Beale and Beale were handling the business. Names like Baston and Maynard-Arnold spoken in the same breath as Cornell Motors would be enough.

"You think I can do it?"

"You can drop a little Beale and Beale secret. *Cornells and C.O.s are a good thing. They're the good oil, and only the élite are going to be let in on it* . . . That sort of thing. You're a smart girl, Laura. You could do it. Preston can go along for social position and the dignity of the thing. Dirk thrown in adds to the picture. It's a brilliant idea!"

The idea had been developing in Mr. Rushton Beale's mind as he talked. Now that it was there and firm he slapped his hand on the table.

"We only want Maynard-Arnold to walk into the office and inquire after Cornells or C.O.s and we're right. Then at the next party you mention to one or two of the *t'other-siders* that Maynard-Arnold was around inquiring after Cornells, and we've got the money. We'd like Maynard-Arnold's money, but his name is good enough.'

"It's better to have his money."

"Anybody's money will do."

"No it won't," said Laura. "You can use the *t'other-siders* to fill up the crevices but if you use West Australian money you'll have as tight and sound a set-up as the pastoral companies have got. They'll stick together and they own the land. They've got security that will weather any market storm. Your *t'other-siders* will get out at the first blow of a summer breeze."

Mr. Rushton listened to Laura with half-closed eyes.

"By God, you're right," he said. "By God, you're right."

He put both hands on the table and, pressing against them, tilted his chair back. He appeared to look down his nose as he stared at the young woman sitting opposite him.

"Do you reckon we're on the threshold of the motor-car age, Laura?"

"Of course," she said scornfully. "Who's going to take a week to ride into Carnarvon from Iduna Station when they can drive in in two days? Besides look what's happening to General Motors!"

"By God, you're right. By God, you're right."

When Laura went out Mr. Rushton Beale went into the Terrace. There he met his brother just coming from the underwriters.

"Paul," he said, "that girl's got brains. She's worth double her salary. And, by God, she knows the right people."

"What's she going to do now?"

"Spill Cornells and C.O.s to the Freshwater Bay crowd."

"For Pete's sake don't let her, or anyone else, spill Coolgardie Mines to anyone. Let's hope we can trust William Montgomery to keep his mouth closed."

"He will. There's too much at stake for him."

"Then double her salary. And for Chrissake send Preston to a decent tailor."

Thus Laura, arrayed like something out of a midsummer night's dream, went to the fiesta at Freshwater Bay.

It was a dream of a night in midsummer. The lights swung like large coloured stars from the tree-tops, the Club house was silhouetted in a string of golden lights, the launches formed a dazzling diamond necklace around the curve of the bay, and the river was a mirror that repeated the scene again and again.

The deep armchairs on the wide verandahs were filled with the male side of the Bastons, Maynard-Arnolds, Cooles, Lessiers, their friends, relatives, fellow pastoralists and hangers-on.

Their harsh north-west voices and their bellowing laughs rang out over the river. Around them flitted the distaff side like moths in chiffons and satins. The young girls and the young men laughed and flirted their way between the launches, the jetty, the Club house, the lawns and the barbecues. The river lay still and smiled under the stars, keeping whatever secrets it was necessary for it to keep. It had known the age-old people of the dream-time, and kept their secrets.

Laura, young, with the extra poise that brains give to natural good looks and wit, was once again, as she had been on that sports day that now seemed years ago, the centre of a court of young men. Again she felt that power of conquest in her, and she rose to the occasion.

There was something cruel in the pleasure she took in being first among the young men.

It was only Mr. Preston's sorrowful and anxious gaze that suddenly brought her back to the reality of her purpose here tonight.

For one shocking moment she thought, "To hell with it! I'm going to enjoy myself." She took another glass of wine from Dirk and another chicken leg from the loaded table beside her.

But Mr. Preston's gaze had taken the edge off her appetite. Her brain began to work and she could not deny the fascination of its possibilities.

She made an excuse to those around her and went towards the verandah where the kings of the earth—at least the owners of

West Australian earth—still sat putting the country and the empire to rights.

"Hallo, Uncle Dreary," she said. This was usurping the privileges of Mr. Maynard-Arnold's own relatives, but Laura had addressed him thus as a child, and she took the right to do so in her adult years with that kind of risk in social aplomb that pulls so many social climbers one step up in the ladder.

"Well, Laura," bellowed Mr. Maynard-Arnold. "So you've come to bother your pretty head with the old codgers, the arm-chair politicians, hey?"

But he was flattered because someone young and pretty had sat down on the arm of his chair and let her soft rounded arm rest along his shoulders.

"By golly, Laura!" he roared, turning his body a little so he could look at her. "How's the family? How's those ruddy gold-mines, hey? How's William getting on up there in that flaming heat? Sand and flies. God-damnit, he'd do better in the north-west!"

Laura's quick eyes had taken in that Papa Baston sat on one side of Mr. Maynard-Arnold and Mr. Coole on the other. Two of the Baston nephews, bronzed north-west

men, were sitting on the edge of the verandah, leaning against the pillars, one eye on
the river and one ear on the verandah conversation. Mr. Lessier sat next to Mr. Coole.
The grouping was perfect.

She cast a quick glance along the verandah
at Mr. Preston's gentlemanly figure as he
walked away. Such chicanery was not for Mr.
Preston. He did not understand the principles of enticement. Like the ostrich he
would rather put his shaggy head under the
sand.

"Not in the north-west, Uncle Dreary,"
she said, giving him a tiny hug. "You big
boys own all the land that matters in the
north-west. Clever, weren't you, when you
were young men? Took the pick . . ."

"Clever? By golly, Laura, you're an
ignorant young sweep! Damned hard work.
Years and years of damned hard work. Look
at Baston here. Overlanded the first mob of
sheep ever went into the north-west. Call that
clever?"

"I suppose it was more than that," she conceded. "The clever ones don't go so much
for hard work. They turn their money over.
Don't I know. You'd be surprised, Uncle
Dreary, how much some of those *t'other-siders*

241

make by just walking in and out again of Beale and Beale."

"*T'other-siders*! By golly!" roared Mr. Maynard-Arnold. "What you make of that, Baston? You and me can fight the damned drought and floods in the north and all these fellows do is come over here and take the pickings."

"They're not making any money out of land, anyway," Papa Baston said. "Take a millionaire to clear the scrub out of the south-west, and we can keep the blighters out of the north."

"But they don't want to make it out of land," Laura said. "That's too much hard work. They want to make it out of the city."

"The city? Do you hear that, Coole?" shouted Mr. Maynard-Arnold. "Bludging on the farmers and station owners . . ."

"How do they do it? That's what I'd like to know," said Mr. Coole. "How do they get here? Where do they get their money from? Who's paying the piper?"

"I fear it you are, darling Mr. Coole," said Laura. "You'll buy machinery and motor cars and tractors, and they'll finance the companies that sell them. The city will grow and they'll run the buses and taxis and build the houses. All they've got to do is sit at an office desk and watch their money grow."

"They're not the only ones," said Mr. Lessier suddenly. "You know what, Arnold? I made two thousand last year out of the Midland Railway Company." He suddenly roared with laughter. "Freights my wool down," he said. "I pay railage to myself." He roared again.

"That crowd of yours got any Midland Railway shares, Laura?" asked Mr. Maynard-Arnold, half interested.

"Not a chance. It's an English company. You must have picked yours up on the London market, Mr. Lessier."

"I did that." Mr. Lessier laughed again. "You fellows are all asleep," he said.

Laura neatly pleated the chiffon of her skirt with her free hand.

"That's how Mr. Beale feels," she said. "He doesn't want to let the *t'other-siders* in either. He's got two companies now and he's trying to keep them out." She sighed. "But they've got all the money. They'll make money out of these, just as those who risked buying General Motors did when they were two and six."

"What sort of companies?" growled Mr. Maynard-Arnold.

"Well, that's confidential," said Laura. "You wouldn't like me to talk the firm's business, would you? But it's motor cars and motor transport. I'll tell you that much."

"Motor cars!" grumbled Mr. Baston. "The old horse and buggy's good enough for me. Started me off . . ."

"You've got a hell of a big car out the front right now, Baston," said Maynard-Arnold.

"Well, haven't we all . . ." said Mr. Coole.

His words dropped like several stones into a pool of silence and thought.

Laura stood up and shook out her beautiful skirt.

"I'll get the cane from Mr. Beale," she said. "I'd better go and talk to Mrs. Preston."

"Yes; you go on off, Laura. Mrs. Preston likes to have someone talk to her."

There was a silence on the verandah as she moved away.

In the small hours of the morning the gaiety dimmed and people began to drift home.

Mr. Preston, out of his newly won entertainment allowance, had hired a taxi and the four of them, Mr. and Mrs. Preston, Dirk and Laura, were making their way across the lawns towards it.

Mr. Maynard-Arnold was shouting at his chauffeur to bring his own car up. Laura ran across the lawn towards him.

"Goodnight, darling Uncle Dreary," she said. She leaned impulsively forward and kissed him on the cheek. "Buy Cornell Motors," she whispered in his ear. "But please, please don't tell Mr. Beale I said anything."

"Eh? What's that?"

But like the night moths she had gone silently across the lawn.

245

11

WHEN Laura told me about the night at the Freshwater Bay Club I asked her did she buy any Cornell Motors herself.

"No," she said. "I bought Coolgardie Mines. I took six months' advance on my new salary and bought Coolgardie Mines."

"If you believed in the motor-car age why did you buy into mining? It was dead as a doornail then."

"That's why. And I believed in myself. I knew there was gold there and I'd worked out the price of gold had to rise by sixpence an ounce to make it payable. On the law of probability the price had to rise. Cornell Motors were good, but long distant, and the big quick money is always made in gold or oil."

Such was Laura's pleasure in herself as a business woman that to a certain extent it mitigated the emptiness of her love life.

It was no use pretending that love didn't matter to Laura. It did. She was restless. She craved admiration and when she got it she revelled in it. Her life became a rush of social engagements between bouts of study with her University instructor, shopping with dressmakers and milliners, occasional teas with Marion Perrent, and a constant vigil against the spying propensities of Robert Doule.

"He drives me mad," she told Marion Perrent. "What am I going to do with him?"

"You don't encourage him?"

"Of course I don't. But I've got to work in the same office with him. I can't escape him. I know it sounds absurd to say it, but sometimes I feel trapped by him."

"Tell him to go to hell, and mean it. One good explosion ought to settle him for all time."

"I can't."

"Why?"

"I don't know."

"There must be a reason."

"I'm sorry about him . . ."

"You can't afford to be. That's dangerous." Marion spoke sharply and out of a depth of worldly knowledge.

"Does it sound melodramatic to say I'm sometimes afraid of him?"

"All love affairs are melodramatic. Love is

an obsession—a state of the glands and has nothing to do with the mind. That's why some men marry pretty faces and find they have to spend the rest of their lives with morons. Why are you afraid of him? Does he bother you?"

"No. He only watches me. And he looks funny, gets a red rim round the pupils of his eyes."

"You'd better change your job."

Laura looked at Marion aghast.

"Leave Beale and Beale? But it's my life . . ."

"Other stockbroking firms would pay you just as much."

"No they wouldn't. They don't know the work I'm doing either. Confidential work; I couldn't do it anywhere else." Laura's bottom lip jutted. "I'm not going to be driven from my job by an ass like Robert Doule anyway."

"How do you stand with your bosses? Get them to shift *him* on."

Laura's shoulder drooped.

"I couldn't do that," she said. "He's got a life too. If I won't go because of him, why should he go because of me?"

"In that case you'd better get married."

"Who to?"

Marion looked at Laura speculatively.

"Is it against the laws of the Church of England to marry your own cousin?" she asked at length. She did not fail to notice the quiver that rippled over Laura's face.

"I haven't asked the Church of England, and I haven't any occasion to ask it," she said. Then because Marion had stabbed her in the heart she stabbed back. "You might find out a way of introducing me to that airman."

Marion Perrent picked up a box of cigarettes from the table and threw it at Laura.

"Get out!" she said. "Get out, and stay out! I told you he was rubbish."

Laura was astonished enough to pick up her things and get out. Marion's face had gone a dark red and the rims of the pupils of her eyes had been like Robert Doule's—fire.

Laura was mystified. Fortunately she was too busy to think about the strangeness of it for long. Danny was back in Perth and the social life of the Montgomeries was in full swing.

Laura, heady with the wine of social and business success, might have played a winning hand with Danny in this period, if she had set her mind to it. When she was on top of the world she was dazzling and irresistible. Besides it was in her nature to be ruthless and to take. There was only one person in the whole world who could have stood between her and the assault of Danny. And fate had ordained that that one person, Sylvia, should stand there.

It irritated me beyond endurance because I thought of the senselessness of it.

I often wondered why Laura, essentially selfish in many habits of her life, should have stood aside so effortlessly for Sylvia. It wasn't that she loved her sister to any great degree. They had never appeared to be close, and they had seen little enough of one another in recent years.

I believe myself that Laura had a neurosis about death. For instance she would never take the bus route to Fremantle that passed the cemetery. She always took the longer and more costly one that went round the river. I think that the angel of death always stood beside Sylvia, and Laura would never approach. It was not unselfishness that kept her from rifling Sylvia's possessions, but a neurosis.

Her scrupulousness was very apparent in

the last two months of Danny's stay in Australia.

There he was, ensconced at "Forty-Five". At hand. Sylvia was four hundred miles away in the middle of the desert.

Danny was extrovertish by nature and he loved a crowd. Mama thought "Forty-Five" with its family of girls, its hustle, its shabbiness, and its lodgers, would be intolerable to Danny. More than once she suggested other accommodation for him.

"I like it here," he said. "I can put my boots up on the fireplace."

This was a thing he never did so one presumed he meant he liked the atmosphere of "Don't-care" and "Tomorrow-will-do".

Denny and Gerry couldn't stay for ever in the country and they had come back to the side room that had been so clinically prepared for Danny. He moved himself outside to a little wooden annexe that was no more than a stableman's room, and proceeded to live like one of his own grooms. Since no one was home during the day-time he fended for himself in the kitchen.

I'm quite sure he loved every moment of it.

To begin with, once the family was home the place was alive not only with Montgomeries but with their friends. And the friends of us older three girls were mostly students. They sat about on the back lawn with Danny, ties and shoes off, hair rumpled, and fingernails not too clean. They arranged the affairs of the Empire.

These people, the Australian Montgomeries and the students, could talk. Danny loved to talk and be talked at by this sort of people. Politics, religion, world personalities, he had opinions on them all. He was not wordy as were his Australian cousins but he had a sophisticated wit and a knack of putting things neatly in six words that was amusing as well as pungent comment.

His listeners formed a court about him just as Laura's male admirers formed a court about her when she went out and about.

Though for a good deal of the time he wore an open-necked shirt and a very old pair of pants he always looked as if he had just taken a shower. Quite often he had not.

He bought himself a small second-hand motor car and went out into the country. He found odd circles of people who were arty-crafty groups or semi-intellectuals. He discovered emigrants from England and Ireland who once had adorned the Backs of Cambridge or the meadows of Oxford. None of us had ever known these people to exist.

If he had any money he didn't look as if he had, but we never knew him to be quite without it.

Laura sat for hours on the old dilapidated box ottoman in the vestibule and talked to him about the market.

"Danny," she implored him, "buy Coolgardie Mines, and wait."

"What with?" he asked.

"Anything. Sell that car. You could pick up ten thousand at one and a penny for the price of that car."

"I can use a car and I can't use paper, except to light the bath heater."

"I'll show you . . ."

And she brought up to "Forty-Five" her graphs and tables of statistics. None of us could be bothered unravelling them. Mary, to begin with, was the only one who had the brains to understand them, but none of us had the price of a new heater for the bathroom, let alone for a packet of seemingly worthless gold-mine shares.

"I once had my fingers burnt with gold shares," Mama said. "Never again. Why don't you learn from what's happened to your father, Laura?"

"He put his eggs into too many baskets," Laura said. "If he'd stuck to General Motors he'd have been all right."

"But you're trying to sell *gold*."

"Because they're at pit bottom. That's when you buy."

But Mama was incapable of believing in gold or believing that in Laura's dark head there could be all she assumed to know.

"Why try to tease Danny into it?" we wanted to know.

"Because of Magillicuddy."

This brought a pensive silence. Though none of us would ever own one blade of grass on Magillicuddy it seemed a family religion to save it. Yet none of us could do that. Only Danny.

"Why don't you farm it, Danny?" Mama asked. "In Australia the owner works his paddocks with his own hands. He's had to . . ."

"I couldn't take the bread out of the men's mouths," Danny said with a smile. "They've got to live too."

"Bread?" said Mary. "I thought it was potatoes."

"Horses," Laura said bitterly. "They do

254

everything with horses, except eat them. Lazy beggars."

Laura had been years in Ireland and she knew, but it didn't stop us being shocked at these words falling so bitterly from her lips. Her eyes were dark and angry.

"I wish I could have Magillicuddy for five years."

Danny looked at her. He had the air of so many Irishmen that said, "We are so right"; but never argued the issue.

Mary once said, "How do you argue with an Irishman when all he'll do is look superior?"

"Do the same," said Laura. "It's the most devastating form of argument. The next best thing is to take out a newspaper and read it. It's the same as putting up a stone wall."

"Don't buy gold . . ." Mama said.

"I'm not," said Danny. He put out his hand and took hold of Laura's wrist. "Come on, old thing. Let's go and eat. Far from this madding crowd. Let's go down to the beach and eat fish fry and meringue cakes."

And they went, Danny as he was, his fine sun-tanned throat rising out of his open-necked shirt, an old snake belt he'd picked up somewhere out in the country holding up his dilapidated pants; Laura looking as if she had stepped out of *Vogue* instead of off the hot pavements of the Terrace.

"Anyone would think she was going out with a hobo," Denny said sarcastically.

"Even if he was covered in coal dust Danny would still look what he is," Mama said. "An Irish gentleman."

"Mama!" we all shrieked in unison. It wasn't that what she said lacked truth, but that it was the kind of thing nobody dared to say in Australia. "A gentleman from overseas" often meant a ne'er-do-well who had left his country for his country's good. In Australia a man was a man, and there weren't any "kinds".

Though Laura went with Danny when he carried her away like that she was very meticulous when she took him out to her dances and parties. She took the faithful but innocuous Dirk and insisted that one or other of us came to partner Danny. No one could ever say that Laura tried to take Danny away from Sylvia.

Sometimes we would suggest one of the more scintillating talkers for Danny's sake, but Laura stuck to Dirk.

"Why Dirk?"

"He's so safe."

"Does that matter?"

"My God, yes."

"You don't like being pawed?"

"Damn being pawed."

None of us at that stage knew much about Robert Doule and that his obsession had had the effect of frightening Laura not only of him, but of the potential in other young men.

Again and again some young man would invite Laura to go out with him. She would go once, perhaps twice. Then drop him.

"But why?" I asked her, puzzled.

Laura would shake her head, shrug her shoulders.

"Not interested," would be all she would vouchsafe.

Years afterwards she told me that when a man got to the stage of flirtation she felt nothing but a sudden fear. She felt as if she stood in the doorway of a trap. Common sense told her that all men were not like Robert Doule, but she had had her lesson in dalliance and had it too young. She could only step over that threshold with someone *she* loved. Never mind whether he loved her or not.

257

There had to be one more emotional experience in Laura's life, however, before the pattern of her temperament was fixed for all time.

It was Danny who inadvertently brought it about, then, being Danny, went away and left the consequences to themselves.

12

DANNY'S mixed bag of acquaintances proved an endless source of amusement and conjecture in the family. He was not musical yet knew musicians. He was not literary yet he discovered people who not only read books, but wrote them. His only politics were Irish politics yet he unearthed people who were ready to lay down their lives for their own brand of Australian politics.

He sat about on Mr. Maynard-Arnold's front verandah and with equal ease lounged in the Trades Hall with the foundry workers or railway gangers.

"Where does he pick them all up? What's he doing with them?" we would ask one another.

"Perhaps he's learning about Australia," Mama said.

"Learning my foot," I said rudely. "Danny doesn't want to learn anything. It's just his way of having a good time."

How he got to know the people he knew, heaven only knows. And why they liked him

259

the way they did, heaven nor they ever divulged.

He went up the north-west with the crew of a cray-fishing boat. He went out to the market-gardens with the Italian growers. He spent a week-end on a poultry farm in the hills with a Cockney immigrant from Fulham. He packed a swag and spent three days with some aborigines in the bush east of Moora. In between times he ate dinner or lunch in the best clubs and with the best ladies or the most conservative of land-owners in the State.

When he was asked "Why?" he simply replied, "Something to do."

He never turned down an invitation of any kind whatever, whether it was in the highest or the lowest society.

"Why do they all like him?" I asked, puzzled. His accent, his polished manners, and that recurring "Oh really!" ought to have damned him with the more implacable types in the coalmines and on the wharfs. But for some reason he was welcome everywhere.

"Charm," Mama said. "Charm. They're born with it, like Laura and Theodora were born with cauls on their faces."

This comment induced in me a new train of thought.

"Danny," I said across the tea-table that night. "People born with cauls on their faces have second sight. Right?"

"So they say."

"Then if Laura says buy Coolgardie Mines, you ought to buy them."

Strangely enough, Danny did not pooh-pooh this as the rest of the family immediately did.

"Who's going to win the Melbourne Cup this year?" Vicky asked me across the table. "Just tell us, Theodora, and we'll all make a fortune."

"What do *you* say about Coolgardie Mines?" Danny asked me.

I shrugged.

"I don't know anything about them. But I've an urge to think that Laura's right. Maybe it's because of those graphs and figures and things. I just wish I had ten pounds. I'd buy Coolgardie Mines."

"The only thing a caul is good for is going to sea," said Mama. "You'll never drown, Theodora."

This Mama firmly believed, though she

261

absolutely refused to believe there was any future in gold.

It was shortly after this conversation that Danny arrived at Beale and Beale's with a young man called Peter Stevenson. Danny had persuaded him to buy Coolgardie Mines.

This was the only time Laura ever had an unpleasant scene with her employers. She told me afterwards they were very angry with Danny. Nobody was supposed to know anything about those particular mines. The partners were picking up small parcels of shares here and there and didn't want the price to rise.

Laura scolded Danny and the firm grudgingly managed to buy a thousand shares for Peter. Whether this attitude had a salutary effect on Danny or not, I do not know. Laura reported that Danny later spent an hour in Mr. Paul Beale's office and after that the subject of gold was dropped. Laura didn't know what had taken place because she and the Beale brothers had all sent one another to Coventry. Only the memory of Mr. Maynard-Arnold leading the rush to buy Cornells and C.O.s saved Laura from a very long session in Coventry.

There were too many thunder-clouds on too many faces in the offices of Beale and Beale that day for Laura to notice that the advent of Danny and the very respectable Peter Stevenson had induced such transports of rage in Robert Doule's eyes that Mr. Preston had pulled his eye-shade so far down on his brow he couldn't see anything but the ledger in front of him.

Several days after this memorable visit Laura was lunching alone in a small café when a young man sat down opposite her. She returned his smile, feeling sure she'd met him somewhere, but couldn't remember where.

"You're Dennis Montgomery's cousin," he said. "We met the other day in Beale's."

"Oh yes," Laura's smile gave him a friendly welcome.

He consulted the menu card while Laura took stock of him.

She liked him. She liked his air which was a mixture of friendliness and detachment. She recognized it as Danny's air. He had dark hair and dark eyes where Danny had fair hair and blue eyes but his face was the same shape and the bones of his hands were even and fine. His wrists were narrow and Laura was ready to bet a pretty penny his ankles were just the same. He had a kind of masculine magnetism that is as undefinable as it is effective.

Laura hated the fact that her parents had taught her to tell breeding by the shape of a person's ankles, but she could never help noticing them. It was a legacy of knowledge for which she was not thankful. It was a rule of thumb that didn't work out in this country where men and women had to walk too far to keep their ankles slim. Besides it was snobbery, and Laura said she hated snobs the same way as she hated snakes.

But she liked Peter Stevenson because his voice was good, he was masculine, and his ankles were certain to be good.

When he put down the menu he caught her eyes and his smile said he knew she'd been scrutinizing him. If Laura had looked deeper she might have understood it to say he was used to being scrutinized by young women.

"You never want to eat much in this country, do you?" he said. "Too hot."

"Where do you come from?" Laura asked politely, trying to mask the real curiosity in her eyes.

"Darlington."

"Oh, up in the hills."

This was the infuriating kind of answer that an Englishman always gave. He said from whence he had come immediately, that day, and withheld the more important information. Laura had to bow to his reticence, for she herself deplored the people who on first acquaintance sketched their life-history for a stranger's ear.

"Are you in Perth for the day?" she asked with the same air of polite disinterest.

When Peter smiled the grooves in his cheeks became deeper.

"Danny and I are having dinner together, then he's coming up to my place for some music."

"Music?" said Laura, astonished. "I didn't know Danny liked music."

"I don't suppose he does, but I do. And if he wants to come up to the shack he's got to listen. Which he does, very politely."

"Do you live alone in the shack?"

"I'm trying to make an orchard grow. One has to rough it to start off with, you know."

"Of course," said Laura.

She noticed again the long fine bones of his hands and his well-kept fingers and nails. They didn't look like an orchardist's hands.

"Would you like to come with Danny?"

265

His dark eyes were a sudden challenge. Laura said "Yes" instantly because she knew that was just exactly what she would like to do.

"We're having dinner at the Metropolitan."

"I won't have dinner with you if you don't mind. I'll go home to my apartment and get things ready for tomorrow. I'm a working girl. Pick me up after dinner. Danny knows where."

"Good."

He picked up Laura's chit and paid for both their lunches. In the doorway he stood looking at her a moment before he smiled again. There was something intimate about his smile. This time Laura did not feel afraid. She did not feel here goes a young man who might trap me. She felt, rather than thought, that here goes a young man who's master of any situation. He's always on top, this one. There'd be no haunting threats behind any bunch of flowers this Peter Stevenson might give away. He'd crack the whip, and that didn't matter because Laura jumped for no man.

It just meant he wouldn't jump for her.

At seven-thirty Laura heard the peep of

Danny's second-hand sports car in the Terrace outside her room.

She had been troubled about what to wear. She wanted to look well, possibly at her best, but she must not look overdressed. In the end she decided on Danny's standards: something comfortably old that still had the hallmarks of a good dressmaker. She wore a dark blue silk dress with a cream guipure lace collar. The collar and her string of small pearls were her only ornament. She brushed her hair till it shone and was very careful about her make-up. Just enough to improve . . . and not enough to be seeking for effect. For the life of her she didn't know why she felt like this, for never in all her life did she waver from her love for Danny. Yet for Danny alone she had never troubled to be different from what she always was.

Tonight, she had decided, her role was to be silent and inscrutable. The second sight with which the caul had endowed her forewarned her that Peter Stevenson would see through most mascaraed disguises. Only the enigmatic or unattainable would rouse his interest.

This pose was almost destroyed from the start.

267

Having stopped his car, Danny could not start it again without getting out and saying things to the engine. Laura in the front seat, about to be wedged between the two of them, could not help joining Danny in his wordy debate with the car. Silence was as impossible to Laura as it was to any Montgomery.

When Danny got back into the car he wiped one oily finger on his trouser leg and said, "Move over, Laura. Sit on Peter. I want to move the gears."

Moving over very nearly did mean sitting on Peter. He had perforce to put his arm out along the back of the seat, almost around Laura, to make room for it.

"Smoke?" he said.

"Please," Laura answered.

She tried not to catch his eyes as he struck a match for her and she bent her head to draw on the cigarette. She knew that he knew she had avoided his eyes. That was worse than looking right in them.

Then she said "Damn" to herself and snuggled against Danny. She had never dared to do that before and suddenly it seemed to be very all right to do it. The man the other side of her just became a bony figure of a man who kept her from making a complete fool of herself as she felt the powerful pull of Danny's muscles when he moved to change the gears.

Danny and Peter talked across her and Laura smoked with half-closed eyes and thought of Danny. The thinking brought tears to her eyes. She had never been so close to him before and the tears were because she knew he didn't notice. He was wrapped up in a political argument with the man the other side of her.

The night was black and moonless but the stars were incredibly bright. When they left the main road and weaved and jolted their way along a road little better than a bush track all conversation, as such, stopped. Peter was directing Danny and Danny was feeling his way from bump to bump with deep concentration.

When they arrived at the shack Laura had to shake herself back into the world in which so short a time before she had wished to appear enigmatically alluring to a man called Peter.

"Keep your head-lights on the door while I find the keyhole," said Peter.

He went into the shack and turned on a

light. Danny turned off the head-lights and they went inside.

It was a two-roomed wood-and-iron structure. It was well, but barely, furnished and scrupulously neat and tidy. It was the room of a musician rather than an orchardist. There were no evidences of toiling with the earth.

There was an old leather sofa, but covered with a particularly fine paisley shawl. There were two armchairs that looked older than the sofa but were made interesting by tapestried cushions. There was a carpet on the floor that was not old and looked expensive. There were two pictures, Monet prints; there were several ornaments on the mantelpiece that Laura knew were "art" but couldn't place. And dominating the whole small room was a glorious rosewood Lipp piano with a music cabinet beside it.

"Ha!" said Peter. "Come in. The sofa's yours, Laura. Lie on it if you like. What do you like to drink? Beer, wine, whiskey?"

"Claret," said Laura, just to be difficult and because she thought Peter was too self-assured. One hour pressed to Danny's side had put this young man right in the place he belonged.

Danny sat in one armchair, crossed one

270

knee over the other and hunched one shoulder a little in front of the other. He peered at the carpet.

"Could be Savronnie, but it's an imitation," he said.

Peter went outside and came in with glasses. He had in his hand a bottle of claret.

His dark eyes sought and challenged Laura.

"You didn't think I had it, did you?" he said.

"No," said Laura. "I didn't. Is this the right hour for drinking claret?"

"I wouldn't know. I understand those who prefer it drink it when they like."

"Drink anything you like any time you like," said Danny. "I hope you brought the whiskey in for me."

"I did," said Peter. He stood above Laura, the bottle in one hand and the glass in the other. "Do you drink a little, a lot, or all the time?"

"A little. And so does Danny, if he's going to drive me home."

Peter filled a claret glass for Laura and then put the bottle on a table. He pushed a whiskey bottle and a jug of water in Danny's direction and said, "You know when to stop."

He took off his coat, rolled up his sleeves and sat down at the piano.

From the first chord Laura knew he could play. The little room thundered with music. After a quarter of an hour he had forgotten he had guests.

Laura half reclined on the sofa and listened. Danny picked up one magazine after another and leafed through them. The music went on and on.

Laura put her feet up on the sofa and lay back, full length. She began to get drowsy and she went into a daydream about herself and Danny, about herself and the winning of a fortune in Coolgardie Mines. About herself making a triumphal return to Ireland, the saviour of Magillicuddy.

After an hour and a half Danny, who had been here before, got up and went outside and put a kettle on the primus stove. When the kettle had boiled and he'd made the tea he made toast on top of the flame. He came in licking his buttery fingers and said, "Well, what about it? Tea?"

Peter let his hands drop from the keyboard. He sat drooped forward a minute, then straightened and shook himself. He swung round on the piano stool and looked at Laura.

"Asleep?"

"Nearly."

"You don't like music?"

"I do but I don't understand it. I just lie and think about myself, to a beautiful accompaniment. I think you ought to play a little softer in so small a room."

"I'm not playing for the room. I'm playing for myself."

He got up and went out into the kitchen and rattled cups and saucers while Danny brought in the tea and toast.

Laura also shook herself and sat up. When Peter brought a cup of tea to her he stood looking down the way he had done when he had poured the claret for her. His eyes deliberately challenged hers. She let one little eyebrow flicker, answered his look with a blank stare and helped herself to sugar.

"So much for you," she thought.

They sat and talked Australia, Australiana and Australian people for another hour, then Danny rose, stretched himself and yawned.

"Coming home, Laura?"

"Yes," she said. "I've a day's work to do tomorrow."

When they went outside to the car Peter held the door open for her. As she turned to

273

say goodnight he picked up her hand and kissed it.

"Not done," Laura said, shaking her head gently. "Not done in Australia."

"Is that where we are?" said Peter. In the glow of the headlights she could see he was smiling. His eyes were dark pools. He, thought Laura, is the enigmatic one.

He held her hand tight so that for a moment she could not get in the car. He bent his head forward a little so the light shone full on his face.

"I'll see you again," he said.

Laura felt a tiny thrill of anticipation go through her. She immediately banished it.

"Maybe . . ." was all she replied.

She and Danny drove down the hills in silence. Laura thought about how she had leaned against him all the way up. There was a lump in her throat. Then she thought about those powerful dark eyes of Peter Stevenson. He had done something to her, that man. What was it? A challenge?

She felt torn in two. Her one and true love was on her right. On her left stood Mephistopheles.

Danny stirred.

"Laura?"

"Mm."

"You liked that man."

"Why, yes. You meant me to, didn't you?"

"No. Not particularly."

Laura tried to see Danny's face in the half-light.

"You do surprise me."

"Sometimes I surprise myself. I didn't like him looking at you like that. Damned cheek!"

Laura was astonished, but she said nothing. When they reached Laura's apartment Danny turned off the engine, switched off the dashboard lights and took out a packet of cigarettes. He lit one for Laura and handed it to her.

They smoked in silence.

"Laura . . ." Danny said. Then he brushed his hand through his hair and made a sound like a half groan. "Oh well . . . Laura. Goodnight!"

"Goodnight, Danny."

But when she got inside the main entrance of the apartment house she stamped her foot. She didn't know herself whether she was angry with Danny or Peter Stevenson, or both.

The pattern of Laura's life was always repeating itself. She was two selves and each seemed unrelated to the other.

The café in which Laura and Peter had met, for the second time in fact but the first time in reality, was one to which Laura went quite often. She persuaded herself the following day that it was not the least unusual for her to go there again. She argued this momentous question to herself all the way down the Terrace yet when she reached the opening into the arcade in which was the café, she turned away. She bought a packet of sandwiches and went down to the foreshore of the river and ate them there. She watched the ferries shuttling backwards and forwards and reflected on the nature of things as she saw them within herself.

It would have been quite in order for her to go to the café if she hadn't had the half-excited, half-expectant feeling of doing something very unusual. To have said to herself, "This is quite customary" would have been a lie. At the entrance to the arcade she admitted it to herself.

She told herself, as she sat by the river, she had done the right and obvious thing. She had, by turning away, dismissed Peter

Stevenson from her mind. She proceeded to dismiss him from her thoughts, but she could not dismiss from her body the strange tingling feeling she had had all the morning.

She thought about figures, and graphs and gold shares. The tingling persisted. So she thought about Danny.

In her mind this was forbidden territory upon which she only rarely trespassed, and then haltingly and not without a sense of guilt. Today everything gave way to a sense of relief and safety.

Open, that is to herself, and without any of the limiting factors of self-discipline, she flew to Danny's image, and inexplicably found safety in it.

She felt as if she had strayed, and found her way home. She felt as if she had seen strange faces and strange places and had suddenly come upon the familiar face in a place well-loved and known.

It all brought smarting tears to the back of her eyes but the tingling feeling had gone. She planned her future with calm. She would have a brilliant career in the world of finance. She even tinkered with the idea of going back to the University. This time she would enrol in economics. She saw herself as economic adviser to great people, great business houses; indeed she carried her dream one step forward, to great *Banks*.

She stood up, shook her skirt and went back to Beale and Beale.

Robert Doule was standing by his desk slitting open the afternoon's letters with a paper-knife. He looked up at her but Laura walked past him, her face still in a dream. Robert Doule noticed it and his own face darkened.

That night Laura went into Marion's flat after she had had her dinner and told Marion about Peter. He was so much nonsense to her since her purging at lunch-time that she laughed as she recounted the odd evening she had spent the night before.

Marion listened to her in silence.

"You mean you just sat and listened to the piano for an hour and a half?"

"I didn't sit. I lay."

"Weren't you bored?"

"Not really. I was tired. He played very well, you know."

"And Danny?"

"Oh, God knows why Danny picked up with him. Danny knows the oddest people."

"And he didn't mind this Whosit kissing your hand?"

Laura was silent.

Marion poured out another cup of coffee each.

"I would say," she said unexpectedly, "that you're on the brink of an 'affair'. A good experience to get behind you. You don't live till you know what it's all about."

Laura was indignant.

"Are you going to say this of everyone I tell you about?"

"No. But the fact you walked away and didn't have lunch in the Café Noir means this particular one has made an impact on you."

Laura tilted her head proudly, a gesture that always amused Marion. "Becoming the great Irish lady," she had once said to Laura. "It won't do, my dear. It's out of character in this country. But not unbecoming, mind you."

"The fact that I walked away meant exactly the opposite." Laura's face was as proud as the tilt of her head. "I was not going to be bothered about seeing him again."

"Or seeing if he was going to be bothered about seeing you? At the back of your conscious thinking you knew damn' well that it would be far more intriguing to him, if he had bothered to go to the Café Noir, to see that you had *not* gone there."

Laura flushed.

"I don't have to go to those extremes," she said. "After all he knows where I live, and where I work."

"You should have stayed home tonight. He might have called." Marion looked up under level brows. "You weren't running away by any chance when you came in here tonight?"

"For an artist," Laura said slowly, "you have a mind strangely preoccupied with other things."

"We don't do anything but fight these days, do we? As a matter of fact I'm sorry about it. I happen to be fond of you, Laura, but you live in a dream of your own world, and it's better to get through the basic experiences as soon as possible. You don't get psychologically complicated that way."

Laura didn't know what being psychologically complicated meant. She assumed it meant collecting a Pekinese and a parrot when one had really abandoned oneself to spinsterhood. She knew nothing of the primeval mire. She didn't even know what her friend knew of it.

She could hardly jump up now and return to her own rooms for fear Marion would think she feared, or hoped, a visit from Peter. So she put on one record after another and wandered restlessly around the flat.

Marion filed her nails, repainted them, and watched her friend out of half-closed eyes.

"You'd better go home and sleep it off," she suggested at length.

"I think I'll go home and sleep, anyway."

The next day Laura quite deliberately went to the Café Noir for lunch. She took a book and engrossed herself in it. She did not admit that Peter might come, but if he did she wasn't going to look for him.

She thought she felt relief when a stout woman sat down in the chair opposite her but in fact she felt that strange tingling again. It wasn't a tingling of anticipation, so much as of disappointment. She could have cried with dismay that she should feel thus.

The next day Peter came. Actually he was inside the café when Laura entered it. He watched her sit down at a table with a vacant seat opposite and when she picked up the menu he left his own table and joined her.

As he sat down he put one finger up and gently levered the menu downwards. There was nothing for Laura to do but look over the top of it. His smile just showed the edge of his teeth and his brown eyes were amused.

Though Laura steeled herself against the unexpected flush that crept up her neck and though she tried to veil the expression in her eyes, she knew that a communication, with which her mind had nothing to do whatsoever, had passed between them.

The waitress was hovering beside them.

"Coffee and salad for two," he said. "And bring the cream separately."

His finger edged the little bowl of sugar lumps towards Laura.

"Do you like sugar in your coffee, Laura, or do you take it black and strong?"

"How do you know I take coffee at all?"

"You'll have to, from now on. Coffee's my drink."

"We had tea on Monday night."

"Tea is Danny's drink. That's the difference between us."

Laura took out her cigarette case and snapped it open.

"Do you know what I think?" she said.

He shook his head slowly from side to side.

"Don't say it," he said. "You'll regret it."

"No I won't. I think you've got a . . . very . . . big . . . opinion . . . of yourself."

"You don't think I play as well as all that?"

"I don't know anything about the piano."

"How do you know I was talking about the piano?"

Laura's eyes flashed and she went a little pale. This was because she felt suddenly afraid, and thought it was because she was suddenly angry.

For a minute she sensed the trap and thought of Robert Doule. Then she looked at Peter's face. He had a strong face, good looking in a clear-cut way. His eyes dominated it and his mouth helped his eyes. No, he would never be a Robert Doule!

"I've been waiting for you every day since Monday," Peter said unexpectedly. "I had three coffees and two salads on Tuesday and you didn't come. Yesterday I got bunged into that other room and only saw the tail of your skirt as you disappeared out of the door. What were you doing when I came in? Hiding behind a book?"

"I might have been behind a book. But not hiding."

The salads were in front of them now and they began to eat.

"By the way, if you don't mind my asking," Laura said, "what happens to the orchard while you pay your daily visits to Perth?"

"Nothing much happens to it any of the time anyway. The piano takes up too much room . . ."

"And too much time?"

"Not enough time."

"You don't find it necessary to earn a living in the meantime?"

"That's a highly personal question, young lady. If my guess is right about your upbringing you were taught never to ask another his politics, his religion or his bank balance."

"Quite right, but you've pushed yourself on me. I'm entitled to know who I'm lunching with. You see I was also taught you never know a man unless he was introduced by a brother or a father, because it's a brother's or a father's business to find out about politics, religion and bank roll."

"And Dennis Hara Montgomery?"

"Danny did not introduce us. He merely brought you into Beale and Beale on business."

"And now you've answered your own question about the living, so far unearned. I have a pittance—a small pittance—left to me by an indulgent mother. It will keep me and the piano but not a wife, or domestic appendages such as a horse, dog, or cow. Hence my minor plunge in Coolgardie Mines. I'd like a dog for company, a well-bred dog."

"You'll wait a long time," Laura said scornfully.

Peter raised his eyebrows.

"Here's hoping," he said, and lifted his coffee cup.

They sparred in this manner until the lunch was eaten. Again Peter picked up both lunch chits.

"Can the pittance cover it?" Laura asked.

Peter grinned.

"For you, the pittance will cover anything."

He walked along the Terrace with her as far as Beale and Beale.

"See you tomorrow," he said, and before she could reply he had turned and walked rapidly away.

Laura spent several hours that night, before she went to sleep, wondering whether she was going to be choked off going to the Café

Noir for lunch by Peter's possessive manner or whether she might as well give in now and be done with it.

When her feet took her to the Café Noir the following day will-power had nothing to do with it. The die was cast.

She felt happy about it. She had an attitude of "who cares anyway" which banished scruple.

Peter was there first and again he ordered coffee and salad without consulting her. Again they sparred without animus, and again he walked with her as far as Beale and Beale.

Robert Doule passed them in the doorway and his face was very white. Laura noticed it but didn't think about it. Her thoughts were tumultuously elsewhere.

Every day she spent her lunch hour with Peter and on Friday he said, "I'll call for you after lunch tomorrow. We'll go up to the shack."

Laura's heart took a plunge. She knew this was one of those irrevocable steps a girl sometimes took that altered the course of her life.

She was brought up in a family and in a circle in which a young woman did not go unaccompanied to a lonely house in the hills with a strange man. Other people did it, she was aware of that. She lived in a modern age of greater freedom for the female and there was no reason why she shouldn't be the same as everyone else of her own age in the same world. But she was different. The Montgomeries had made her different. To go with Peter involved a tremendous step, not necessarily forward but very much to the side.

Nevertheless she went. By continuing to lunch at the Café Noir she had committed herself. One doubts if she could have withdrawn even if her habits had counselled her otherwise. She was already in thrall. The tingling feeling she had experienced the day following her visit to the shack with Danny persisted. Her heart leapt forward to these daily meetings. When they were over the pulse in her throat made itself known to her for the first time.

When she looked at Peter she could not drag her eyes away from his though something in her made her angry that he should look into her eyes and hold them the way he did. She resisted him, yet she went gladly. Underneath it all there was a sorrow. He was the wrong man.

Peter had acquired a small sports car and on Saturday afternoon he called for Laura and drove her into the hills. All the way there she pretended it was an outing like any other outing. She talked gaily of her own affairs and such of Beale and Beale affairs as were not confidential. She told Peter of the parties she went to accompanied by the Preston family, which were a camouflage for selling ideas. She told him about Marion Perrent.

She did not tell him about her family, about Danny, or any of the Montgomeries. This was inviolate territory and had something to do with a sense of betrayal, of treason.

When they arrived at the shack Peter pulled on the handbrake sharply and putting his arm along the back of the seat turned to her.

"What are you afraid of?" he asked, again holding her eyes with his, a small smile pulling in the corners of his mouth.

"Afraid?"

"You haven't stopped talking. I don't care a damn about Perrents and Prestons, or Beale and Beale for that matter. I'm interested in you."

Laura's mouth drew in angrily.

"I think you are interested in you."

"Are you afraid I'm going to seduce you?"

"Not afraid. Though I had thought of it."

The arm along the seat closed around her shoulder. He took her chin with his right hand and bent his head down and kissed her on the mouth. His hand left her chin and slid around her body. He did not so much gather her to him as bear down on her so she felt crushed, exhausted. Yet the tingling in her rose like a wave. It crawled up her limbs and body and burst through her lips as his mouth clung to hers.

Then he let her go.

"Now what?" he said.

"Very nice, thank you." She looked down at her bag as she opened it and took out a cigarette case. Her eyes were not so much turned down as veiled.

Peter took one of her cigarettes and struck a match for her. When he sought some kind of answer in her eyes she was ready. The look she returned was as challenging as his. He would never know she had never been kissed like that before. He would never know she had not known that blood could pour through one's veins like that and almost suffocate one.

He would never know that her head swam, that her body had become some kind of violent force that shocked as well as amazed her. He would never know she had not known what passion was.

Peter leaned across her and opened the door.

"Let's go inside," he said.

They went up the three wooden steps to the shack and Laura stood aside while he opened the door. When she went in she automatically went to the window and opened it. She stood in front of it breathing deeply. When she turned round she was ready.

"Do we drink tea, coffee or claret?"

"Claret's your drink, I think."

He went out into the lean-to kitchen and brought in two glasses and a bottle of claret. He filled them up.

Laura sat down on the sofa and he came and sat down beside her. They sipped the claret in silence.

"You know I'm going to make love to you?"

Laura laughed.

"I thought you'd begun."

She didn't care about anything any more. She was whirling round in an eddy. She had to keep going. The only important thing was not to let Peter know she had never had this experience before. She did not wish to appear sophisticated for the sake of vanity. Some instinctive sense of self-preservation told her that Peter would lose his own fire if he thought he was dealing with a child. And she needed his fire. She needed it as desperately as a man lost in the desert needs water. Even if it is rotten water.

He reached past her and put the glasses on a small table. He took the cigarette out of her hand and stubbed it on a tray. He put his arms around her, crushed her back against the head of the sofa and kissed her again.

He made love to her in a manner that seared and transported her, that awoke her in amazement to the world of senses. He touched her body and she felt as if her flesh burned under his fingers.

She felt drunk.

"Oh God," she said.

He sat up and looked at her.

"Now we'll have some piano."

He ran his fingers through his hair, stood up and went to the piano. In a minute chords were crashing through the air and the wooden walls of the room were vibrating and the claret glasses on the small table trembling.

Laura was beyond thinking. He had not violated her last privacy. She was still whole and a maiden, but he had shattered all her defences. He had lifted her out of her own world into one of wonder, and desire.

Then he had got up and gone to the piano.

He played till she couldn't stand it any longer and had to shout to make herself heard.

"Shall I make some tea?"

"Coffee."

When she had made it and brought it in he got up from the piano. He sat in one of the armchairs, sipped his coffee and looked across the room at her.

"Quite a way to spend Saturday afternoon, huh?"

"Quite a way," said Laura. Why could he look at her like that as if nothing had happened? Was this so very ordinary an experience for him? Would it not occur to him he had shattered the glass darkly in which she had, till this afternoon, lived?

"You have an element of surprise about you," said Peter, "Quite fascinating."

"Meaning what?"

"So much old-world dignity, or is that a

façade? And underneath you're just woman, like anyone else."

Laura felt as if she had had a slap in the face.

"At least one is spared the indignity of being obvious."

He burst out laughing.

"Meaning me?"

He got up and went to the piano. He put his coffee cup on the top of it and began to play an air with one finger.

"If I start that I won't stop for an hour," he said. "Let's go across to Kalamunda and have tea at the pub. It's a nice drive."

"Yes. Can I go somewhere and make-up my face? You don't seem to have a bedroom."

"No, only a bed and an iron tub on the back verandah. You'll find my shaving glass hanging over the tub."

Laura went outside and repaired the ravages of his love-making. She felt as if she had taken a drug, not the soporific kind but the opposite. She would have given anything for him to have put his arms around her, and offered her love. Whatever it was he had given her, she wanted more, and was ashamed that it was without love.

When they were in the car, the wind blowing the hair back from their faces and the smell of fallen gum leaves pungent in their nostrils, his mood changed. This time it was he who did the talking. He told her about the music he had been playing. About its composer and his extraordinary life.

"It's music he thinks about. Music and the senses," Laura thought. "He doesn't think about the human beings involved. Only as instruments. I am an instrument, the same as his piano is."

Her thoughts calmed in the healing touch of wind on her face.

"Why should he talk, or even think, of love? You can only love someone you *know* because it is what you know about them that you love, like Danny."

Thought of Danny sobered her. It touched off that little ache at the back of her throat and the tight feeling behind her eyes.

Would or could Danny make love the way Peter had done? When she tried to conjure up a vision of Danny in love the vision melted away into the nothingness of a shadow. Danny with his arms around her? She could not feel them. Danny with passion in his lips? She could not taste them. Danny was forever the nebulous dream. The unattainable. The figure in a minuet.

They had tea at Kalamunda, sat on a wooden bench under the trees by the railway line, and talked about men and women, and why they were different. Quite early in the evening Peter drove her back down on to the plain and home.

When he had pulled up outside her apartment he put his arm round her again and kissed her. He took quite a long time about it but his kiss was more sensual than passionate. The fire had gone out of him.

Every day the following week Laura had lunch with Peter in the Café Noir. She wondered if he would ask her again to go to the shack on Saturday afternoon. At first she decided she didn't want to go and if he asked her she would decline. By Wednesday she decided that if she was in for a penny she might as well be in for a pound and if he invited her, she would go.

By Thursday she felt anxious because Peter had said nothing. She wanted to go now. She wanted to experience again that tingling sensation that crept over her body until it became a storming of all the outer surfaces of her skin. She was ashamed of it so she did not admit it to herself. Instead she told herself she was becoming interested in Peter as a personality. She *liked* him. When he left her in the Terrace and there had been no mention of Saturday afternoon, Laura felt bad-tempered and irritable. When she saw Robert Doule hovering in the doorway she was sharp with him.

"Why are you everywhere I am?" she demanded. "I always seem to be falling over you. Don't you ever do any work?"

Robert's face was thunderous.

"Who's the bloke?" he said.

"What bloke? Oh, you mean Peter Stevenson? He's just a friend. Why don't you mind your own business, Robert?"

She flounced through the outer office and shut the door with a small bang. Only Mr. Preston, sitting stuffily at his desk, noticed that Robert's hand trembled as he pushed back the letters from his desk and that he sat down and buried his head in his hands.

Peter had said he might be remaining in Perth for the evening and if so would meet Laura outside in the Terrace when she left Beale and Beale's at the end of the afternoon.

She was nearly sick with disappointment when he was not there.

She went home to eat a lonely supper in her own rooms. She felt badly enough to know she had to look this thing in the face. What was she doing? Where was it leading? There was no talk of love. There could be no future. Was this one of those things that was a case of living from one day to another and letting next year take care of itself? Had some madness taken possession of her?

She could not bear her own company for a whole evening, and came up to "Forty-Five".

She came into the dining-room where only Mama and I were sitting. I was reading and Mama was making coat-hangers for Christmas presents.

"What's the matter with you?" I said. "You look like you hate someone."

"Maybe I do," said Laura. "But thanks for the welcome all the same."

She sat down as if she was about to take a meal and drummed her fingers on the table.

"You look very nice indeed, Laura," said Mama. "Would you like a cup of tea?" She was trying to pour oil on troubled waters.

"In a minute, Aunty. I just want to sit. I'm tired. Where's Danny?"

"Out," I said. "He's gone to some dinner at the Perth Club. All dressed up too. You ought to see our Danny when he's out of those old pants and into his tails . . . ."

I caught Laura's angry eye and stopped talking about Danny.

"How's Sylvia?" Mama asked. "Have you had a letter this week?"

This question pricked the bubble of Laura's anger. Suddenly she had a deflated, defeated look. Her face was tired. I had never thought Laura could look sad before, but tonight her face was sad.

At that moment Danny came in. I heard him coming in the front door and his footsteps coming down the hall. I saw Laura stiffen and her eyes go to the door. They were haunted eyes.

Danny came in. He stood just inside the door and lit himself a cigarette.

I was right when I said one should see Danny in his evening clothes. His appearance was one of extreme dignity. His hair, parted well over to one side, shone like polished gold. He held his cigarette in his left hand and "shot" his cuffs by first shaking his right hand and then pushing the cuff of his left hand.

It was a funny yet touching mannerism. It made one think of the courts of kings, or at the least, of fashionable night clubs. His golden cuff-links gleamed like his hair. He looked so very polished himself. For the first time I noticed his eyelids, too, could droop. He had a touch of other-worldliness. Not so much an alien air as one that touched memories of that immortality that came into the world with us, trailing clouds of glory.

Danny brushed his hand through his hair and came into the room. He came easily and without constraint and sat in one of the leather chairs. He crossed one knee over the other and said,

"How's big business in the world today, Laura?" with a smile that disappeared as quickly as it came. It was a shadow that flitted over his face.

Laura's finger drew a line along the edge of the table. She looked as if she was suffering.

"It goes well, Danny," she said, lifting her eyes. "You should buy Coolgardie Mines. But you won't, just because I tell you."

Danny took out his cigarette case and offered Laura a cigarette. He lit it for her. When he did this he had a quick nervous movement, with a touch of ingenuousness, something that was really quite foreign to his nature. It was probably mannerism. No more.

"Who knows?" he said. "I might come back in a year or two, and think about it."

We were all startled.

"Aren't you going to stay in Australia, Danny?" Mama asked.

"No," Danny said. "I don't think it's my climate."

"You mean the heat and the flies?" I asked.

"I mean everything. Do you think I belong here?" He flicked his eyebrows up.

"Nobody belongs here when they first come," Mama said severely. "Everyone is a stranger in a strange land. They have to make their own way."

"Have to?" Danny's eyebrows flicked again. "Nobody has to do anything, Aunt Helen, if they don't *want* to."

"You want to do something for Magillicuddy," Laura said bitterly.

"Yes, but not thirteen thousand miles away. I think I'll leave on the *Mooltan* on the fourteenth. That gives me a fortnight in which to round things off and run up to Kalgoorlie to say goodbye to Uncle William."

This was cruel of Danny. It was all said so non-committally, as if it was a matter of no great moment.

He was going home. He had made up his mind like the snap of his fingers. That it struck a blow to all our hearts did not occur to him. Danny had no need for love so he did not comprehend our need to love. He would not have understood that we loved him, or why.

Laura sat looking at the table.

"I don't think I'll wait for that tea, Aunt Helen," she said, standing up. "I think I'll go."

She went to the door.

"Goodbye . . ." She could not get anything else out. Her face was rigid but her eyes were stricken.

Danny with his usual formality had stood up when Laura stood up. He made a half step towards the door as Laura went out so abruptly. Then he sat down again.

He listened to what Mama was saying about "Laura's temperamental behaviour these days", but his eyes had the sightless stare of the polite Irishman whose thoughts are miles away.

13

IT might seem that Danny's departure from Australia precipitated Laura into Peter's arms. Possibly she was half-way there and the same thing would have happened with or without Danny's presence in Australia.

It was quite certain she was never happy with Peter. In fact those were her words, "I never knew a moment's happiness. I was tormented from the start. I hated him . . . and I was drawn to him as if to a magnet. I prayed for Danny to deliver me . . . and even if there hadn't been his feeling for Sylvia, he would never have saved me. To throw oneself on Danny's mercy was to throw a thirsty man into a mirage to slake his thirst."

Fate did not help her, for when she arrived home there was a note slipped under her door.

Will pick you up at two-thirty on Saturday. Peter.

Her reaction to that short note was one of defeat. She had wanted Peter. Inwardly she had been fighting this want because she knew the whole thing was dead-sea fruit. She had come to "Forty-Five" perhaps instinctively looking for harbourage. We had not understood, and had not given it to her. Then Danny had come in . . .

She had no more strength.

At the appointed time she was outside on the footpath waiting under the gum trees that shaded the Terrace from the blaze of the Australian sun. She didn't care any more whether Peter might think her over-anxious. He could think what he pleased. She would take what he had to offer, for what it was worth.

Peter's car swerved round the corner from a side street. He did not get out of the car but leaned across and let open the door. It swung outwards and Laura got in.

"Let's go to Lesmurdie and look at the waterfall," she said.

He looked at her speculatively.

"A passion for scenery, or a reluctance to be the subject of love addresses?" he asked.

"Today's mood is for scenery. I'll probably regret it by tomorrow, but at the moment I can do nothing about it."

He passed her a packet of cigarettes and a box of matches.

"Light one for me," he said as he started the car and released the brake.

Laura lit a cigarette and handed it to Peter. It was the kind of intimate gesture that only lovers can make and she was surprised at the pleasure it gave her.

Unexpectedly her mood changed. She would have liked to sit closer to Peter. To have touched him and have him touch her. She realized she was committed to an afternoon of scenery or conversation. Suddenly and inexplicably she wanted love.

But she made no gesture. Pride was as stiff a pain in her throat as love was an ache there.

She could have cried with relief when Peter drove straight past the Lesmurdie turn-off from the main road and proceeded up the Greenmount Hill towards Darlington. Then she could have cried with the sorrow of it all. This was not what life had intended for her. It had meant her to stand forever portraited, a lady in a blue silk dress, beside Danny in his fine dress clothes, the green fields of Meath around her. Life had meant a twilight hour in which Danny took her hand and they ascended into a gallery where a log fire burned, dogs lay on the mat, and memories of a hundred years of hunting and shooting hung about a house like a faint aromatic scent. When Laura saw what life had meant for her she saw a portrait and a minuet.

Here she was, away across the world, almost sick for the love of a man she neither liked nor understood.

He slewed his eyes round and looked at her. There was a wicked grin in his eyes.

"Any more orders?" he asked.

"With what object? You still go where you please."

She knew he saw the small light in the deep recesses of her eyes. Once again something had sprung to life, and that tingling was spreading like a faint warm glow over her body.

What was she doing here? Some inward compulsion had brought her hither. Why was she here? Because in the first place Uncle Tim, who would have seen that life had arranged itself properly around her, had died. And Danny, the other figure in the portrait and the minuet, was going away.

Sylvia, death hovering in the background, Danny, and Uncle Tim, they were all to blame. They had left Laura, the girl who was born with a caul on her face, with a great natural beauty, with poise, position and brains; a girl born with ribbons in her hair, to become flotsam and jetsam in the wayward eddies of her own emotional make-up.

Uncle Tim should never have died.

Thus she thought as she longed to press her face on Peter's sleeve, on somebody's sleeve, and when ultimately he let his hand leave the steering-wheel and he put his arm round her to draw her against him, unresisting, relieved, and even grateful, she curled into the nest that was bounded by his arm and his body.

She did not know what next was to happen to her. Nor did she care very much.

Until now the group behaviourism of people of Aunt Sheilagh's and Uncle William's generation, of the Prestons, the Bastons and Maynard-Arnolds, had kept at bay any of the newer age that might have made overtures on the virginity of a young and attractive girl. Nevertheless Laura had eyes and ears and more than average intelligence. She knew what went on in the world. She knew now what might happen next.

And she did not care. Uncle Tim had died and Danny was going away. There are wells of loneliness into which even a young girl with all life's gifts strewn along her path might sink. Anything could happen now.

It follows that it did happen. Laura was neither ashamed nor frightened, because the overwhelming excitement of her senses prevented her thinking of anything except that this extra phenomenon of sex was the most overwhelmingly pleasurable thing that could ever happen. Curiosity, astonishment and pleasure were her only feelings. Thought was banished.

Peter lifted himself up from the sofa and reached for a packet of cigarettes. He took two, lighted them both at once and put one in Laura's mouth.

He inhaled deeply and looked through the spiral of escaping smoke from his nostrils at Laura.

His free hand took hers and gently rubbed the knuckles of her hand with his thumb.

"What an enigma you are, Laura," he said.

"Why?"

"Such an air! Such a lady of manners, and of the world! Such challenge in a pair of brilliant blue eyes! And . . ." He shrugged.

"And what?"

"So untampered with. How come?"

"You thought I was just a lass on the loose?"

"No. But I thought you knew what you were doing."

"I did. I wanted it this way."

He put his cigarette in his mouth and ran his fingers through her dark hair, pushing it back from her forehead and then curling and entangling his fingers in it.

He looked at her through half-closed eyes.

"The perfect pattern of beauty," he said. "Square forehead . . . nose very good . . . eyes quite big enough . . . and mouth . . ." He put his head on one side and considered her mouth. "The eyes challenge, and the mouth says a prayer. Laura, you fascinate me."

"You don't sound very fascinated, Peter."

"I am. What fascinates me about you is why you look the way you do, and come to be different."

"Does it matter very much?"

"It just interests me. I'm interested in people. I like putting my nose against some-body else's window-pane and watching to see what happens inside. And then wondering why."

Laura felt chilled. She wanted Peter to be tender and not objective. She wanted him to put his arms around her, all passion past, and be gentle and loving and kind. She wanted to shed a tear or two, not for maidenhead lost, but for all things past.

The chill was like a cold hand on her heart.

She lifted her shoulders up from the headrest and kissed him on the mouth.

"It's a time for kissing," she said. "And not philosophizing."

He grinned and flipped his fingers through her hair again.

He stubbed out his cigarette and stood up. He hitched his pants up round his waist and went over to the piano. He stood letting his fingers trill an air.

"Oh *no*," said Laura. "*No.* Don't play, Peter. I couldn't stand it."

"You'll have to. I'm going to write a song to you. A lyric. To Laura . . ."

He moved the piano-stool into place with his foot and sat down. He picked at an air with his fingers.

Was composing a song Peter's way of being tender? She lay and watched him.

He turned round on the piano-stool. He looked at her with far-away eyes.

"What was it? How does it go? You know . . . that poem about Laura. Written by an Irishman too . . . something stolen from Petrarch."

He frowned. Then he got up and went to the bookcase and pulled out a small green book. He went back to the piano-stool and sat leafing through it.

"Ah! Here it is!"

"*'In the years of her age the most beautiful and the most flowery—the time Love has his mastery—Laura, who was my life, has gone away leaving the earth stripped and desolate.'*"*

As he read he raised his voice, lifted a declamatory hand and gave himself up to rendering poetry.

"Bravo!" he applauded himself when he had finished. "We must have music to it."

He swung round again to the piano and began to rumble the bass end of the keyboard with his fingers. Laura had the unhappy feeling he was not as good a player as he had seemed at first. There were too many

*J. M. Synge (from Petrarch)

310

discords, even for one in the throes of composition. And she hadn't cared for the poetry.

Peter grew exasperated and his fingers accidentally found a chord or two that struck a chord or two in him. Within a minute composition was banished and he was away in his own interpretation of masters, one of whom he could never become.

Laura wrinkled her brow and listened hard. If she had to bear much of this she had to know whether he was good. He could *play*, he could do what Denney irreverently called "Bashing the keyboard about". But did he play correctly? There were so many obvious corrections and an occasional fumble. How many faults there might be that Laura would know nothing of, she could not tell.

"Peter . . ." she said.

He took no notice. His head was bowed over the keyboard and a lock of hair had fallen across his eyes. His playing was pounding. Perhaps it was good. Laura didn't know.

At last he crashed into a finale and let his hands drop, exhausted, from the keyboard.

He turned slowly round and looked at her.

"Was that 'To Laura'?" Laura asked.

"That," he said, his voice heavy with

sarcasm, "was the second movement of Beethoven's C Minor Concerto."

"Then I think you should practise it, Peter. You should never make a mistake. When I was teaching myself the typewriter I would not pass on to the next exercise until I had typed the present one eight times perfectly. When I made a mistake, I started again."

"*Typewriter*! *My God*!" He crashed his fist down on the piano keys. "Did God send this woman into the world to compare a piano with a typewriter? What have I done, thus to be visited?"

"The principle of practice, Peter. That's what I was talking about."

He looked at her savagely.

"You wouldn't know a right note from a wrong. Go and get the coffee. That's all women are good for."

Laura laughed.

"Touché?" she asked. She went up behind him and put her arms round his neck so that her hands lay on his on the keyboard. Her lips were pressed near his ear.

"If you're going to put the piano before me," she said softly, "you'd better make it good."

He turned and kissed her on the cheek. In a

minute their arms were round one another. He stood up and half carried her to the door into the kitchen.

"Get the coffee, my darling."

The chill had gone and Laura was suddenly and inexplicably happy. She liked being pushed into the kitchen. She liked getting Peter's coffee for him. She liked domesticity. She liked the day outside and the sound of the piano coming from inside. She liked the smell of Peter's shaving-soap when she had had her face pressed in his neck. She liked the feeling that it would all happen again, and that she wanted it to happen again. She did not ask herself why she felt as if she were on the edge of a precipice and didn't care—even liked it. If she had asked herself she would have replied, "Because I'm about to take off on wings, into wider, unknown and thrilling realms."

If she had asked herself, "Can you love two people?" she would have replied, "Yes. I know. Because I do." She did not admit the deep sorrow that was in her nor that a world was lost. She called that deep incorrigible despair that was really with her *impending excitement*.

When Peter drove her home to her apartment that night she was hoping and expecting him to make an arrangement for them to meet the following day, Sunday. It seemed unthinkable that even the few hours left of night should have to separate them.

"When will I see you, Peter?"

"I'll be in the Café Noir for lunch on Monday. I'll bring you a book to read. About Beethoven."

"A book to read? I don't want a book to read. I just want you."

"You shall have me, my darling. Me and a salad and two cups of coffee."

"Peter, what are you doing tomorrow?"

He hesitated for a fraction of a minute.

"I've got a trio practice. There are three of us, piano, violin, 'cello. We spend most of Sunday that way. I might drop in late, if I can shed the others."

"Oh yes. Please darling. I'd love that."

"Can't promise, but I'll try and make it."

Thus Laura entered upon the first day upon which she endured hours of mental agony *waiting* for Peter.

All the morning she thought about his coming. She washed her hair and turned out her small apartment. She went in to see Marion Perrent and told her about Peter.

Marion looked at the other's heightened colour and the brilliant eyes, once so challenging and frank, now evasive.

"You're in love, Laura. Watch out you don't get your fingers burnt."

"I'm not a child," said Laura with a touch of hauteur.

"In which case you've slept with him already. Oh well, the sooner the better. Then you stop wondering what it's all about."

Laura looked at her friend, troubled.

"I think that's cynical, and just a little low."

"You can call it what you like. I call it the facts of life. If you've slept with him to begin with you'd better get some new clothes to keep him."

Laura felt the cold hand on her heart.

"You love a person for what he or she is, not what they wear."

Marion shook her head slowly. She smiled.

"Do what Momma says," she said. "A man runs till he's caught the bus. Then he rides along till he gets bored. Then he gets off and tries a new stream-lined motor car. Buy yourself a new dress and a new hair-do. And darling, be *aloof*. It pays dividends. Besides, this dewy-eyed humility doesn't suit you. It's

315

like seeing a mountain pony do a one-step in a circus ring."

Laura felt real anger welling in her.

"Where do you get all that worldly knowledge from, Marion? It stinks a bit."

"That's a very unpleasant expression for you to use, Laura. The first step down-hill—or is it merely into the highroad of life?—is to get common in your speech. The best thing about you has been your 'quality' if I may use such a word. Don't lose that between the blankets. Or weren't there any blankets? Don't say it was under a tree or in the middle of a haystack?"

Laura's anger died cold. Somehow Marion made her feel defiled. The colour rose high in her cheeks.

"I thought you advocated experience," she said bitterly.

"With discretion, my dear. And good taste. You see, I've been through it all myself. I *know*."

"As a result you can forecast?"

Marion turned away. She put the kettle on the electric ring.

"Yes. One has to *learn*, Laura. But it's a sorry business. I happen to be fond of you."

"Then why were you anxious for me to find out about life?"

"Because you wouldn't stay in the warm parental nest. You wanted to go out in the world and compete. You're in business. So you've got to have an armour. Armour is a thing that grows on you like a tough outer skin. You don't just put it on like the ladies of old put on their chastity belts. Want some tea or coffee?"

"Tea, please. When I'm with Peter I have to drink coffee."

When Laura said that she felt a lifting of spirits. She savoured for the first time the pleasure of talking about Peter in a familiar domestic way. She would have liked to go on talking about him but was afraid of Marion's caustic tongue. Instead she drank her tea, borrowed a lace collar to put on her bluest blue silk dress and went back to her apartment.

She had not forgotten Danny. She had locked him away and barricaded the door against herself.

When she had had her lunch she lay down on her divan bed with a book. But she couldn't read. First she lay pleasurably thinking about

Peter's coming. She was certain he would come. Her very certainty was a challenge to the possibility that he might not come. She pooh-poohed this idea to herself but it set up a new train of thoughts. Marion's cynicism. How could Marion know, or not know, whether this affair of Peter might not be the love of Laura's life? Of course she, Marion, knew about Danny. She had seen the sun shining out of Laura's face, and out of the faces of all the Montgomeries, when the last of the line had come back to Australia. She had challenged Laura once.

"This Danny? This cousin? How does he stand with you? Some kind of Celtic myth come to life? Or have you got special feelings?"

"Both," Laura had answered simply. Marion had looked closely at Laura and changed the subject.

Would Peter come? For the first time Laura admitted that question.

She felt restless and got up and made herself a cup of tea. She looked at the clock. Half-past three. If he came it would hardly be before half-past five. Two hours.

She would mend the lace on two of her

318

petticoats. God knows they needed it and ordinarily she never had time. Laura tidied her drawers in the process of finding her petticoats. She tidied her work-basket in the process of finding needle and thread. She put her sewing things together ready for use and then decided to rinse out a blouse. As she hung it out on the small verandah she looked across the river. She really ought to go out. She should have gone up to "Forty-Five" and had tea with the cousins. If she did she might miss Peter. But he wouldn't come before half-past five anyway. It was four o'clock. An hour and a half. She could be back before half-past five. But supposing he came? Supposing they ended their practice early or one of the instrumentalists had failed to turn up?

She had better write a letter to Mama. Supposing she wrote one to Da instead?

She allowed herself a wry smile. She could see her father reading her letter and exclaiming at every third sentence,

"Why doesn't she come to me? Now if she had listened to me I would have told her she'd get no research information from the Chamber of Mines. Fools and rapscallions! Well, she can get on with it. But don't let her come to me when she's in trouble."

No, Da wasn't any help. And Mama belonged to another life and another world. Laura would write about the daily nothings of food and clothes and the fact that Mr. Preston had got a new suit for party-going. The first in twenty years.

The letter was finished and the sewing was untouched. It was a quarter to five.

Laura could at least take a walk along Adelaide Terrace. She would see Peter's car if it drew up.

She dressed, carefully made up her face, and went downstairs. Out in the street it was still in the first hush of approaching evening. The sun was shining out on the river but here, in the Terrace, the tall houses and the trees cut off its rays. It was in that quiet secretive shadow of an early evening in autumn. There was something sad about sundown in autumn in Australia. It didn't have the beauty of turning and falling leaves. It was merely still and shadowed and very lonely. Filled with an ineffable sadness, because of the places in shadow where the sun did not shine.

One ought to have a home into which to turn. A home with a fire and muffins and dogs lying on the mat. The smell of tweeds and turf in the air.

But autumn in Australia was not cold enough for fires. It was merely chill. And forlorn.

Half-past five. Six o'clock. Half-past six. Seven.

"I shall go mad," Laura said to herself. "I shall never do this again. Hanging around! *Waiting*! Oh God, could anything be worse!"

It was better now the sun was gone and the world was darkling. There was no sharp comparison between the places where the sun still shone brightly, and the deep purple shadowed places.

She boiled an egg and made some toast. She sat down at the table in front of them and buried her face in her hands.

"What have I come to? Is this me, Laura, waiting like a miserable nobody for a man I don't even care about. He's selfish, egotistical and not even very competent at the piano. He's a poseur, an empty sheath. And who is he? No family. *Nothing*."

She went to the mirror and looked at her face. She could see she didn't look very well.

The bloom was off her confidence and off her beauty.

She went back to the table and her untouched egg.

"Uncle Tim," her heart cried. "Why did you go away? Why did you die?"

Because she was in need she wept for someone she believed would have enveloped her in his protecting arms and taken care of her.

At half-past eight Peter came.

"Saw your light," he said. "Thought you might be in."

Laura looked at him savagely. Thought she might be in?

Careful. Don't make a fool of yourself. He doesn't really care. As Marion said, you'll never hold him if you don't look good, and play a part.

"Come in," she said. "I suppose you want some coffee." She could not keep the strain out of her voice.

"What's up, Beautiful? You look as if I'm a nightmare instead of the man of your dreams."

"As a matter of fact I was just going to bed. I've a big day tomorrow."

Don't believe me, Peter. Don't go. If you turn

322

round and go towards the door I'll cry out. Please spare me that last indignity.

She turned her back and put the kettle on the electric ring and took out two cups and saucers.

"Pretty mad, aren't you? Well, I couldn't get here any earlier. Car broke down."

Thank God for a car. It makes the perfect excuse.

She did not answer aloud but put coffee in a saucepan ready to pour the boiling water on it. Peter came across the room and put his arm around her. She shrugged him off. Yet she longed for him to keep his arm there, for him to turn her round and kiss her, not passionately but lovingly, tenderly. If he did she knew her eyes would give her away.

When she turned round she was a little white, but under control. She carried the saucepan of boiling coffee to a small table and strained it through into the cups. Peter was sitting on the lounge smoking a cigarette.

"Hell of a way to make coffee!" he said. "I'll buy you a percolator tomorrow."

"Were you thinking of coming again?" she said. "Otherwise it wouldn't be worth while."

"Of course I'm coming again, silly ass." He laughed.

When he got up as if to take the coffee cup he put his arms around her. He pressed her head against his shoulder and ran his fingers through her hair.

"Beautiful, proud Laura," he said gently.

She stiffened in her effort to control a sob. Gradually she eased. She leaned against him, her face found its warm nest between his jaw and his shoulder.

"Never mind the coffee, sweet. We can have it afterwards."

That was it, of course. He interspersed casualness with tenderness.

14

LAURA had known frustration and those minor unhappinesses of childhood and youth, but now she knew real unalloyed unhappiness.

More than anything else, more than her need to love and be loved, to express herself as God made her, a woman of charm and conquest, was the bitter disintegration of her pride. Every hour of every day she told herself that Peter was not worth while, that he was an impudent upstart. To the rest of the world she may have been just one more girl, a little over-endowed with beauty and brains. But to herself she was proud. She had integrity, she had taste, and she had disdain. That she also had a body working on certain principles of chemistry as well as a heart longing to love was something that had not occurred to her. If it had she would have thought that personal dignity should have put her above these things.

But what are the powers of dignity compared with the powers of a glandular system?

Laura was desperate for love and she writhed in the toils of that desperation.

Sometimes Peter came down from the hills and appeared in the Café Noir for lunch. Sometimes he was waiting for her after office hours. Sometimes he transported her to the shack in Darlington. But always he reserved the right of coming or going according to his mood or his other activities. He could never keep an appointment as a point of honour, so he rarely made them. On just enough occasions to keep Laura wondering and waiting.

She writhed against the indignity of that waiting. She told herself she would not put up with it. No self-respecting person, least of all Laura Montgomery, could put up with such a situation.

On one such occasion she came up to "Forty-Five". I was alone at home. It was a wet blustery day in early winter and there was nothing to do but sit before a fire and make tea and toast. I knew that Laura was troubled. She had a pallor. Her usual self-possessed manner was gone. She was very quiet and sat looking into the fire. There was no liveliness in her.

I always felt I had understood Laura. That

did not mean I was particularly close to her. Laura was too independent for close friendship, let alone with a cousin. Moreover, there was an inherent, perhaps even unconscious, rivalry that kept us apart. We were alike. That was one rivalry. The matter of the caul was another. And last, there had been Uncle Tim. Each rejected the idea that the other had claims to favouritism with Uncle Tim. Yet each had had it from him. Each had mourned Uncle Tim as her own possessed and possessing grief.

Perhaps on this day, because I too was troubled with affairs of the heart, my manner softened. Perhaps Laura, though formerly she would never have admitted it, realized we were alike and that I would understand, and would not be critical.

"Do you know anything worse than a wet day when you're feeling low?" she said. She was still staring into the fire.

"No. And as I feel low today, I'm glad you've come."

She looked up curiously.

"Why?"

"The wrong man," I said shortly.

Laura's gaze went back to the fire.

"It always is," she said sadly.

We both sat pensive for a minute.

"You know," said Laura. "Old Mrs. Preston said to me the last time we went out together, 'Prize your youth, Laura. When you're my age you'll wonder why you didn't cherish it!'" She gave a short laugh. "Can you imagine Mrs. Preston ever having had youth?"

"She must have had it, and something more too. At least one man fell in love with her. And married her."

"Perhaps she had a good youth. You know, met the right man first and married him straight away. No problems there. They seem happy enough, but I wouldn't change places."

"Even to get rid of whatever it is that's wrong with you now?"

Laura shook her head slowly from side to side.

"Even to get rid of him."

"Is it that dark-eyed Peter person you get around with sometimes?"

She looked at me.

"Yes. He's a beast. I hate him."

"Then why?"

She spread her hands.

"Obsession, I suppose. The droop of his

328

eyelids, the way he lets one leg stretch straight out in front of him when he sits down, the pulled-in-at-the-corners look his mouth has when he smiles. It's all got nothing to do with love, yet when I'm at my maddest I see him, his leg, or his mouth, or his eyelids. And my heart drops. Have you ever wondered why the poets put the seat of love in the heart? It's certainly in that organ one has all the physical feelings of love. It's got nothing to do with the mind, or the brain."

"The heart's a very volatile organ," I admitted. "It moves up and down several inches in the course of an hour's conversation."

Again we were silent. I leaned forward and rescued another piece of toast from the fork which I had rested at a convenient distance from the coals, leaning against a warming brick. I buttered it from the crock which was standing at the side of the fireplace. I cut it and put it on a plate and handed it to Laura. She began to eat it without enjoyment.

"Can't you give him up?"

She looked at me with sombre eyes.

"I'll have to, but God knows where the strength will come from."

It was then she told me all that I have set down in the foregoing chapters. She began slowly, with only little snippets of information, withholding far more than she told. Yet I saw the whole picture. Presently as she warmed to the healing powers of talking-it-out she told me more, even of that crucifying afternoon in her apartment when she had longed and waited for him. And hated him.

"Of course Aunt Helen would say 'Wipe him off'," she finished sadly.

I nodded. Yes, that is what Mama would have said, "Forget him. He's not worth the trouble." It's what everyone says when they see someone unhappily embroiled with some other person who can never do them any good.

Finish! Kaput!

But they never tell you how. They never tell you how, weak and foolish as you are, you can fight forces within yourself that are stronger than yourself.

They can never tell you how, when you see the face of the loved and despised one, you can prevent your heart, and it is the actual organic heart, from turning upside-down.

"I know," I said to Laura. "I know."

She looked at me curiously.

"Then you too think that youth is an awful burden?"

I nodded.

"When one is old," I said, "one is either happily married, or one is not. There may be regrets, but at least the struggle is over."

"Already, as I sit here, I am getting restive. I'm saying to myself, *If I go home he may be there. He might come.* But if I go home the chances are I'm going to put in a thoroughly miserable evening."

"Then stay here."

"I think I will. Do you think I could have a bed for the night?"

"There's always the box ottoman in the lobby."

We both laughed. How many people over the years had the box ottoman given a night's rest?

Perhaps the release of talking helped Laura because after that she seemed happier and talked quite brightly of other things. She told me a lot about Beale and Beale, about Robert Doule, about dear old Mr. Preston (an archaic ornament, in and out of office hours), about her researches into the history of various mines on the gold-fields.

"You really believe that one day you'll

redeem a fortune in the fields?" I asked.

"I don't have to find the gold," Laura said. "It's there. I just have to watch the cycle of prices and the relationships of costs. I'm not the only person who's doing that now. There's quite a lot of men on the Terrace picking up parcels of gold shares on the cheap. But Beale and Beale were in first. And thanks to Da we know where the gold really is. Beale and Beale's real problem is, of course, to keep Da quiet."

I laughed.

"I can't imagine anyone telling Uncle William to keep quiet. Least of all his own daughter."

"He owes Beale and Beale an awful lot of money . . ."

When Mama and the others came in they were all pleased to see Laura. They stood in front of the fire and castigated her for not coming more often and then they began to get the tea in the kind of vociferous milling crowd that used to irritate Laura when she stayed with us. Now it pleased her. I could see her colour had come back. There was a sparkle in her eyes and her voice was full of those rich cadences that had always been more than half her charm. She laughed as heartily as anyone over the usual kind of personal anecdotes that we delighted in telling and she told us one or two of her own. She told us about the three dogs in the City Gardens.

"I'm always afraid that some day someone will put them in the dog-cart and take them away," she said. "Sometimes I walk down to the Gardens just to see if they are there. When they are not, I'm full of anxiety. Then next day, there they are. I could almost cry with relief."

"They'll come to a bad end," said Mama.

"I know," said Laura. "But oh! Life is grand while it lasts."

Laura's preoccupation with three mongrel dogs was something that puzzled Mama. She liked dogs and wished these particular dogs no harm, but that someone should lie awake at night and think about them was something that passed her understanding.

"You'll get bitten by one of them one day," Mama said warningly.

"When I do I'll beg leave to withdraw my sympathy," said Laura.

After tea we all played coon-can and made an awful lot of noise about it. Laura remembered she had a packet of mint toffees in her bag and produced them. Mama watched her passing them around.

"You shouldn't bring them here. They'll pull the fillings out of everybody's teeth."

"Who's got fillings?" Denney asked feelingly. She had been suffering from toothache and there hadn't been enough money to send her to the dentist to have her teeth filled.

We pooh-poohed Mama and went on eating mint toffees.

"Don't complain," said Mama, "when the worst happens."

"You sound like Uncle William," said Vicky.

"Don't always be looking for the nigger in the woodpile," I said. "We never can afford to buy toffees ourselves."

"It won't be a nigger in a woodpile so much as a filling in the mint," said Gerry. She had dug a lump of toffee out of her mouth and sat looking at it ruefully. There embedded in it was a nice piece of amalgam filling.

"Told you so," said Mama with an air of victory.

"I'd have swallowed it first," said Laura crossly to Gerry. "Do you have to bring everything out of your mouth to exhibit?"

334

She was back to her old self. Perhaps, I thought, she would now have the courage to deal with Peter which she had so feared she lacked. The abrasive quality of the Montgomery wit, I thought. It removes adhesions.

The next day Laura went to work feeling like a being rejuvenated. Mama would have said, "like a giant refreshed by rain." This was Mama's favourite saying after a satisfying meal.

Laura was cheerful and brisk with Robert Doule, with Mr. Preston and the stringy stenographer, Miss Smythson. She was clever and authoritative with the partners when she discussed market trends with them. At lunch time she went out and bought a new winter suit.

"I feel good," she said to herself. "Why do I feel different? Well, it doesn't matter why. Thank God that I do."

She had not looked up and down the street at lunch time or at five o'clock to see if Peter was waiting for her. She had not gone to the Café Noir for lunch. She felt proud of herself. She felt released.

When she'd had her evening meal she went into Marion Perrent's flat.

"I'm just going up to Mount Lawley to some friends. We're going to have some music. Like to come?"

Yes, Laura would like to come very much. Then she couldn't possibly be waiting in for Peter, could she?

Laura went back to her apartment and changed her dress. She took particular care with her make-up, still very light in those days, and chose a simple but well-cut dress in a light navy blue.

When she went back to Marion's flat the latter stood looking at her with an air of speculation.

"What's happened to you, Laura? You look lovely. What's more, you look as if you've got some kind of heavenly secret. What is it?"

Laura shrugged.

"Must be the weather," she said. "I like it cool. I never could stand the hot summer the way my cousins do. I spent too many years in Ireland, I suppose."

She wasn't ready to tell Marion yet about this wonderful sense of release from Peter. Perhaps she still doubted it herself.

They took a taxi to Mount Lawley.

Immediately Laura entered the Leperts'

house she had a sense of warmth and home-coming. Her hosts were simple, hospitable and natural in their manner. They were very Jewish in their appearance and particularly in the speech of Mr. Lepert, whom everyone called Dada. He was a European Jew, fat, comfortable and with an aura of loving-kindness about him that warmed Laura's heart. She noticed how affectionately his son and daughter spoke to him, and how affectionately he spoke to them. His wife was not quite so stout but very fashionably dressed. She did not have quite the same air of boundless love to all people but she was extremely kind.

Laura had always heard that Jews were wonderful home lovers and here was every evidence of it. They, the Leperts, were obviously very fond of Marion. They spoke to her in the same tone they used towards their own children. They were delighted to have Laura with them.

"Go and sit down by Dada," said Mrs. Lepert. "He would like to talk to you."

Laura sat in a low chair beside Mr. Lepert's prodigious one. It had to be prodigious to hold his bulk.

"You must come often, often," Mr. Lepert

said as if this was of utmost importance to Laura's well-being. "We like to have you. Do not wait for Marion. Just come. If it is too far I could get Sonny to go for you in the car."

It was the sort of welcome one imagined given to the prodigal son. It seemed to say, "Here she is at last, the loved one. She has come home." This did not so much bewilder Laura as make her feel misty behind the eyes. Why should she come into this house of strangers and be given this welcome? Why did she feel she had come home? Why did she feel that the benign fatherhood of this stout hook-nosed Jew was something personal to herself? And what she needed.

Mr. Lepert touched her arm.

"You like music? My wife, she is very fond of music. And Sonny, you shall hear him play the piano. Miriam sings. You shall hear them. They have some new Berlioz records. The Fantastic Symphony. You know it? It is very good. At first the young man is very sad. Love is killing his heart. Then there is the pastoral movement. It is very quiet, very sweet. Like the country in spring. His heart is peaceful. But it is only a dream. The pain all comes back. That is like life, yes? We are lulled, soothed. But the pain is there. It all comes back . . ."

"Dada, what are you talking about?" his wife said. "You must let Laura listen for herself. Do you like Berlioz, Laura? Very unorthodox, but we are very fond, in this house."

"I don't know if I know Berlioz or not," Laura confessed. "I do not know much about music at all. I have a friend who plays a good deal. Sometimes it seems very wonderful to me. Sometimes I just do not understand."

When she said this she thought of Peter and her heart gave that old unhappy lurch. She felt the chain tighten around her. Had she never really been free at all? Had it all this day just been a question of slackened chains? All the time they were there, they were there.

She glanced unhappily at Dada Lepert. What had he said about the Berlioz symphony? The pastoral phase . . . peace . . . calm . . . quiet. But it all came back!

A dark-haired girl with a very striking face came in at that moment. She carried an instrument case under her arm. There were cries of delight from all the people in the big drawing-room.

"Dolly!" they cried. "Dolly is here. Now we can have the trio."

"Dolly, come here and talk to Dada," said Mr. Lepert. He was too big and cumbersome to rise from his chair for anyone who was not his own age. "Come and say hallo to Dada," he repeated. He was beaming from ear to ear.

Dolly went up to him and kissed him as lovingly as if she had been his daughter.

"Hallo Dada! How are you?"

He let his hand slip along her arm and come to rest on her instrument case.

"Ah," he said. "You have brought it. That is a good girl, Dolly. Now open the case and let Dada play with it."

"Play with it but not on it," cautioned his daughter Miriam. She turned to Laura. "Dada can't play anything, but he likes to pretend."

While Mr. Lepert fondled the viola Miriam introduced Laura to Dolly Mendle. When Dolly heard Laura's name she looked at her with sudden interest. Later, when she took her viola from Mr. Lepert and was tuning it beside the piano, Laura could see she was looking at her, as if trying to read something special in her face. Laura was a little puzzled. Why should this extremely good looking and vivacious girl take so much interest in herself?

"The Mozart, Dolly?" asked Sonny, and he swung round on the piano stool and played a few bars.

"Come, Miriam," said Dolly. "You must try your violin."

"Oh, but I can't. I'd rather sing. I'm only learning."

"Go along, Miriam," said Mr. Lepert firmly.

"Dada says," said Mrs. Lepert warningly.

Miriam obediently picked up her violin from the top of the piano and tuned it against the piano. Sonny tried a few bars again and both strings joined in with him. Then they all stopped. They started again. This time they played the piece right through.

Mr. Lepert nodded his big head approvingly.

"You see?" he said. "It can be done. Soon, soon, you will make a very good trio."

"I am a better accompanist than Peter," said Sonny to Dolly. "You must give him up and come here. When Miriam has had some more lessons, we will do very well."

"Peter can be brilliant, when he's not being absolutely foul," Dolly said.

Laura stiffened at the name. Mr. Lepert

341

was talking to her again and she tried to concentrate on what he was saying and not overhear the conversation at the piano. Yet she felt startled. Peter played in a trio. Of course she knew that. But he had never mentioned a girl playing with them. Laura had always believed Peter's two musical friends were men. She tried to think, while still politely listening to Mr. Lepert, had Peter deceived her or had she deceived herself?

"You are in love with him," Sonny said with exasperation to Dolly. "And what good is it? He is very careless with girls, and not at all kind to them. You are wasting your time. You must come here on Sundays in future."

"We'll see. We'll see," said Dolly with pursed lips. She cast a fleeting glance at Laura. "Now let us have the Berlioz. After that Miriam must sing."

They all three went to the gramophone and the record cabinet.

Laura could see that Marion was now looking at her across the room. Her eyebrows were faintly raised and there was a small sardonic smile in the corner of her mouth.

Mrs. Lepert came and took Laura to that part of the room to talk to her sister.

"You cannot have Laura all the time, Dada," she said. "You are very old and very selfish."

Mr. Lepert made a deprecating gesture.

"But you will come back, won't you?" he said kindly.

Laura smiled at him.

"Of course I will."

Where she now sat she had Marion on one hand and Mrs. Lepert's sister on the other. Behind her was a huge Chinese floor vase and now she could see the lovely cluttered ornaments over the fireplace. She thought it might be necessary to examine each individual piece to appreciate the beauty.

As Sonny Lepert put the record on the gramophone and began to adjust the timing Laura turned to Marion.

"Was it Peter Stevenson they were talking about?"

"Who else?"

Laura turned back, her face towards the gramophone. The music began and Miriam turned off all the lights except two small shaded ones in opposite corners of the room. They sat in a warm muted gloom and listened to the music. Laura remembered what Mr. Lepert had said about the symphony and she listened more consciously than she had ever done when listening to music before. Yes, she could feel the reveries and passions. She was conscious of the idée fixe without knowing what it was. She only knew the whole thing touched a chord in herself. It was profoundly true because she knew it. Knew it in her own experience. In the third movement she recognized the serenity and false peace of interlude. This was how it had been with her all day. It was nothing but an interlude. Something had to follow.

When it was over Laura could feel a fine damp perspiration on her brow.

The lights were turned up.

"You like that?" Mrs. Lepert asked. "Sometimes, with some people, they do not like programme music, but we like it."

"Yes . . ." Laura said. "Yes. I liked it very much."

"Some nightmare!" said Sonny. "Would you like to have a nightmare like that?"

Laura felt her eyes might be haggard as she lifted them up to Sonny who was standing over her as he carefully returned the records to their covers.

"Did he wake up? Was it only a bad dream?

What happens in the end?" she asked in a low voice.

Sonny shrugged.

"When you go through a love affair, as Berlioz did—it was an Irish actress—you always go through a nightmare. The whole thing's a nightmare. Eh Dada? What do you think? Is a love affair a nightmare, or is it a heavenly prank played on foolish mortals?"

Mr. Lepert shrugged and spread his hands.

"Like this . . . like that . . ." he said. "It all depends on who loves who."

Everybody laughed and Mrs. Lepert went to assist a maid wheel in a table with coffee cups set on it. Miriam leafed through her music.

They had coffee and cakes, fare so rich that Laura could only take a little of it, and Miriam came and sat down beside her when Marion moved away.

"You play very well," Laura said.

"Oh no. Not me. It's very good of Dolly to come and play with me. They say she will play with the new Symphony Orchestra they are just forming. Of course Sonny is good at the piano. Better than that wretched Peter Stevenson Dolly can't divorce herself from."

"Oh? Why not?" Laura hated herself for asking the question.

"Like Sonny said, she's in love with him. He's that sort. Makes use of her. Goes off with other girls when it suits him, but he always comes back to her because of the music. If she would only see it is because of the music, that he is utterly selfish."

"She doesn't look unhappy," Laura said, wondering if her own unhappiness was blooming around her like a dank fungus.

"She's philosophic. Besides she knows he can't do without her, without her viola, that is . . ."

Laura felt she must change the conversation. This was like peeping in bedroom keyholes.

"Will you sing when we've had supper?" she asked. "What will you sing?"

"Yes, I will have to sing. Dada would be angry if I did not. But I should sing first, instead of the trio. Now I have to do it on a cup of coffee and two cakes. I won't be good, I promise you."

She was, however, very good. She had an unexpectedly powerful contralto and if Laura hadn't been feeling so unhappy she would have enjoyed Miriam's singing more than the other musical performances. The Berlioz, she thought, she would never forget. She would remember it with pain.

Sonny, after elaborate farewells and many petitions from the family to "Come again, come often!" drove them home. Laura was thankful for this. It spared her Marion's comments.

She went to bed, sore inside and out. Her skin felt taut and her muscles ached. Her heart, the physical seat of the affections, was heavier than a stone twice its size.

Why had Marion known and not told her? Where was the limit to the things that Marion knew, and did not tell? There was the silent immaculate airman. And now Peter. Had Marion known that Dolly Mendle would be there tonight?

What if she did! What did it matter? If only the pain, the physical pain, would leave her so she could go to sleep. *To sleep, perchance to dream.* She had learned that at school. And have Berlioz-kind of nightmares?

Laura groaned aloud as she turned over and buried her face in her pillow.

The next day, after work, she came up to "Forty-Five" for tea.

"Theodora, come to the pictures with me. I can't bear my own company."

I went gladly because I couldn't bear my own.

When we sat in the Piccadilly afterwards drinking coffee she told me of the previous evening.

"What are you going to do?" I asked.

"Nothing. Just let it go. Just let time pass. Remember how Uncle Tim used to say when we fell down and barked our knees, *Wear it out, wear it out, chickabiddy. Pain wears out just like everything else. Even time.*"

As she said it I could hear Uncle Tim's voice, "*Never mind*," he would say. "*You'll be surprised. One morning you will wake up and the hurt will be all gone. It always is.*"

"*Always, Uncle Tim?*"

"*Always. Time heals everything. Look at the old gum tree with a scar on its trunk. The tree doesn't feel the scar any more.*"

"*But the scar is still there.*"

"*The scar stays, but it doesn't hurt any more.*"

Laura and I sat there in the dimly lit restaurant and looked into our coffee cups. We had youth and great good health, both of us.

The world wandering by would have thought of us as being amongst the world's blessed. Yet our hearts were heavy and we believed our only hope of happiness lay in the words of a loved man who had died and left us, leaving us only the memory of his tender and inexhaustible fatherly love.

15

FOR some time Laura felt quite ill. When she stood up her knees were weak. She had a shivery pain in the back of her head that was with her day and night.

She worked hard at the office but in an impersonal way. She did not notice that whenever she passed through the outer office Mr. Preston would look up from under his eye-shade and watch her. His eyes, a little faded and old, would follow her as she passed from one door to the other. Then they would turn slowly round to where Robert Doule sat, his own eyes dark and angry.

One day Robert had occasion to bring some files into Laura's own den-like office.

She was sitting staring in front of her, hardly aware that Robert had come in, that he had placed the files in front of her and that he now stood looking down at her.

She gave a little sigh and shook herself. She looked up at Robert. Their eyes met. Each read the deep unhappiness in the other.

It came as a shock to Laura to realize how

unhappy Robert was. She had known well enough he languished because of his unrequited love for herself. She had been vaguely sorry about this but of late months had not bothered to take note of it. She had been wrapped up in herself. She had not encouraged Robert's affection but had nevertheless taken it for granted much as she took for granted the kind of watch-dog affection Dirk Preston and several others of the Pepper Tree Bay contingent gave her. She had accepted all that as a kind of regal right and never looked deep into it.

Now she suffered and she understood suffering. Moreover it shocked her to discover someone felt and suffered *about her* the way she suffered about her own love affairs. It was an incredible thing, but here it was, staring down at her.

She felt a wave of pity.

Robert's hand was still on the table. He rested his weight on it as he leaned forward slightly, looking down at her.

She sighed and, half unconsciously, her hand went out and rested a moment on his.

In that instant and in that gesture each confessed something to the other.

Robert jerked up straight. He bit his lip.

Then he turned and walked rapidly through the door.

Laura's eyes followed him.

"Poor Robert," she said. "Poor silly Robert. As if I'm worth it. As if anybody's worth it."

At five minutes to the lunch hour Robert came back into the room.

"Laura, shall we go into the Gardens?"

Pity and understanding were still with her.

"Yes. I haven't been to the Gardens for ages." She blinked and forced a smile. "I wonder if the dogs are still there. Do you know I haven't thought of the dogs for ages."

"They're still there as far as I know. They were a few days ago."

Laura put on her light wool coat and her beret.

"You go and buy some sandwiches," she said. "I'll walk on."

"We'll go together as far as the sandwich bar," said Robert firmly.

His manner was quite bright for him, and his step light. Laura didn't notice it any more than to think, "Thank God, he's not going to gloom."

They walked down the Terrace together and when Robert dived off into a small shop that dealt in daily lunches for workers she went on to the corner alone. She did not so much as glance over the road where was the entrance to the arcade in which stood the Café Noir. She never wanted to see Peter Stevenson again. She knew that if she did she would never conquer her obsession. As it was, every time she saw someone who looked like him, or saw the same make of car that he drove, she felt ill. Would there ever come a day when such a face or such a manner of walking, or such a make of car, would not turn a gimlet in her heart?

For these feelings she despised herself. She did not love Peter. She never had loved him. The whole thing was an unhealthy obsession. She hadn't the slightest doubt about that. She thought it was an incredible thing to make oneself ill over someone who wasn't worth a moment's thought, or that she, Laura Montgomery, should be cast into this hideous Berlioz nightmare.

She shook her head.

"It can't be true . . ." she muttered to herself.

The three dogs stood like a guard right in the entrance to the Gardens. The black-and-white one in the middle, a foot in front of the other two. His ears were cocked, his tongue lolled and his tail swished slowly from side to side. He appraised each newcomer who passed him going into the Gardens.

Laura stopped in front of them and smiled.

"You bad eggs," she said. "You're still here!"

They all approached. They sniffed a little. The black-and-white dog walked disdainfully to the other side and threw himself down on the ground. His tongue lolled and his eyes watched her with interest. His two followers did what he did. Laura went into the Gardens and found a vacant seat where she could see the entrance, wait for Robert and watch the dogs.

"They care for no one but themselves," she thought. "They suffer everyone and they exploit everyone. And they're sublimely happy."

Such happiness, she thought, was enviable. Her heart softened as she watched them. What a wonderful life!

Presently Robert came and he sat down beside Laura. He fed her sandwiches one by one and then produced a special, though generally forbidden treat, a carton of ice-cream with two little wooden spoons.

"Lovely but naughty," said Laura.

"It's a special day. This is celebrating."

Laura looked at him curiously.

"Because we're having lunch in the Gardens again?"

"Because we're together again. The way we used to be. You've got rid of that fellow . . ." He looked at her suddenly and sharply jealous. "There isn't anyone else is there?"

Laura shook her head.

"No one else, ever. I'm just going to stay the way I am. No love affairs for me, Robert. I mean that."

He was content. So long as he could pick up the crumbs from the rich man's table that was all he required at the moment. So long as there was no one else. So long as Laura came fresh and untouched to the office every day. So long as she was his exclusively in thought, if in no other way, he was content. Even happy.

Thus daily they fell again into the habit of walking to the Gardens for luncheon. Laura looked forward to it because she looked forward to seeing the dogs. She felt a great tenderness towards them, and a great admiration. This was the life she envied, independence of others. The dogs loved no one. They were bad when they wanted to be bad and were friendly when their mood was softened after much physical activity or when they wanted to scavenge about those eating their lunches. They were supremely happy. They had one another. They had no need to love anyone but themselves.

Laura did not notice that Robert's manner had subtly changed. She was still wrapped up in herself. She was still feeling unwell. She did not notice, or if she did, did not mind that Robert's manner had become a little authoritative. He decided what sandwiches they would eat for lunch. He decided where they would sit in the Gardens. He spoke sharply to Laura when she went to step off the footpath in the road of an oncoming motor car. He also spoke firmly to her when she stopped in the Terrace to speak to someone of whom he did not approve.

Laura did not mind because she did not care. She was not observant enough to notice the subtle changes in Robert Doule. If anything it was a relief to her to be taken care of—even by Robert Doule.

One day as they walked along in the warm sunshine of a late winter's day they passed Mr. Preston. As usual Mr. Preston completely removed his hat from his head—most Australians merely tipped them or raised them half an inch—and he bowed deeply right from the hips. As he bowed the hand carrying his hat swept to one side and his wife's shopping bag, laden with the domestic shopping which he had been doing, swept to the other.

Such courtliness was noteworthy and nearly everyone who promenaded the Terrace regarded him as "quite a character".

"Damned old fool," said Robert.

Laura started.

"Don't say that. He's really an old darling."

"My foot. Ponderous ass. Slow and muddled. Who does he think he is with those grand-manner airs?"

"Outside Beale and Beale, he's quite somebody, Robert. He is an identity in Pepper Tree Bay, and in his own right."

"How would you know? You left Pepper Tree Bay years ago."

Robert was speaking with an egotistical

superiority and Laura looked at him in surprise.

"You don't know what you're talking about," she said, but without sharpness. "My friends are all in Pepper Tree Bay. I often go there, and very often with Mr. Preston, and Dirk. It's partly business as well as friendship."

This was an aspect of Beale and Beale business of which Robert had known nothing, just as Laura's continued connection with her parents' friends had not been apparent to him. Laura's life, he had surmised, had been bounded on the east by the apartment in Adelaide Terrace and on the west by Beale and Beale in St. George's Terrace. That she ventured six miles round the river to the famous bay where lay the homes of the plutocracy was something in his ignorance that had not occurred to him.

He scowled now. He became preoccupied. His slight bossiness remained but it was accompanied by moodiness and a tendency occasionally to be rude to Laura.

She began to wish she had not renewed the lunch hour loitering in the Gardens.

Once or twice she made an excuse of personal shopping to avoid going to the

Gardens, but she always found Robert loitering around the Terrace waiting for her. Once or twice Dirk Preston rang her at the office and because the girl on the switchboard chose to make a mild joke about it in the public section of the office, Robert showed signs of anger.

On a certain day, a week or two later, Robert came into Laura's office.

"There's a car ordered by Mr. Rushton Beale to pick you up tonight?"

His manner was heavily suspicious.

"Yes, I know. I'm going to the Pastoralists' Club Ball. It's business, don't look so peeved. It suits Beale and Beale for me to go to those things."

"The Pastoralists' Club?" said Robert rudely. "Is Mr. Beale a member of the Pastoralists' Club?"

"No," Laura said. "I don't think he is. But Mr. Preston is. I'm going with Mr. Preston."

"And Dirk?"

"And Dirk. Don't be so damned rude, Robert. As I said, this is purely business."

"You're trying to tell me Mr. Preston is a member of a Club that Mr. Beale couldn't make?"

"Look Robert, I don't suppose Mr. Beale

has even tried to 'make' the Club. His own club is suitable to his needs. The Pastoralists' Club is Mr. Preston's sort of club. His family have been members ever since it was founded. But that's not the point. The sort of people who are members of the Pastoralists' Club like advice about their investments. In spite of what you think about Mr. Preston they take a lot more notice of him, because he is their own kind, than they would of Mr. Beale because they know Mr. Beale is a business man with a vested interest in advice. Now stop talking about something you don't know anything about."

"And how much does Mr. Dirk Preston know about business?"

"Nothing. He's my partner."

"Ha!" Robert's voice was shaking with suppressed jealousy, "So the whole thing is just a rig-up for you and Dirk Preston to go to a ball . . ."

"Shut up!" said Laura in exasperation.

At that moment Mr. Rushton Beale came into the room.

"What's the matter?" he said, looking at Robert's white face and the black angry glow in his eyes. "Lost something?"

Robert opened his mouth, hesitated, swung

round on his heel and plunged out of the room.

Mr. Beale's eyebrows raised themselves to extraordinary heights. Then he looked at Laura.

"You haven't been pulling that young man's leg, Laura?"

"No," she said, still exasperated. "But I think he thinks he owns me or something. I just don't know how to handle him . . ."

"Don't fool him. That's not fair game, you know."

Laura was indignant.

"I don't fool him. He fools himself. How can I stop him? I work here; so does he."

"I'll get Preston to have a word with him."

"No, please don't do that, Mr. Beale. He wouldn't take it from Mr. Preston. I'll do it myself. I promise you."

"Well, I don't want the office upset because I happen to have a very attractive female in it."

"You won't," said Laura slowly. "Did you want something more, Mr. Beale?"

"Don't look so haughty either, Laura. You look much nicer when you're friendly. Yes, I did want you. I want you to take some of these quotes down to Tomas and Co. Do you

361

think you can talk the drift of things convincingly enough for old Tomas? He's as stiff and conservative as they make them. He'll probably think I've sent the junior typist along."

Laura smiled.

"I'll handle him," she said.

Mr. Beale looked at Laura closely a minute.

"I believe you will," he said. "You'll be the talk of the Terrace, you know, if you get old Tomas playing along."

Mr. Beale, friendly to his staff, but coldly urbane in the matter of business, knew the advantages of suddenly confronting an elderly die-hard with Laura, when Laura was cold and efficient. He knew men found themselves weakened by the encounter. They had no way of picking themselves up after the count of nine which was the first effect of coming face to face with Laura and being told their business by her. There were no prepared replies adequate.

Actually the next day Laura *was* the talk of the Terrace, not only because of her success with old Tomas—she had been seen lunching amiably with him at the Esplanade—but because she had been the most striking and successful young woman at the exclusive Pastoralists' Club Ball. Laura's sorrows had lent a touch of dignity to her celebrated natural handsomeness and no matter how much Dirk Preston was thought to have only sawdust in his head his superb good looks and the curious reverence with which his father was always treated had made him the perfect partner for Laura's night-moth beauty in her deep blue and spangled gown.

Mr. Beale was very pleased with her. He actually rubbed his hands together as he smiled on her.

"You'd better look out, Laura. We might have to raise your salary."

"By how much?"

"Fifty pounds a year?"

"Then deduct fifty pounds a year from what my father owes the firm."

Mr. Beale looked at Laura through serious eyes.

"It would take a great many years, Laura. Is it worth it?"

"Please do it. It's just a gesture, but has meaning."

"Better to invest it. It's bad business not to draw a dividend, even an infinitesimal one."

"What do you suggest? Cornell Motors?"

"You couldn't pick up a small packet. Coolgardie Mines, I think."

Their eyes met.

"We're all due to get rich, one day," Laura said softly.

"Provided war keeps out of the picture . . ."

"Predictions only hold while the economic direction holds its course. There could be legislation too . . ."

"Hmm. I don't think we've got too long to wait."

"The price of gold is up to the point of making Coolgardie Mines pay their way, once we've got machinery installed."

"I know. That's the rub. Let Great Coolgardie or the Great Sandstone boost its dividends—and they will in the next six months—and we can form a subsidiary company to raise the capital."

All this Laura had discussed with her principals before. It was a dream of the future they kept turning over in their minds. Somehow when they talked their dreams out of their systems they thought they were one step nearer realization. Mr. Beale, on such days, always went to his club and ordered the best of possible lunches. Mr. Preston he dispatched to his own club to do likewise.

"Gives confidence," said Mr. Beale. "Gives confidence to the onlookers!"

The country needed confidence at the moment. Wall Street was rocking and economy was on the downward slide.

Oddly enough it gave Laura a tinge of conscience. To boom the gold-fields the country had to be desperate for money.

She was thoughtful and preoccupied and forgot to take any notice of Robert Doule. Once again he became a piece of furniture around the office.

She was not entirely free from what she called the "pain of a pianist", meaning Peter Stevenson. But she had arrived at the state when she could see him in the distance, or even close at hand, and not let it deflect her course. She did not now leave the office by the side door, as she had done for weeks. Neither did she deliberately walk on the other side of the Terrace from the Café Noir. She did not go into it, but she did not avoid its presence.

On one occasion, within twenty yards of Beale and Beale, she all but ran into him in the Terrace. She wondered, but did not care, if he had deliberately walked that way at that

hour with the intention of meeting her. She
didn't want to know. Knowledge of that kind
led to no future. The only future was the *time*
of which Uncle Tim had spoken with such
confidence. The *time* that draws an asbestos
sheet between fire and those who get burnt by
fire. The *time* that heals.

When Peter put out his hand and stopped
her she was a little pale, but only because she
had the shivery pain again at the back of her
head.

She looked at him and thought,

*There's nothing to him. Conceit and egotism
ooze from him. Why should . . . how could . . . I
feel like this?*

"Where have you been, Laura? Are you
avoiding me?"

She was looking at his face and thinking,
There's nothing in it but conceit! Then,
because of the pain at the back of her head,
admitting the humiliating fact that he still
had a certain compelling magnetism.

Because she was looking at his face and
thinking these things she did not answer.
Perhaps Peter put another construction on
her silence.

"Poor Laura!" he said. "Beautiful, proud
Laura! Shall I call? If I do, will you come?"

He was smiling into her eyes. There was a certain tenderness there but also a self-assertion and a knowingness. It was this Laura could not bear. Peter underestimated her strength. It was her own fault that he knew how great his fascination for her had been, but it was nobody's fault but his own conceit that he did not know Laura had a steeliness in her . . . greater even than her pride. She had escaped him. She would never go back. He had yet to learn that.

At that moment Dirk Preston, tall, Peter-Pannish, and very happy-go-lucky, came down the Terrace.

Laura put out her hand to make sure he stopped.

"You know Dirk?" she said to Peter by way of introduction.

"Sort of," said Peter. He grinned. It was clear he didn't believe Laura was going to pretend he had been supplanted by this amiable play-boy.

"Peter Stevenson, Dirk," Laura said, smiling at him.

"Great ball the other night, eh?" said Dirk, all happy recollection. "Great band! Everybody a bloke knows there. You looked swell, Laura. Golly! I was proud of you."

"I was proud of you, Dirk. I always am."
Her smile showed the gleaming whiteness of
her teeth and the blue spangling light of her
eyes.

"Shoot along, darling," she added. "I'll see
you later."

"Sure thing. Be seeing you. 'Bye, Stevenson. See you some time."

They watched him progressing down the
Terrace, smiling on all and being smiled on
by all.

"What are you trying to put over me,
Laura? You don't think I'm falling for the
ruse that *that* has supplanted me?"

"You don't have to fall for anything, Peter.
He just happens to have supplanted everybody." She saw the disbelief in Peter's eyes.
She knew he knew she had too many brains to
be in love with anyone as simple as Dirk. She
also knew that nothing hurt a snob like real
hard-handed snobbery. She was now quite
coldly ruthless.

"You see, Peter, he happens to belong to
the right people. My people. One may stray,
temporarily, but one always returns to one's
own kind. Don't you think?"

Laura's "Don't you think?" was so exactly

Danny Hara Montgomery that it went for genuine with Peter.

Peter's smile turned to scorn.

"Good God!" he said. "In this age, and this country."

"Sorry, Peter. But thanks for a lovely time, all the same."

She smiled, and her smile was so exactly Aunt Sheilagh that again Peter took it for meant. It was a perfect smile. It had a hint of condescension and more than a hint of correct politeness. Moreover it was well bred and friendly. It bunged Laura right back into Pepper Tree Bay and banished Peter Stevenson for ever.

All the same Laura's pain in the back of her head increased as she walked away, and she would have liked to go into some quiet corner, and *faint*.

The whole scene had only taken a few minutes but it had taken all Laura's attention. She did not see Robert Doule hovering on the steps of Beale and Beale twenty yards away. She did not see that Robert probably got the full brunt of the brilliant smile she gave Dirk as she turned and waved Dirk on his way.

When she returned to the office later in the

369

afternoon she had occasion to look up some files in the main office. She sat down at a spare table with the files in front of her. Robert Doule sat at his desk, white and rigid, doing nothing. Mr. Preston sat at his desk and looked at him from under his eye-shade. Laura studied her files and didn't think of either of them. The pain was still there at the back of her head and she was trying to concentrate on the files to forget its cause.

The telephone on her table tinkled. She picked it up.

"Yes, it's me," she said. She paused. Evidently the switchboard girl was talking to her. "Yes. Put him through."

She looked up and glanced at Mr. Preston. She smiled at him and made a gesture to suggest he turn his head away and stop up his ears. Laura was receiving a private telephone call in the main office again. From Mr. Preston's son.

She went on doing something with a pencil on the file in front of her as she listened.

"Yes," she said. "Yes, I'll be there. What . . . that blue ball dress again? Dirk darling, aren't you sick of it? . . . All the same I'd like another one, just for the fun of it . . .

Okay, to please you . . . I'd do anything to please you, sweet . . ."

She did not see Robert Doule push back his chair. But she heard him. Dirk was still speaking on the phone and Laura could not hear him because of the noise Robert Doule was making. She frowned, pressing her ear closer to the earpiece and looking at the wall in front of her.

"Say it again. Some silly ass in the office is making a racket . . ."

It was all Robert Doule could stand. He had come to the end of his tether. One imagines things went black before his eyes because as he lurched across the office towards Laura, he did not lurch straight. He knocked into the side of Mr. Preston's table and steadied himself with his two hands on it. His breathing was like an animal's in pain.

Mr. Preston was an elderly man, and not very agile. So he wasn't quick enough to grab the paper-knife before Robert grabbed it. He was quick enough, however, to know this was drama and not play-acting. He pushed his table from under his knees and it knocked Robert slightly off his balance.

Laura put down the telephone receiver and sat looking at them in amazement. At that moment she had no idea what it was all about.

The typist, Miss Smythson, gave a little scream and put her hand over her mouth.

Robert regained his balance. The knife was in his hand and he was suddenly standing over Laura.

She didn't know what she felt at that moment. Not so much fear as astonishment as she realized what Robert felt; perhaps the tragedy of what she had done to him.

She hardly perceived that Robert was grasped from behind. She saw a blurred picture of Robert doubling forward from the middle like a jack-knife. The hand holding the paper-knife struck the table in front of her. Mr. Preston's head, still with the eye-shade in place, somehow was getting in the way around Robert's right shoulder.

Then there was an awful crash and Robert was backwards on the floor and Mr. Preston was sitting, a little stunned, under Laura's table.

Miss Smythson screamed in real earnest. The door from Mr. Rushton Beale's office flew open, also the door leading from the main corridor.

Mr. Rushton Beale and two clerks from the

offices opposite were in the room. The two clerks were struggling with Robert Doule on the floor.

"Preston," said Mr. Beale, "*what* are you doing there?"

Mr. Preston scrambled out from under the table, holding his hand to the seat of his pants. They were torn from side to side, and a great deal of cotton vest was protruding.

The two clerks from the adjoining office had Robert Doule spread-eagled on the floor. He lay there, his head rolling from side to side, and he cried.

It was a terrible crying. Loud, and quite crazy.

Laura, sitting in waxen silence, put her hands over her ears and closed her eyes.

The two young men released Robert but he tried to leap up in a frenzy, so they spread-eagled him again.

"What happened?" said Mr. Beale.

Miss Smythson, still sitting at her desk, pointed to Laura.

"She drove him to it," she said. "He tried to kill her."

Mr. Beale's eyes narrowed.

"Preston," he said, "what happened?"

Mr. Preston backed modestly towards his

desk. His hand still held his pants together. He sat down heavily. He pushed his eye-shade back and sighed.

"The young man has had a nervous breakdown," he said. "He's been quite that way for some time . . ."

"Why didn't I know?"

His eyes met Mr. Preston's faded and gentle ones. The message said this was a gentleman's explanation, and that there should be a gentleman's agreement between them.

"Miss Smythson," Mr. Beale said sharply, "ring Dr. Benton. He'll be in his surgery farther up the Terrace. Then ring an ambulance."

He walked over to where Robert Doule was lying, still rolling his head from side to side and sobbing. Mr. Beale bent over him and wiped his nose. He looked at the two young men from over the way.

"I'm sorry to trouble you," he said. "Do you mind holding him until we can get some relief?"

Miss Smythson finished telephoning. She came and stood over Robert and looked down at him.

"You should ring the police," she said

374

quite sharply to Mr. Beale. "She drove him to it . . . but he tried to . . ."

"Be quiet, Miss Smythson. If I hear another word you will leave the office. You heard what Mr. Preston said. Mr. Doule is under nervous strain."

He stared hard into her eyes. She tried to defy him but eventually her eyes dropped.

"Very well, Mr. Beale. I'll get on with my work, if you'll excuse me."

She sat down in front of her typewriter and didn't stop pounding the keys until after Robert Doule had been removed.

Mr. Paul Beale came into the office and said, "What the hell?"

Laura sat in white and graven silence. Mr. Preston kept twisting his head to examine the amount of damage done to his posterior.

"Laura, go into my office," Mr. Beale said.

When she went to get up he had to help her. She stood up straight by her table then walked with stiff legs to the door. When she went through she heard Mr. Rushton Beale say to his brother,

"Preston is always the perfect gentleman. Even when he hasn't got a seat to his pants."

16

LAURA was never quite the same again.

I suppose we are what life makes of the material with which God and our parents—very much behind one another's backs—present life.

Laura I am sure would have been quite a different person if she had never come to Australia. In fact the whole Montgomery family would have been different, except perhaps Aunt Sheilagh.

Nothing changed Aunt Sheilagh. She was exactly the same the day she left Australia as she was when I was a child. Not wealth, position, hard times nor the dry winds of years in a gold-mining town in the Australian desert changed her. She remained sweet, a little shallow, but very kind. She was loving and loved. Everyone else changed. Uncle Tim and my father had changed to dust and bones. Sylvia might have lived longer if it had not been so important for her to go to meet Danny when he came back to Australia for the third and last time. We five children of

Joe Montgomery became entirely Australian with no vestiges left of our Irish heritage.

And Laura? Beautiful clever Laura, who if she had reigned in her own country would have become a whole person. As it was, Australia and events in Australia tore her asunder. The affair of Peter Stevenson and the affair of Robert Doule left their marks on her spirit. When pain was finished with— there remained the scar. It was a thing in Laura's temperament that appeared a blemish instead of what it really was—a memory of the past.

She was called superficial. A flirt. She was afraid to be loved and afraid to be kind. So superficially she became a little cruel.

The naturally kind heart she inherited from her mother suffered a terrible blow when Robert Doule cracked up. This event and the final defection of Marion Perrent from the role of wholesome friend drove Laura back into the fold at Pepper Tree Bay. She had already established herself in the business world and she might have climbed to great heights therein. As it was, she took refuge, and like the canary in his cage she longed for liberty from her refuge but when the door was left open she no longer had taste to suffer the jungle law in St. George's Terrace.

That is not to say Laura gave up her business activities. Far from it. She became quite a personage in the realm of the Terrace. But she became objective, cold and often very hard. Of course business men admired her for these qualities and when those who dealt with her were mildly chiacked by their colleagues in the city clubs they invariably retorted, "She has a masculine mind."

This explanation of Laura's ability made both Mama and Laura grind their teeth.

"The vanity of it," Mama would say.

Laura would put on an extra layer of epidermis and at the same time buy a new suit and "lay on the charm". This the men liked, though in self defence they had to excuse their interest,

"She has a masculine mind."

After Laura had found a bust photograph, naked, of the silent airman in Marion Perrent's studio one day, she gave up Marion and the apartment in Adelaide Terrace.

There were things here deeper than she wished to probe. The photograph, taken in a Rupert Brooke pose, though not indecent, sickened her. The secretiveness of Marion's knowledge of the young man also sickened her.

"Where are you going to live, Laura?" I asked.

"With Mrs. Preston."

This silenced the family. There was mixed consternation and surprise.

Mrs. Preston? Back to Pepper Tree Bay? Away from the city?

"But will you like it? You're so fastidious. Mrs. Preston is nice and very kind, but Laura! That house! It's shabby!"

Laura shrugged.

"I won't be in it very often."

Aunt Sheilagh and Uncle William were delighted. This move, they thought, would put an end to Laura's undignified capers amongst stockbrokers on the Terrace. Uncle William said he had never heard of anything so preposterous as a young woman working in an office. "Like a common nobody . . ." He never conceded at any point that Laura had done anything towards resolving his own financial affairs. He talked big about making an allowance available to Laura and then pronounced,

"She won't need anything beyond pin money living in that Preston household.

There's enough social life in Pepper Tree Bay to keep her happy. If she doesn't like it she can come home, where she belongs."

Aunt Sheilagh said,

"Darling, I'm so happy for you. Now you've got Dirk, and the river. Of course the Bastons and the Maynard-Arnolds will look after you. Don't come up to Kalgoorlie in the summer, it will ruin your skin. And darling, don't go bathing too much. A good skin is absolutely essential to the making of a good marriage."

It didn't occur to either of them that living in Pepper Tree Bay was going to make no difference to Laura attending at Beale and Beale at nine in the morning every working day in the week.

Her continuation at Beale and Beale was only made possible by the transferring of Robert Doule, after a three months' illness, to the Adelaide office, the other side of the desert and the Nullabor Plain.

The Robert Doule affair might have died, except in the Terrace office colony, which after all is a world of its own, and its gossip tit-bits never likely to reach the drawing-rooms of Pepper Tree Bay, if it hadn't been for Mr. Preston's disaster to the seat of his pants.

They say that in all comedy there is some seed of tragedy. Certainly the reverse was the case in the Robert Doule affair. When Mr. Rushton Beale had got over the purely practical side of the affair he had time to reflect on the scene in the main office when he had first opened the door.

Laura was on one side of the proscenium, as it were, and Robert Doule prostrate on the other. Dead centre, however, was Mr. Preston sitting under Laura's table and feeling for the seat of his pants.

The story was too funny for Mr. Beale to keep to himself and he repeatedly told it in his club.

Within a few days everyone in Pepper Tree Bay, as well as in the main financial citadels of the Terrace, knew that a young man had tried to throw away his life, or Laura's, nobody was quite sure which, for love of her brilliant blue eyes.

The city savoured the tit-bit and looked at Laura with freshened respect, but not so Pepper Tree Bay. It looked as if Laura might be banned from the drawing-rooms around the river bay. Aunt Sheilagh's friends hoped, for her sake, she would not make the social mistake of bringing Laura with her when next she came down from the gold-fields and paid her round of calls in Pepper Tree Bay.

Laura's move to the Prestons' household, however, confused the intentions to cut Laura loose from the fold. This put everyone in a quandary. They decided to "wait and see". They waited long enough to forget, and soon it was never remembered that it had been intended to banish Laura.

The fact that Laura went everywhere with Dirk satisfied everyone.

"Such a nice sensible boy. Healthy, you know."

In the city it was different. Laura, because of her fine appearance, her proud arrogant carriage, and her reputation for a "head for figures", could not pass up and down the Terrace unnoticed. Soon she became "that woman the young man blew himself up over", or "There she goes, you know, the one the young fellow took a dose of arsenic about".

"Callous, I reckon."

"Couldn't care less, could she? Look at the way she walks along. Thinks she owns the world."

"Golly, I'd like her fur coat, all the same."

"Perhaps the bloke left it to her in his will."

Laura knew of these stories and they made her colder, more aloof.

Because, underneath, she was a young woman, vibrant with life and aching to love and be loved, she sometimes dropped the pose and became alive. Then real charm, not the façade she "stacked on" to get her own way with business deals in the Terrace, would come into its own again. She would laugh and be witty and merry at some social gathering, dance or launch party. Then once again the young men would gather around and Laura would hold court.

Nevertheless as soon as anyone showed too much interest Laura froze up. She gained the further reputation of being a flirt.

"Always trying to dangle some man after her, and as soon as she gets him cuts him and returns to old Dirk."

"Dear old Dirk! What he puts up with from Laura!"

"Let's hope he won't be the next one to put a pistol to his head."

No one suspected Dirk of being short of the sexual impulses, which he was, so that it was

383

unlikely he would put a pistol to his head for anyone. It was precisely this absence of impulse in Dirk that made him such a reliable companion for Laura.

At one stage even the denizens of Pepper Tree Bay, who were anxious for Aunt Sheilagh and Uncle William's sake to omit from the records Laura's love-history, were afraid that since Dirk Preston and Laura were living in the same house they might be sleeping together. Behind Mr. and Mrs. Preston's back, of course.

But since it was much more convenient for all social relationships in Pepper Tree Bay *not* to hold this theory for any length of time, in due course Dirk and Laura were taken for granted and people forgot to comment.

"One supposes they'll marry some day."

"When Dirk has made enough money, of course. Laura is likely to be expensive."

Nobody would have dreamed of thinking, let alone suggesting aloud, that Dirk didn't have it in him ever to make more money than enough to keep him a pleasant and harmless play-boy.

On the surface Laura emerged from the Doule affair more poised, but hard. Sophisticated in an apparently self-seeking way.

384

Nobody, not even me, born with a caul on my face, knew what really went on underneath. But of this I am sure: Laura suffered. I saw too many evidences of a deeper side.

One day we walked through Pepper Tree Bay up Swanbourne hill to the sand dunes behind the fire station where we could see the Indian Ocean on one side and the near reaches of the river on the other.

As we passed the place where Oliver Harding had saved Sylvia from the consequences of heart strain by holding her up and massaging her back, Laura said,

"Remember Oliver holding Sylvia?"

"Yes. And Danny and Oliver making a seat of their hands and carrying her home."

Laura was silent and when I saw her hand go up to her face I stole a look at her. There were tears in her eyes.

I tried to take her mind off her thoughts by talking about the view. We sat down on the sand dunes and Laura, her hands clasped around her knees, sat with her face to the sea.

"I often wonder if I'll ever go back," she said.

"Back to Magillicuddy?"

"Yes."

"Do you want to?"

"I don't know. I hated Australia when I

385

came back last time. I hated the grey colour of the bush and the trees. And the way everyone spoke. I used to dream, night after night, I was back in Meath. It was like dreaming of an unattainable land. Then I got sorry for those spindly trees, because they were such poor cousins to the elms up the driveway of Magillicuddy. Then I got to admiring them. Now I love them. I love their enduring quality. I think of what they have suffered and endured to survive. I think of the pitiless sun, and the paucity of rain, and I think I'd like to be like one of those old gum trees. They've got *character*."

"Someone or other said, 'It's not the country. It's the people that live in it'."

"You're right," Laura said slowly. "It's the people. But they're like the country. They're gnarled and enduring too. They've got character. I hate to admit it, but I'd rather have old Uncle Dreary Maynard-Arnold, and old Papa Baston, than Da. Look what they've endured. After all Da, and all the Montgomeries, were brought up soft."

"It hasn't been 'soft' in Australia."

"No. But they don't know it. They don't live in a world of reality. They live in a world of 'what will be'."

386

"Except us. Our generation."

Laura looked at me for a minute.

"You're all right," she said. "You're an Australian. You don't have to struggle inside yourself."

A look of such sadness came over Laura's face that I was taken aback.

Then she jumped up and brushed the white sand from her skirt.

"I hate this place," she said. "When I look at the sea I *long*. And I don't want to long for something I'm not sure I want any more."

"But if you had the opportunity to go back, you would go back?"

Laura shook her head gravely.

"I don't know," she said. "I really don't know."

"I wonder what Danny is like now," I said thoughtlessly.

There was such pain in Laura's eyes I felt frightened for her. One does not like to see one so young and so able and battling, like the gum trees, show such signs of inward pain.

On another occasion Laura told me she had repeatedly gone back to the Gardens to see if the dogs were still there. When day after day they were absent she plucked up the courage to ask the gardener.

"We sent for the dog-cart," he said. "They got to be too big a nuisance. Barking at everyone comin' in, and one day the big one, the leader, got an old bloke in the calf of the leg. That was the end of 'im. We had the dog-cart fetch 'em away."

Laura went home and that night she cried herself to sleep.

"Could you cry so much as that over three strange dogs, Laura?"

"It wasn't the dogs. It was what they stood for."

What had they stood for? Courage? Independence? Pride in themselves? Were these the things in Laura's own character she mourned as if lost? Were these the things of which Marion Perrent, Peter Stevenson and Robert Doule had deprived her? Or had it all been Australia's fault?

As far as Uncle William was concerned, everything was Australia's fault.

"No one in the whole country knows how to boil an egg decently! Knaves and rapscallions! Frightful manners! Now, if they'd listen to me . . ."

With so much inoculation from our father

and uncle we, though we'd known no other country, also thought it must be a dreadful country, but it never occurred to us to want to go anywhere else, even though the depression had set in with a vengeance and from being poor we got to being very poor. But the strange enduring trees, the vast desolate landscape, the placid shining river remained the same. They did things to one's heart as a dream sometimes does . . . a dream of things very old and long gone but not entirely forgotten.

It was the depression, however, that brought Uncle William's affairs back to life.

Exactly as Laura had predicted, when the balance of trade remained consistently against the country, the country had to buy everything from overseas with gold. The market value of gold rose and the government price for it rose. Coolgardie Mines could now pay their way. This was honest gold. Gold brought out of the land and sold fair and square on a fair and square market. But it was first cousin to all the dummy mines that sprang up everywhere and the host of minor companies floated to explore for new shows and re-explore old mines for what would now be payable gold. Moreover the boom in gold served to absorb a considerable number of the otherwise unemployed.

The *t'other-siders* became the number one enemy of all Westralians again. They poured across the border either with some capital to exploit the situation, or, being without capital, to find work.

The character of the miners themselves changed. Engineers, school teachers, musicians competed with Italian migrants and the old Cornish miners for any kind of work at all.

Kalgoorlie became a flourishing centre again and Aunt Sheilagh was torn between the desirability of buying a new Pepper Tree Bay house, returning to riverside civilization, or remaining in Kalgoorlie, the only place in the whole vast State where money flowed and music and conversation were good.

Uncle William paid excited and flying visits to Perth. Laura implored him to sell some of his paper gold and pay his debts. She emphasized the necessity of converting some of his new wealth from shares in gold to land and houses. The latter, in any place but the gold-fields, were dirt cheap. But Uncle William had dreams of Midas. Already he was a wealthy man again, on paper. Besides he wasn't going to be told, by his own daughter, "Bog-Irish habits from living with *t'other-siders* in the city", what to do on the share market. He'd been dealing in the share market before Laura was born.

Beale and Beale who were, when all was said and done, a good solid and responsible firm, took a hand in this attitude. They insisted Uncle William recoup them in cash for their labour of years in carrying him on their books.

They applied pressure on him to sell some of his holdings and very scrupulously did not buy these holdings themselves. They tried to persuade Uncle William to reinvest some money in Cornell Motors and City Omnibuses.

"Ha!" exploded Uncle William. "Companies *they* floated!"

"They're long distant but solid, Da," Laura said. "Look at the list of shareholders and you'll see how solid. The land is behind them, and the landowners own the earth when all the wheat and gold is dug out of it."

"Utter nonsense!" said Uncle William and threatened if he heard another word from Laura he would sever his connection with the firm altogether, and put her back to school where she'd learn to respect her parents.

Laura learned from inside the firm that Danny, after all, had become a minor shareholder in Coolgardie Mines. Without saying a word to her he had taken her advice all those years back—was it so very long ago—and bought two thousand shares.

Laura watched the market till she thought it had reached unreal heights. She sold three-quarters of her own shares in Coolgardie Mines and invested some in Cornells and City Omnibuses.

She cabled to Danny to sell, but didn't get a reply.

Uncle William came down again from Koolgardie and offered to buy Mama a house and set us all up again in Pepper Tree Bay. But Mama shook her head.

"I've had my fingers burnt in gold shares," she said. "I don't believe in money that is not in the Bank. We'll make out . . ."

"One more year, Helen, and we'll all pack up and go back to Ireland."

Mama puckered up her mouth and looked up from her needle-work at Uncle William.

"What would we do in Ireland?" she said. "We wouldn't know anybody."

"You wouldn't have to know anyone.

They'd come and know you. You're a Montgomery, aren't you?"

Mama shook her head.

"I'm not," she said. "I'm the only one who
is not a Montgomery."

"For God's sake, Helen, stop thinking
about yourself. Think about the girls.
They're all Montgomeries, all five of them."

"They're Australians," Mama said shortly.
"They couldn't help it, but that's what they
are. This is their country."

"Damned nonsense," Uncle William said,
and stamped out of the house.

Going to Ireland sounded an interesting
proposition to us. After all, we'd been
brought up to believe we were Irish and that
it was a grave misfortune to have been born in
Australia. This was a dreadful country . . .
and Ireland was heaven . . . hadn't we been
told!

I remembered later how my father, when
he had come back from the war, seemed to
have changed his opinion about Ireland. He
had stopped talking about it, except to say it
was a dirty place, and had stopped talking
about his friends and relatives except to say
they should all be stood up against a wall and
shot.

It was all quite bewildering but we did not struggle very hard against Mama's attitude. We had been fascinated, even charmed, by our Irish relatives but our one security had been Mama. We believed in her blindly. She was our rock and our refuge. Whatever Mama did and said was right. It was impossible that she could be mistaken or wrong. Anyhow she was too bossy to have let us have our own way about our own destinies.

Basically we knew it was pride spelt with a capital "P" that kept Mama from accepting Uncle William's proposition. She had fought the fight with Fate too hardly to give in to any man. Like the old gum trees, she was enduring. Also she held the theory that those who came out to Australia and later returned to their own countries were "no-hopers". They gave in. It was the Bastons and Maynard-Arnolds of the world who Mama admired. People who stuck it out the hard way and won through.

Aunt Sheilagh came down to Perth with Sylvia and rented a large house overlooking the water in Pepper Tree Bay. The dinner-parties and drawing-room musicales began again. The emeralds came out of the Bank and Laura took to wearing her mother's pearls because Aunt Sheilagh was always wearing her emeralds now and someone had to wear the pearls to keep the lustre on them.

Once Laura left them on the small table in our bathroom at "Forty-Five".

"For goodness' sake, Laura," I said. "Someone might steal them."

"No, they wouldn't. They're just the same as every typist's in the city. The only difference is that mine are real, but nobody'd guess. Half a guinea at Woolworth's and you can have the same."

Thus Laura of a two-thousand-pound string of pearls!

Aunt Sheilagh was much in demand in Pepper Tree Bay. She could give better dinner-parties than anyone else because only those who were "in gold" had any money these days. Farmers were walking off their properties and wheat was *1s. 6d.* a bushel. The sheep and cattle in the north were dead from drought anyway.

The Bastons, Maynard-Arnolds, Lessiers and Cooles, their relatives and hangers-on had their money, such as was left, in motors and omnibuses and no one could afford to buy a motor car or ride in an omnibus.

Uncle Dreary Maynard-Arnold was cross with Laura and crosser still with Beale and Beale.

"Hang on, Uncle Dreary," Laura pleaded. "The gold market has got out of hand. It will crash. The depression won't last for ever and the motor-car age will live again, only much brighter and for much longer."

Oddly enough, Mr. Maynard-Arnold, who believed that women were only fit for child-bearing, house management and gossiping, believed in Laura. It was more than her own father or Danny appeared to do.

She sent Danny a second cable.

Sell C.M. now.

She received no answer at all.

Laura drafted out a cable to herself, on a pilfered cablegram form, instructing herself, care of Beale and Beale, to sell two thousand shares in Coolgardie Mines for Dennis Hara Montgomery. Beale and Beale were holding the script so she had no difficulty, until such a time as the rush of business eased in the firm and the partners or Mr. Preston got around to checking the orders and their origins.

"Sufficient unto the day is the evil thereof," said Laura, and cheerfully banked £5,500 in Danny's name. He had invested £100.

The next day Coolgardie Mines went up a shilling and stayed that way for a week. The following week they fell a shilling. The week after they fell two shillings. Everything else except shares in the big old-fashioned mines began to drop. The dud shows closed down and the market began to fall. The recession was in.

When Coolgardie Mines had lost six shillings on the downward slide Danny obliged by cabling Beale and Beale to sell.

Laura sent a laconic reply.

Sold.

She had a bad half-hour with the Beale partners but emerged unruffled. She had sinned against the firm and caused them to sin against the ethics of the Stock Exchange but nobody knew it but herself. And she saved Danny's money for him.

Uncle William started to sell but he was selling too late. He would never be a wealthy man now. His debts were paid, true. He had recovered some money but not a great deal.

The only one who really mourned was Mama.

"But Mama, he *wouldn't* be told," we said. "No one can help a man who *won't* help himself."

Mama shook her head.

"They weren't meant to manage their own affairs," she said sadly. "They were meant to have silver spoons held in their mouths all their lives, by someone else. All of them . . . they were all the same. Joe, Dennis, Rory . . . and now William."

"Not Uncle Tim?"

"No. Not Uncle Tim. He was different from them."

"And Danny?"

At this stage none of us knew that Laura had saved Danny's money for him. We thought he'd done it himself.

Mama pursed up her lips and thought.

"Maybe Danny will be different. Maybe he'll be more like Uncle Tim." This was a new thought and a new hope to Mama. She spent the rest of her life believing in Danny.

The catastrophe did not seem to upset Aunt Sheilagh very much.

"Darlings," she said. "Money always turns up from somewhere, in the end. Only this time I really don't think I can go back into the desert for another ten years. William will have to put his money into something else. Now Sylvia and I are back in Pepper Tree Bay, we don't feel like moving away."

Nobody felt like telling Aunt Sheilagh Uncle William didn't appear to have much money to put into anything else anyway.

"I think we ought to buy a sheep station," Aunt Sheilagh said. "There are so many empty ones now, with all these people walking off . . ."

"What with?" asked Gerry. "And if you do, who'll you sell your sheep and cattle to?"

"The Banks, darling. None of you children seem to read the papers. Don't you see . . . the Banks have everything nowadays. They advance the money, and they buy the stock. I suppose that sounds complicated to you . . . but darlings, we've been dealing with Banks all our lives. We *understand* them."

There was nothing for us to do but shake our heads and Mama went out and made some tea.

The next day when I came home from the school where I was teaching I found a note on the dining-room table.

Gone to Uncle William. He's ill. Bring my white uniform and cap down after dinner. Mama.

"Now what's the matter with Uncle William?" I thought. And added unkindly, "I suppose the Banks have told him just what they think of him and he's gone to bed to sulk."

Then as I got the dinner I remembered about Mama's cap and uniform. She never took those when she went nursing unless she intended to stay on a case. And Mama only stayed on cases that were serious. She was nursing in the Schools Nursing Service now and rarely took an odd case.

Of course Uncle William would be different. She would give him of her best.

But I felt uneasy. I went to the telephone and rang up the Pepper Tree Bay house. Laura answered the phone.

"How is Uncle William?" I asked. "What's the matter with him, Laura?"

She was silent a moment and when her voice did come through it didn't sound like her voice any more.

"I don't know how he is . . . he's bad. Oh Theodora . . . do come down. I don't like it. I

400

don't like it. Dr. Riley says it's his heart. He's here now. Mama is out in the kitchen showing Sarey how to make a mustard plaster as her Nana used to make them in Galway. She doesn't seem to *realize* . . ."

"I'm coming at once," I said.

I hung up, wrote a note for the others and left it on the dining-room table and went out and caught a bus to Pepper Tree Bay.

As I walked up the road towards the house I saw Dr. Riley's car moving away. I walked round the path and went into the house through the side verandah door. Laura was standing in the passage, leaning against the wall. Her face was very white.

"Laura?"

She nodded.

"He's gone . . ." she said. "He's gone."

I knew she meant Uncle William was dead.

For a moment I didn't feel anything at all, and found myself saying to myself,

"Three down to Australia."

Then suddenly I thought of Uncle Tim, and the tears packed up behind my eyes.

"Why did they all have to die . . . *here?*" I said.

Laura nodded.

"They hated it so . . . ."
Here was the tragedy. It did not lie in death but in the geography of their graves.

17

AUNT SHEILAGH said,
"Darlings, the climate of this country is bad for the heart. In Ireland the
climate is so soft. People never die of heart
failure in Ireland."

Gerry barely suppressed a "What, never?"

"You brought Sylvia out here . . ." began
Vicky.

"Yes, darling. But you see Sylvia's heart
trouble is congenital. That's quite different.
It means there's something wrong with a
valve. With Tim and Joe and my darling
William . . . there was nothing wrong with
their hearts at all. They just broke . . . their
hearts, I mean."

It seemed funny that everyone in the Montgomery family should die from heart attacks.
Being neurotic, Denney and I were often to
be seen, thereafter, feeling our pulses. We
even thought it wouldn't be such a bad idea
to go back to Ireland after all. Only seemingly
nobody had any money now.

Laura explained Aunt Sheilagh's position

to her patiently. Aunt Sheilagh showed no inclination to do anything about the house in Kalgoorlie which she owned or the house in Pepper Tree Bay which she rented. She appeared to go on living the same way . . . two servants in the house and two men in the garden. There was also a paid caretaker in the house in Kalgoorlie.

When Laura showed a tendency to push Aunt Sheilagh into doing something Mama took a hand.

"I suppose it is eating up money, Laura, but you can't do anything with your mother just at the moment. She doesn't *realize*. You'll have to be patient."

This Laura was not.

"Aunt Helen," she said. "Mama never realizes. She has always lived in an unreal world. She lives in a little Ireland transported to Australia. She thinks, if she thinks at all, that her homes here are the same as Mount Clare in Galway, or Magillicuddy in Meath. Places she owns by right of residence."

"You are very unkind to your mother."

"I can't afford to be kind. I'm faced with the hard facts of life. If I thought by waiting Mama would realize her financial position, I'd wait."

It was true that Aunt Sheilagh was a little unreal. Uncle William's funeral would have been funny, if there had ever been anything but tragedy in death.

To begin with there weren't any Montgomery men left. We were a world of women. Yet Aunt Sheilagh had sat quietly and done nothing at all about burying Uncle William. She just waited for some man to appear from somewhere and make decisions. Of course it was Mama and Laura who did everything. All the men of Pepper Tree Bay and some from Kalgoorlie who had been Uncle William's friends came to the funeral and were pall-bearers, and things like that. But there was no one but Laura to decide who were to be pall-bearers. And there was no one but Laura and Mama and Vicky and me to be chief mourners.

This was quite shocking because none of the men of Pepper Tree Bay or Kalgoorlie believed in women going to funerals, let alone taking precedence in these affairs.

Yet what else was there to do? Was Uncle William to go to the grave liked and respected, but unloved?

Also, Aunt Sheilagh hadn't sent a wreath.

She had expected some nebulous person to do it for her. When Laura had said,

"Mama, shall I send a wreath for you?"

Aunt Sheilagh had replied,

"I do wish you would stop doing things for me, Laura. This is the wrong time to be bossy. You have lived too long away from home . . ."

"But you must have a wreath, Mama."

"Of course I'll have a wreath. I always have the biggest and most beautiful wreath at funerals. It will have the pride of place. It will be attended to, just as everything else will be attended to by . . ."

One had a dreadful moment when one was afraid Aunt Sheilagh had been going to add, "William".

So Laura, afraid there might be the embarrassment of two wreaths, did not send one on her mother's behalf.

When the coffin left the old Church in Pepper Tree Bay there was no wreath from Aunt Sheilagh.

Laura tore the card off the very spectacular wreath sent by the Chamber of Mines and wrote "From your loving wife" on the back of it and pinned it back amongst the flowers.

No one in Pepper Tree Bay was going to say Aunt Sheilagh had not loved Uncle William.

Then when we came back from the funeral Aunt Sheilagh said some of the pall-bearers had been wrong ones.

"Why, *he* . . ." she said, pointing to one card. "*He* was William's enemy. William wouldn't permit him standing room at his funeral."

"When people die, Mama, even their enemies forgive them," Sylvia said.

"What could you possibly know about it, Sylvia?"

"I know that Da hated that man more than he hated Da."

"My dear child, you do talk nonsense. What could you who have led such a secluded life know whom your father hated? As a matter of fact William hated no one. There never lived a more gentle and kind man. He never said a hard word in all his life. His voice was ever soft, gentle . . . and low . . ."

"That was Cordelia's voice, Mama," Laura said. "The quotation finishes with 'An excellent thing in *woman*'."

"Laura, I'll do what I like with my own quotations."

Mama said, "Laura, come and help me make the tea." Outside she said, "Dear, don't argue with your mother. She doesn't understand . . ."

"I know," said Laura. For the first and only time the tears sprang into her eyes. "I don't know what to do with her. I don't know how we'll manage, unless she does understand."

For eight weeks Laura, restive on the bit, refrained from worrying her mother about their future. By that time she and Beale and Beale, though not finished untangling Uncle William's affairs, got a fairly clear idea of where his finances stood. By selling the bulk of his gold shares they could *realize* a little more capital, but very little. They thought Aunt Sheilagh should hold on to her Industrials. They would reap a pittance, but it was something secure. The house in Kalgoorlie was freehold and might bring a good price.

"Mama," Laura said, "if you and Sylvia are going to stay here you must either sell the Kalgoorlie house and buy this one, or rent it out to pay for the rent of this house, or some other smaller house in Pepper Tree Bay."

"Darling, you are a worrier, aren't you?

Something will turn up. I've a brother in Galway, and there's Danny at Magilli-cuddy."

Laura drew in a deep breath.

"Mama, there's a depression on in the world. Nobody, not even Uncle Brian or Danny, has any capital money to spare. Either might offer you a home, if you want to go back to Ireland. In the meantime you *must* do something about your property here. Also you can't keep Sarey and Ann in the house. Nor the men in the garden."

"Don't be absurd, Laura. I couldn't do all that garden myself. And I've always had a maid for Sylvia. Even in Kalgoorlie after we lost our money, I had a maid."

Laura sat and gazed helplessly out of the window.

"Aunt Helen," she said afterwards to Mama, "do you think it is a good idea to let reality face Mama? I mean, supposing I let her run up bills and wages and then let the hordes in to dun her? Would that make her *see*?"

Mama was worried. It might make Aunt Sheilagh *see* but in the end it would cost her either her own little bit of capital money or

Laura's. It was the kind of expensive lesson none of them could indulge in.

Salvation came in the form of a letter from Danny. He was coming back to Australia to settle Uncle William's affairs. We could all go back to Magillicuddy with him.

Laura received this news in silence, as did we, Mama and the five daughters of Joe Montgomery.

If Aunt Sheilagh and Sylvia went back to Ireland with Danny, at least they would have a home. As for the rest of us . . . Well, it was nice of Danny to suggest it, but being poor in a ramshackle Magillicuddy would be much worse than being poor on the banks of the Swan. In Australia you could always shoot a rabbit if you were hungry.

Besides where were we, or Danny for that matter, going to get the money to transplant us across the world?

"You must all come," said Aunt Sheilagh with finality. "None of you will die of heart failure in Ireland."

This, of course, set Denney and me to feeling our pulses again.

Nevertheless, Danny's imminent visit took the tension out of everything. Here was a man, and a Montgomery to boot, on his way to settle affairs for us. Aunt Sheilagh smiled sweetly and just a little tearfully.

"I told you something would turn up," she said to Laura reproachfully. "Now everything will be straightened up."

Not a word about the fact that Laura had already straightened everything up, except Aunt Sheilagh herself.

We put away from us such queries as "Would Laura go too?" "How would Sylvia stand up to the journey through the tropics?" "How much money, if any, did Danny have to take on the load?" And last but somehow more sadly, "Was he going to marry Sylvia?"

The colour, so long absent, came back into Sylvia's cheeks. She sat, very still and dreamy, but obviously happy.

Dr. Riley said there was a new approach to the treatment of such cases as Sylvia's.

"The heart is a muscle," he said. "Experiments abroad have shown some very good effects from mild exercise. The heart must work, a little."

He prescribed a short slow walk for Sylvia twice a day.

So twice a day Sylvia walked along the banks of the river, not very far, and not very fast.

She certainly looked very much better and her prettiness took on a new radiant quality.

I saw it and noted it, alas, a little sadly. Sylvia well was a Sylvia fit to marry.

And my heart ached for Laura.

One day I tentatively suggested this to Mama. She was quite shocked at my attitude.

"Laura can have half a dozen men dangling after her, any time," Mama said crossly. "Why take Danny from Sylvia? Besides, Sylvia suits Danny. Laura is too competent, too hard. And an outrageous flirt."

"Mama, how can you be so blind!" I said. "She's competent because she has to be. You are, for the same reason. You used to praise and admire women who were capable. And as for being a *flirt*—why, that's only a façade."

"A façade for what? Laura has had a wonderful life so far. Of course the wretched Doule affair was unpleasant. But the young man was a paranoic and bound to break down over someone or something sooner or later."

"Underneath Laura is very kind. And she *feels* things."

"I'm glad to hear it. But you don't have to be sorry for her. Laura will go a long way. I only hope when she gets to the top of the tree

412

she devotes some of her energies and ability to doing community things."

Did Laura want to get to the top of the tree? What tree?

The only tree Laura and I ever talked about was Uncle Tim's tree with the scar on it.

Laura had bought a block of land in the hills and she was worrying about an old red gum tree that stood on the boundary of her block. On which side of the boundary line did the tree stand? If on Laura's side, then the tree would stand. If on the neighbour's side, then the tree was to come down.

It was a big old tree, raddled with gum holes, and I think there were white ants in one dead root. It had been blackened by fire and the main trunk had broken off about fifteen feet from the ground. The branches were green and leafy except where the die-back on the topmost branch left it with long thin crooked fingers pointing leafless as a fleshless crone's old hand to the sky.

At evening time, when the western sky was blood red with sunset over the plain and the distant sea, the crooked fingers stood out black, pointing resolutely to a pitiless sky.

Laura loved the tree the same way as she loved the dogs. It had survived centuries. It

413

had endured the depredations of fire, drought, blackman's spear and whiteman's axe. It stood on the edge of the range in virgin bush above the place where the earth faulted away down to make a landslide drop to the plain. It had never known white man before.

One Sunday afternoon I went with Laura to the hills to inspect her block. She might build on it, she said.

"Why so far out?" I asked.

"When you get to know the bush," she said, "it's not lonely any more. It's like the glens of Ireland, there's always something there . . ."

I didn't know about the glens of Ireland but I knew about the bush. It was true, what Laura had just said. There was something there, hovering over and through it. Something silent and intangible, a shade of things past, things of which the black-fellows spoke in their tales of the dream-time from which they all came.

We walked along the rut track to Laura's block.

The tree had been felled.

It lay on its side, its roots heaved in the air as if in some last spasm of pain, its branches, the die-back branches and the leafy ones, sprawling across the ground, crushing the undergrowth in a hideous and ungraceful mess.

Laura stood looking at it wordless.

I didn't say anything at all. I knew that this was not the time to utter one single word.

Presently a man came walking down towards the boundary from the shack that was being built on the next block. He didn't have to do more than look at Laura's face to know how she was thinking. He knocked out his pipe against a banksia tree.

"It was an ugly tree," he said.

"About as ugly as Whistler's mother," Laura said between her teeth. As her neighbour did not know Whistler he could hardly be expected to understand the comparison.

As a straw can break a camel's back so I think it was the felling of the old tree that had more to do with Laura's uprooting of herself again. It was always the little things that broke Laura's heart. She who had not wept for her father wept for three vagrant dogs and an old gum tree.

18

THREE months passed before Danny arrived in Australia.

It was spring. That is to say, the winter had ceased and summer had begun, overnight as was its habit on the west side of the great desert.

After one violent outburst the westerly winds, the roaring forties as we called them, died away. They had immediately made room for the east and north-east winds to come in and scorch the abundant grass everywhere. Within a few weeks the green of the earth had turned to a parched and brittle yellow. Over the land was a scent. The air was redolent with drying eucalypt leaves, drying everlastings, and from the deep south the last of the boronia. Within a week the early morning air smelt of the desert.

As a child I had often wondered where that morning east wind had risen. How many thousand miles had it travelled before one heard it coming, a low soft moaning, as it swept in gentle gusts over the hills, down on to the plain, and so out to sea.

One could hear it coming, and one could smell it. Like the bush there was something in it. It whispered of things so old that no man could assess them. It swept over the oldest land on earth, over black people older in race than all other living races, over animals found elsewhere only in the annals of antiquity.

It was a sad wind for it told of things very, very ancient. And it told of new things, the terror of the desert to man and beast, their secret deaths scattered over the vast continent, of nameless graves. And of exploit, and endurance.

Did the east wind know where Leichardt had died? Did it know where Lassiter's lost reef of gold lay hidden? Did it know what happened to my mother's brother, a young man who had set out to walk through the desert to Coolgardie in the early days of the gold rush? And never been heard of again.

The east wind spoke, but it only hinted of things. It never really told.

Life had been going on quietly with us all while we waited for Danny to come.

Laura was no longer living with the

Prestons but had moved home with her mother. If she went on straightening Uncle William's affairs, and bit by bit straightening the little things about the house in Pepper Tree Bay, she said nothing. She did things quietly, fastidiously and without Aunt Sheilagh knowing so much as that a box or a magazine had been moved.

Aunt Sheilagh received all her after-funeral callers dressed in deep mourning and when she went out to return these calls she wore a black widow's-veil, not over her face but draped in a soft loose band around the crown of her wide-brimmed Swiss straw hat. Even in black Aunt Sheilagh looked elegant.

The calling and returning of calls took up a lot of time and energy. It filled in the blank period of waiting for Danny. Laura and Sylvia did not wear black. They wore white or mauve. This shocked some, though others thought it sensible. The thing that really shocked Pepper Tree Bay was Laura continuing to make her daily excursion to the Terrace and Beale and Beale.

"When Papa died," Lorine Coole said, "I did not go out for six months and did not go out to a party or a festive occasion for a year."

"Yes, of course," agreed her friends. "And

when the Baston baby died, they all wore black and white and nobody, not even Susan and Anne, went outside for three months."

"Crazy!" said Gerry. "How do they all think Laura's going to earn her living if she stays home for six months or a year?"

"They don't understand Laura earning a living," I said. "They think she does it all for nothing, just to be different."

"Why don't they . . ."

"Because they're all brought up in an age when the only decent way for a young woman of position to earn a living was either by being mother's help to married sisters, or, if married, like Mama, by taking in lodgers."

Mama said,

"You do talk nonsense."

"You've been so long out in the hard hard world, Mama," I said. "You've forgotten what they all think, and how they think it."

Danny was coming from England on the *Orontes* and it was due in Fremantle on the first of December.

The gloom of Uncle William's death was dispelled in favour of the anticipation of the coming of the last of the Montgomeries. Everyone, even the five daughters of the late

Joe Montgomery, had the same expectation of the arrival of royalty as did Aunt Sheilagh's household. Both houses, the one in Pepper Tree Bay and our own shabby mausoleum, were rejuvenated. Curtains were washed, carpets cleaned, and here and there paint was applied to kitchen cupboards.

"As if Danny would notice," Gerry said scornfully.

"It needed brightening up anyway," said Mama, one hand holding the paint tin while the other stirred the paint with a stick. She spoke through her teeth because they were clenched on the paint-brush while her two hands were occupied elsewhere.

Sylvia, who had looked so well during the winter, did not like the dry spring wind. Her colour waned, except for the high red spots on either cheek. The doctor suggested that now summer was with us she should give up her short evening walk. He took her pulse and sounded her chest and then said he altogether forbade the walking.

Everyone took it for granted Sylvia would be acquiescent. Nobody watched to see what she did when she walked around the lawn on the river side of the house on the night before Danny arrived.

I had gone down to the Pepper Tree Bay house to see if there was anything I could do to help in the celebrations for the morrow. Aunt Sheilagh, a huge white apron over her black silk dress, was in the kitchen showing Sarey how you make Irish tea-cake, and the proper way to cook mutton, which was by pouring wine over it and leaving it all night in a lukewarm oven. Aunt Sheilagh insisted the wine had to be claret because it was claret they used for this purpose in Ireland. She disregarded the fact that while Australia produced some very fine wines she produced only a very discreditable claret.

"Is Sylvia outside?" Laura asked.

"She went out into the garden. She's probably mooning in that cane chair under the pepper tree."

Laura went outside but Sylvia was not in the cane chair under the pepper tree, nor anywhere else in the grounds.

"She couldn't have walked down to the river," I said. "She would never walk up those banks afterwards . . . surely . . ."

"Perhaps she took a little walk. It's such a lovely evening," Aunt Sheilagh said complacently. "After all she's been doing it for three months. It's hard to stop just when the nights are lovely, and Danny's coming."

Half an hour went by and Laura began to worry.

"Come and look for her," she suggested to me.

We went out into the wide gravel pepper-tree-shaded street and looked along its shadows.

A brilliant moon was shining in a cloudless sky and one could have read a newspaper by it, though nothing could penetrate the black obscurity of the shadows.

"She wouldn't go the full length of the street?" I asked anxiously.

"Let's walk to the corner of Bay Road."

We did but there was no sign of Sylvia. As we returned to see if Sylvia had walked the other way old Williams's cab ground along the street beside us. Laura hailed it.

"Have you seen Sylvia, Mr. Williams?"

"That I did. She was walking, very slow, mind you, along the Highway past old Joe Montgomery's school."

"Past the school?" There was a high note of anxiety in Laura's voice. "Are you sure?"

"Certain sure. In this moonshine I could see the nose on her face."

"She was going up the hill?"

"Ay, up the hill, towards the sea."

"Where are you going now, Mr. Williams? Could you take us up to the Highway?"

"I'm going to get old Cameron to catch the eight-fifteen train. I'll drive you far as the corner."

We jumped into the back of the cab and Williams flicked the horse with the tail of his whip.

At the corner we got out as quickly as we'd got in.

"Up that way," Williams pointed up the long slow hill with the handle of his whip.

"How could she . . ." breathed Laura. "Up a hill. Why, she's never done that since . . . since . . ."

"Since Oliver held her up and massaged her back, and Danny and Oliver carried her home."

We looked up and down the moonlit road. There was no sign of Sylvia, or any other person.

"Where could she have gone? And why?" Laura said in exasperation.

"Do you think it's possible she walked up

there to the sand dunes where you can see over the sea? Tonight's paper said the *Orontes* was due in Gage Roads at eight this evening. It will be hove-to before it can berth in the morning."

This I said slowly and uncertainly because somehow it highlighted the relationship between Sylvia and Danny. I couldn't bear to hurt Laura on that subject.

Laura stopped and looked at me. It was as light as daylight and I could see her eyes, now dark, taking my thought and turning it over in her mind.

"Yes . . ." she said at last. "Yes. That is what she has done. Danny's ship out there in the Roads . . . and the day he and Oliver carried her home. It's all in her mind. She's gone up there to see Danny come back."

She turned and began to run up the hill, me after her. We could not run far because although the grade was mild the hill was very long. Presently we slowed down to a breathless walk. At the fire station we turned off the road into the low bush at the place where Oliver had held Sylvia in his arms. There was no one there.

Laura looked towards the sea.

"Those dunes over there . . ." she said.

"One could see the ships anchored in the Roads from there."

We hurried, as best we could through the deep soft white sand towards the highest dunes. There was no one there.

"Let's call," I said.

We coo-eed, but there was silence.

"I don't think she would come right up here," I said at length. "Look how ploughing through that sand made us breathless. If she came here at all, she would have walked round the dune, to the sea side."

We scrambled down the dune on the sea side ourselves, but there was no one, and nothing but moon-washed low bush with silver shining here and there on the leaves. Over us the pale sky was hung with a million blazing lamps. The moon, now high, had lost its fire and was riding small, round, serene and silver.

"*Sylvia!*" I called again.

We waited in silence.

"She couldn't have come," I said, feeling a little foolish. "I think perhaps we're investing Sylvia with a sentiment that might be just peculiar to you and me."

It was when we turned back that Laura found her.

She was lying on the crest of a low round-topped dune.

There had been no Oliver to hold her up to catch the life-giving breath. And no Danny to carry her home.

Danny was out there on the silver sea, perhaps looking to the land just as Sylvia had been looking outward.

She had gone to meet Danny in her own fashion.

Mr. Preston, Dirk and Laura went to meet Danny early the next day when the ship berthed.

When I asked Laura later what Danny had said when they had told him that Sylvia had died, she shrugged her shoulders and said, "I don't remember."

Mr. Preston told me much later. Danny had put his hand to his face. A remote veiled look had come into his rather large eyes and he had said in the soft clipped speech of his, "Oh . . . I'm so sorry."

When they had gone to his cabin to pick up his satchel he had invited Dirk and Mr. Preston to have some Irish whiskey with him. As he and Laura sat side by side on the edge of his bed he had put his hand on hers. There were tears in Laura's eyes. Danny took out his handkerchief and wiped them for her. Then he sat twisting the glass of whiskey in his hand, saying nothing.

When Mr. Preston told me about it he brushed the tears from his own old and gentle eyes and I knew that he too had wept.

It was a funny thing about Sylvia dying. We had waited for it and yet when it came we could believe in it less than when Uncle Tim and Uncle William had died. Because she had never really lived and never been more than a shadow of a person we could not believe in her dead. Her shadow, one felt with a sad prescience, would go on living with us as it always had. Certainly between Danny and Laura.

Aunt Sheilagh with her usual profound lack of insight had dressed Sylvia in her white confirmation dress and on her fair soft still-living hair had put the confirmation veil. There were flowers heaped on the pillow and clasped in her hands. She looked, for all the world, a bride.

This offended me deeply. It seemed to me a travesty of what might have taken place on the morrow. No one else in the family felt that way and perhaps it was because of my feeling for Laura that I accepted the last picture of Sylvia with rebellious pain.

I do not imagine that anyone will ever know what Danny thought.

We had all gone to the Pepper Tree Bay house to await Danny's arrival. Only Aunt Sheilagh wore black, the same black that she was wearing for Uncle William. Mama kept on her white starched linen dress with buttons down the front, her nurse's badge at her throat.

"Waiting for someone else to have a heart attack," Denney said bitterly.

"Shut up," I said.

I knew that Mama felt this kind of presence would keep the family under control in this difficult hour. Her severe professional dress gave her an authority over the house, over Laura and Aunt Sheilagh. And they were in need of it.

"How's *your* pulse?" Denney persisted.

"I couldn't care less," I replied tartly. And at the moment that was true.

Mama had pulled up all the blinds and opened all the doors. The house was loaded with flowers that she and Vicky and Mary had arranged. The trees overshadowing the west side of the house kept it cool and Mama put chairs out on the verandah overlooking the river.

"This is Danny's home-coming," she said. "We're not going to bring him into a house of gloom."

But we were bitter and the only things we could say were acid.

"Home-coming?" said Gerry. "What makes you think Danny's come *home*? Home was never here, where everyone dies. Danny will never stay here. Too shrewd."

It wasn't because Sylvia was dead that we were bitter. She was no more dead to us than she had formerly been alive. It was that they had *all* died. The five Montgomery brothers who had walked about the earth, Ireland, Australia, Canada, as if they had owned the land upon which they trod; who had always known what was right for other people and who had thought they could tell the other people of the earth how they should live, were all dead. There was not one of them left to say, "Didn't I say so . . . ." when things fell out wrongly. Or "Let them do it themselves!

They don't want advice, but don't let them come to me when they're in a mess!"

They were all dead and gone and had not left a mark behind them, except perhaps father's school on the corner of the Highway. They, so possessed of the all-seeing eye and depths of profound wisdom, who, with the exception of Dennis, had set out for far lands to bring the right way of living to lesser mortals, had all died. Having done nothing.

Nothing?

There was Danny. Who knew what Danny was?

There was Laura and me. Had not Uncle Tim left for ever his mark on our characters? We were not to know then that the handful of boys that Uncle Tim had brought each year to the coast would grow up and in memory of that great adventure of their childhood form the Gold-fields Children's Fresh Air League sponsoring the annual evacuation of gold-fields children to the coast each year. Or that Joe Montgomery's school on the corner by the Church under a greater headmaster than the erratic Irishman would one day become one of the renowned schools of Australia. Or that Uncle William's constant and edgy advice to his pastoral peers around the verandahs of Pepper Tree Bay would result in great parklands set around the city precincts, a timeless and living memorial to the visionary pioneers.

I did not dip into the future and at the moment I could not see there were Montgomery footprints in the sands of time.

I shook my head at the thought of the present emptiness. Neither Laura nor I had the seeds of great achievement in us. The best that might be said of us was that we might die without having left a black mark behind. But build empires? No. No Montgomery, for all his exalted idea of himself, would ever do that. So we thought. Thus our tongues were bitter.

It was Gerry who said and did the worst thing while we sat there in Aunt Sheilagh's big square blue-and-gold drawing-room.

She put her head a little on one side, just as Uncle William did before he uttered one of his truisms. She affected the deep timbre of his voice and the soft hint of a roll in the end of his sentences.

"*Four down to Australia,*" she said.

Before anyone had time to throw something at her Danny came in.

He walked over to Aunt Sheilagh, and then

431

Mama, and kissed them on the cheek. He then shook hands with each of us.

We all made inarticulate noises of welcome, but there were tears stinging our eyes. When we looked at him there was that old, misty inexplicable love pouring from our hearts towards him, touching his golden head.

It was difficult to see him for the aura with which we begifted him. I blinked my eyes.

He stood talking to Aunt Sheilagh. He had an elusive air of distinction and authority, both of which qualities were shielded from us by the fine but impenetrable gauze of his reserve. He was the only person we have ever known who caused us one and all to be silent for long stretches.

Presently we all sat down again, and Danny, with that old characteristic gesture, lifted his pants a little above the knee before he sat down and then with a careless movement threw one knee over the other. He took out his cigarette case, offered Laura a cigarette, then lit first hers and then his own. He held his cigarette in his left hand and his right hand with its fine bones lay on his knee. He looked round at us one after the other and smiled.

"Something wrong with this country," he

said. "You'd better all come home with me."

Our tongues were loosened and we began to talk awkwardly. How had he enjoyed the journey? What was Magillicuddy like? How long would he stay?

Laura sat, withdrawn and silent. She had nothing to say. Mama and Vicky went outside to make tea.

"What do you do with yourself, Theodora?" Danny asked politely.

"School teaching," I said. "But I'm going to get married, I think."

"Oh really!"

Would anyone ever tell what a person from Great Britain meant by that non-committal "Oh really!"?

After we had tea Aunt Sheilagh took Danny in to see Sylvia. He did not come back into the drawing-room but later I could see him leaning against the low picket fence looking out over the river. He was talking to Laura. They stayed there a long time and at length I felt I didn't want to stay there any more. I went back to my school.

It was Mama and Laura who went to Sylvia's funeral with Danny. This persistence on the part of the Montgomeries in going to their family funerals distressed their friends in Pepper Tree Bay. A funeral, they thought, was no place for women. But there were only women left to accompany Danny. No one in the family was going to let Danny go alone. Never mind about Sylvia, we all loved Danny too much to bear the thought of his lone distinguished figure standing isolated beside that grave.

Again we had that dreadful after-funeral tea-party. They were becoming part of the social order of things for the Montgomeries.

"If we can't have any weddings or christenings to keep the family together," Vicky said, "then we'll have to put up with funerals."

It was after this period that Mama got into the habit of saying every time there was a family row, "It'll have to be a wedding or a funeral to pull us together again."

We hardly thought about christenings because the future generations ceased to interest us. None born in the next generation to the Australian Montgomeries would bear the name anyway. So why have any children at all?

Our love for Danny might be called by some "ancestor-worship" but at that time nobody could have accused any one of us about caring for posterity.

After the "wake" as Uncle William would have called it we all went home to our own affairs. Mama was adamant about this.

"It's all very well for us to try and manage Aunt Sheilagh," she said. "But we'll only complicate things if we try to run a triumvirate of Danny, Laura and Aunt Sheilagh. They can only work out what's to be done if we leave them alone."

Except for inviting them all for tea on Sunday night, when no family affairs were discussed, we left the Pepper Tree Bay household alone.

It was therefore not till some weeks had passed that I learned that Danny and Laura had gone to Kalgoorlie to settle the house affairs there.

The Pepper Tree Bay circle of friends nodded their heads in approval that something was being done but they made firm arrangements for the proprieties to be observed. In the early nineteen-thirties girls from good families had not yet begun the practice of floating about the world in the company of young men, without the semblance of chaperonage. Not on the West

Australian coast anyway, whatever they did in other parts of the world.

Mr. Maynard-Arnold, who amongst other things had mining interests, had Danny nominated for his club in Kalgoorlie so that Danny would have somewhere respectable to stay. The caretaker in the Kalgoorlie house was not regarded quite enough to safeguard Laura from blacks, Afghans and drink-addicted miners, so Mrs. Preston, amidst nods of approval in the drawing-rooms of Pepper Tree Bay, announced her intention of going to Kalgoorlie, "in case she could be of help to dear Laura."

"Can't see Mrs. Preston holding camel-drivers and fly-blown blacks at bay," said Gerry.

"Don't be silly," said Denney. "That's only a ruse to keep the young men at bay. Even in mourning, Laura still captivates the eye."

As a matter of fact, at that period there had been a young Dutch business man who had been very taken with Laura and had been sending her flowers and leaving his card at regular intervals at the house.

I met him on one occasion at an evening in

a friend's house and he spent most of the time with me trying to get me to unravel what he called the "enigma" of Laura. I don't know that he was so much infatuated with Laura as intrigued.

"She's the most attractive person I've met in years," he told me. "She has true natural beauty. In rags she would be lovely."

Yes, even rags would not have altered Laura's beauty. Except for her pale clear skin and the brilliant blue of her eyes, hers was almost a Semitic beauty. Not even time, let alone rags, would alter that high square forehead and the aquiline nose. Nor, I thought, rob the line of her chin and the abundance of sensual promise in her mouth. For all her pride of carriage there was something compassionate in Laura. Perhaps the Dutchman sensed it.

"She attracts," he said. "Then she puts up the equivalent of a ten-foot wall of protection. Why? And why did a young man throw himself under a railway train?"

The Robert Doule story again, and in a new dust-jacket!

Danny, Peter Stevenson, Robert Doule, Marion Perrent, the three dogs and the old gum tree were, I thought, the reasons why

Laura put up her wall of protection. Not to mention the battle to excel in the business world which was in conflict with the protected and insular drawing-room world of Pepper Tree Bay. So I said,

"I expect it's all the deaths in the family."

"I don't think so," Dorn de Vries replied.

I thought privately it was a pity Laura didn't succumb a little to this man's charm. He was good-looking, obviously well off and he spoke flawless English as if he had been brought up in that country.

"Why is she an enigma?" I asked, looking at him curiously.

"Why not?" He raised quizzical eyebrows. "Doesn't it strike you as unusual that a beautiful young lady, brought up in a fixed social atmosphere, should go off to work like a typist in the city each day, and wearing a four thousand pound string of pearls?"

"Four thousand pounds," I said scornfully. "They were insured for two thousand and I doubt if they cost that much."

"Four thousand," he repeated. "Not including the diamond clip. I should know. I'm a pearl buyer for my firm in Amsterdam. That's what I'm doing in Western Australia. I've just come down from Broome."

I looked at him with interest.

"Would you really know the value of a pearl necklace just from seeing it on someone's neck?"

"Throat, dear Miss Montgomery," he corrected me with a smile. "We speak of pearls as being around a throat and not on a neck. Yes, I would know. Laura's pearls, at any rate."

"You're not thinking of being interested in her because of her pearls, are you?" I asked.

He shook his head gently.

"No," he said. "I have pearls enough of my own." And I believed him.

However, later I told Laura about what he had said of her pearls.

"You shouldn't wear them to work, and leave them about on people's wash-basins," I said. "You might need that money some day."

"So I might, said Laura. "As for the pearls, well, except for the diamond clip, you could get the same for ten and sixpence any day of the week in Woolworth's." This was the second time she had said this.

Such cynicism irritated me and I said so. Laura put her hand to her neck—beg pardon—throat, and touched the pearls.

"I'm sorry," she said. "I don't know what makes me talk that way. I hate cynicism in other people. And I loathe people who are cynical about Australia." She added this last as an afterthought.

"Is Danny being cynical about Australia?" She looked at me curiously.

"Danny's not cynical about anything. Besides, Australia doesn't exist for him. It's just a country he's passing through. And which he doesn't see."

"If Aunt Sheilagh goes back with Danny, what will you do? Are you going to stay in Australia, Laura?"

Laura's eyes shadowed and her lips puckered. She didn't answer for quite a long time.

I was walking beside her along the Terrace so I spoke of other things at random.

"Some of those pastoral companies are folding up," I said, pointing to one or two blank brass places on the outside walls of business blocks.

"Fools," Laura said. "They should be patient." Then added, "I don't know about going home. I can't make up my mind."

"Home" meant Ireland to Laura but it didn't necessarily mean the place in which she would pass the rest of her life, any more than it meant this to the thousands of Australians who always referred to the United Kingdom as "home". They did it because they caught the habit from their fathers or grandfathers who had one and all come to Australia to make their "pile" before going "home". Those who never had returned were either those who never made their "pile" or who had become tied to the new country by families which, being born in Australia, didn't find it such a dreadful place after all. We five daughters of Joseph Montgomery, for instance. We knew Australia was a dreadful place and that the people in it were vulgarians and barbarians because we had had this dinned into us from birth by our father and uncle. But oddly enough we liked it. We even loved it, but would never have said so in the presence of our elders. By and large the idea that Australia was a dreadful place ended up by meaning that any part of the United Kingdom was so beautiful and the people in it so cultivated, so well-bred, so pleasantly mannered that one and all of us regarded it as the glamour dreamland of life. Meantime we got on with loving generously the place where we found ourselves to be.

441

On the following Saturday afternoon Laura asked me if I would like to go up with her to see her block in the hills. As I loved a day in the hills I readily accepted. I knew that Laura's only purpose in going was to reassure herself. I felt she was perhaps on the edge of a critical decision. To go, or to stay. I also felt it was a decision she must make alone and that I must make no gesture to help her. After all Laura *knew* Ireland and what she would be going back to.

We left in mid-morning carrying our lunches with us. When I had suggested Thermos flasks of tea Laura had been almost sharp.

"No," she said. "The best part of the bush is the smell of burning gum leaves, and billy tea."

We took the bus to the last town in the hills and walked the four miles along first a gravel road and finally a bush track to where Laura's block, a full acre of ground, sloped gently on the brow of the range overlooking the coastal plain.

It was a lovely day towards the end of summer. The heat had gone and a few early morning dews had softened the burned aspect of the undergrowth.

Laura seemed happy, almost blithe, as we walked along. We talked of many things but all the time Laura kept coming back to the bush.

"It's so lonely. And so vast . . ." she said. "It would take thousands of years to tame it, the way the Americans have tamed their country. It's not friendly, unless you love it, and understand it."

I began to think that it would be, after all, the lure of the country, this "dreadful" country, that would keep Laura here, if she stayed, and not the prospects of a brilliant business career, in the Terrace. I had wrongly been believing that a career, and its ultimate rewards, had been the tie that might keep Laura with us.

When we arrived at the block we sat on the great old trunk of the tree Laura had so much loved. Her neighbours, having felled it, had evidently no inclination to remove it.

"Why?" she said. "Why?" Her voice was bitter with anger. "It can't be less unsightly to them lying there, than it was when standing."

I looked at the neighbouring piece of land. I could see where a small section in the middle had been cleared and there were pieces of wood driven in at regular intervals that showed the first signs of a house to be built.

"I suppose it interfered with their view," I said.

"View be damned," said Laura. "Look at that . . ." Her arm swept the western horizon. The plain, grey, flat, misty and mysterious, stretched before us, and away to the north and south. The river lay in shining blue pools, and beyond the sand dunes, where Sylvia had died, was the blue rim of the sea.

"It needed that tree," said Laura.

But it was the tree itself, because it was enduring and bore the scars of old battles against the adversities of wind, fire and storm that Laura had loved, and not what it might add to the view.

We boiled our billy and drank our tea and ate our sandwiches. There were no sounds but our own. The neighbours were not on their block this day and there was probably no man or woman within three miles of us. We were alone . . . except for the ghosts of men of a race so ancient they belonged only to their own dream-time.

We sat in silence.

Did Laura hear and see those wraiths, those

stirrings in the grey secret bush, that were all around us?

Its beauty lay in its mystery and its ancient and inscrutable endurance.

Yes, I thought, you have to understand it to love it. And when you do, nothing else could ever take its place.

I glanced at Laura's face. There was a fine frown between her brows and a look of such intense preoccupation in her eyes that I remained silent.

Once again Laura was going through that painful experience of being slowly torn in two.

On the way home I spoke to her about Danny.

"Laura," I said, "what is Danny really like?"

"Like no one but himself. Oh, I suppose he's got the familiar characteristics of the British when they're out of their own terrain. He doesn't talk about himself and he appears to be sceptical of people who do talk about themselves. He doesn't take in Australia because he sees no occasion to do so. He's politely indifferent to people who do not interest him and scrupulously polite and considerate to me and Mama and people who do interest him."

"I know," I said. "That's what we all see about Danny. But inside him. What is our Danny like inside him?"

It was then that Laura made the one and only confession of love in her life.

"I love him," she said simply. Then she paused. "When you love a person you read beauty into him . . . or at least you see only the beauty that's in him. I like his prodigal air of kindness to those he likes. I like the way he hoes into fruit salad and ice-cream like a small schoolboy. I like the unexpected breakdown in his manner when he hears something funny or sees something that interests him. He creases all up, like a child with a bright toy."

"Yes, I know," I said gently.

Laura looked at me sideways out of her brilliant blue eyes.

"I love the way his eyelashes lie like little half-moons on his cheek, and the fact that when he's asleep he has the face of an effigy in Church—so effortless." She laughed. "So smugly serene!"

We both laughed.

"You asked for it," Laura said to me. "That's what *I* think."

This brought a lump to my throat. Not because Laura had done the unexpected thing in suddenly showing me her heart nor because there was pain in the meaning of her words, but because she had touched a place in me that was very tender. We all loved Danny, but it was hard to know why. There was something about him that was heart-touching.

19

IT was now apparent that Aunt Sheilagh was to return to Ireland. Laura was still undecided.

It was absurd, everyone in the family said, for Laura to remain in Australia with her mother so far away. After all, Laura was all that Aunt Sheilagh had left.

But neither Aunt Sheilagh nor Laura showed any feelings on this aspect of things. They had never been very close. Aunt Sheilagh had been wrapped up in Sylvia and her social life in Kalgoorlie and Pepper Tree Bay. Way back when Laura had been a little girl Aunt Sheilagh had found her what she called "difficult" and Uncle William had called "intractable". There was a gap in their relationship that neither time nor events had bridged.

Laura had only had her dogs and her tree and her odd assortment of friends upon whom to visit the overflow of what was really a kind heart. None of these objective things or people had been receptive.

The only time Aunt Sheilagh showed any feelings about what Laura did with her future was one evening when we were all together. She talked of us as "a family" and wouldn't hear of the suggestion that the family would now fall apart.

"How could it?" Mama asked wistfully. "There's Tim and Joe and William always here."

"And Sylvia," added Gerry.

"Sylvia," said Aunt Sheilagh, holding her head up and donning a faint air of hauteur, "is always with me, wherever I go."

Nobody said anything to this because our hateful logical minds could see that this division of places between Sylvia and the older generation meant that Sylvia meant more to her mother than the three Montgomery brothers. This we knew not to be true and it was only because we loved Aunt Sheilagh, as much for her inconsequential thinking as for anything else, that we kept our tongues quiet in our cheeks.

"Of course, Helen," Aunt Sheilagh said, addressing Mama, "you must all come home. That is the only thing to do. It is unthinkable any of us should go on living so far away from Magillicuddy."

449

"Has Laura made up her mind?" Mary asked gently.

"Laura will do what everyone else does," said Aunt Sheilagh firmly. "Such nonsense to think of staying here . . ."

"Well, I'm afraid we're all going to stay here," I said. "It's our home."

This exasperated Aunt Sheilagh.

"Darling," she said. "What nonsense you do talk. Magillicuddy is the only home any of us has."

None of us felt like explaining to Aunt Sheilagh that nobody owned Magillicuddy except Danny.

"We can't go, Sheilagh," Mama said. "And that's all about it. We haven't the money, and if we had we wouldn't go back to live on Danny."

"If Danny were at home he would be very angry with you. You know very well he has invited you all home."

"I'm sure he means it," said Mama. "But it wouldn't work out."

"If you stay here you'll all die," said Aunt Sheilagh tragically.

"Of heart disease I suppose," said Gerry.

Denney and I promptly began feeling our

pulses. Certainly we had both complained of pains in the chest lately.

"Indigestion and imagination," Mama had said bluntly. "Stop thinking about yourselves."

Aunt Sheilagh lifted her face in a slightly theatrical way. She was still a lovely looking woman.

"Darlings," she said. "Your father and uncles died of *broken hearts . . .*"

"And it's all Australia's fault," said Gerry laconically but fortunately so nearly under her breath that Aunt Sheilagh didn't hear.

Aunt Sheilagh's affairs had finally been wound up. She was not penniless but she certainly didn't have enough to live on in her own inimitable style unless Danny could provide that in his home. We were very much under the impression that Magillicuddy was not what it once was and that instead of being about to provide a thousand or two to Aunt Sheilagh's income it really required a thousand or two to be spent on it.

A week or two after this family conversation on the subject of whether we should all go "home" or some of us, at least, stay here, I

451

met Laura coming out of the chief jeweller's shop in the main street.

"Feel like a cup of coffee?" I asked.

We went together to a small café and while the waitress was bringing the café's dreadful version of milk, coffee and water, boiled up for hours together, Laura drew out a jewel case from a packet. She opened it and lifted out a string of pearls. I recognized the diamond clasp and thought I recognized the pearls.

"What happened?" I said. "Have you had them restrung?"

She clasped them round her throat and smiled at me ironically.

"Do they look the same?" she said.

"Have you had them copied?" I asked.

"Yes. And I've sold the originals."

I was shocked.

"But they're Aunt Sheilagh's . . ."

"I've banked the money in her estate. She's none the wiser."

I was doubly shocked.

"Do you mean to say you've sold Aunt Sheilagh's pearls and she doesn't know anything about it?"

"She needs the money. I always said you could get the same for ten and sixpence."

"Is that all you paid for that string of pearls round your neck?" I asked, incredulous.

"Throat!" corrected Laura. "No, they cost quite a little. Ten guineas to be accurate. Dorn de Vries arranged it all for me. He has bought Mama's pearls."

"*Laura!*" I said. "Can't you go to gaol for that?"

She shrugged.

"Mama needed the money," she said.

There was no doubt about it, Laura did things that took my breath away. She was really quite unpredictable.

"And if you stay in Australia you won't be there to see her reaction when she finds out," I said accusingly.

Laura shrugged. She picked up her gloves and fitted them on her long slender hands.

I still hadn't got my answer. Was Laura going or staying?

It was another week before I did get an answer.

I had gone with Mama down to the Pepper Tree Bay house to one of Aunt Sheilagh's sorting-out evenings. Aunt Sheilagh was "going through" things. If there hadn't been so much tragedy in the current doings of the

453

Montgomeries there would have been much comedy in these "sorting-outs" and "going-throughs".

Aunt Sheilagh had instructed the gardener to enter the burning-off season and keep a fire smouldering at the foot of the garden near the river bank. To this fire Aunt Sheilagh made periodic excursions with arms full of things to be thrown away and burnt. Mama, or I, and occasionally Laura, would follow with our bundles of things to be thrown away, and see on the edge of the smouldering fire some treasure of ancient family lore which Aunt Sheilagh thought worthless. We would retrieve it, hide it in our pockets or, if too big, in one of the tool-sheds. We would then cast our share of the rubbish on to the fire. Aunt Sheilagh emerging from the house with another bundle would pounce on an old book or magazine, piece of lace or gee-gaws from an ancient resurrected trinket box.

"Oh naughty, naughty!" she would cry. "There's a recipe in that book. I might need it. And that magazine—I kept it. I've forgotten why, but there's a reason. It *mustn't* be thrown out!"

Amongst the loot that Mama and I retrieved was a wood carved mirror frame of great beauty and a solid silver pepper pot and salt cellar.

Aunt Sheilagh had looked uncertainly at a Queen Anne chair whose tapestry seat was a little frayed and whose legs were more than shaky.

"I suppose the only thing to do with it is to burn it . . ."

Mama and I let out cries like wounded animals.

"Oh *no*, Aunt Sheilagh," I begged. "Uncle Tim brought that out from Ireland."

"Well, you can have it if you want it. There are three others somewhere. As a matter of fact, now that I come to think of it, they belonged to your Uncle Tim's godmother. She lived in Bective. I suppose you'd better have them all. Only for goodness' sake take them away now, else they'll get in the way and be burnt."

"Aunt Sheilagh," I said with tears in my eyes, "I was Uncle Tim's godchild. Please, please give them to *me*. Otherwise there'll be a dreadful family fight over them. I promise you, God's honour, Mama shall have them as long as she lives. But after that they're *mine*."

"Darling, don't get so upset. They're not really valuable, you know. Everyone in

Ireland is cluttered up with Queen Anne chairs. English importations, you know."

Mama and I looked at one another helplessly. Honesty at last won the day.

"Here in Australia they're very valuable. You could get quite a lot of money for them, Aunt Sheilagh."

"Darling, they are yours. After all, you were Tim's godchild."

And Aunt Sheilagh went on airily disposing of old cushions and pillows in the direction of the garden fire.

So on the night of Laura's final decision Mama and I hied ourselves in the direction of Aunt Sheilagh's loot party.

Danny and Laura were there, turning out little drawers and tearing up letters and bits of paper.

Danny had on an open-necked shirt with a hole under the sleeve and an old pair of tweed pants that were frayed at the cuff of the left leg.

How he could achieve such an air of distinction in such old clothes I could never understand.

"Hallo!" he said affably. "Come to work?"

"Come to see you all don't throw out

something I'd like. Specially something of Uncle Tim's," I said.

He looked up at me and smiled.

"Poor Theodora," he said. "Uncle Tim was the saint of the family, eh?"

"Well, wasn't he?" I asked.

"He was the only sane one, anyway."

"Are they all mad? Are you?" I asked.

"It's a pleasant sort of madness. And quite common amongst the Irish."

He bent his head again as his fingers leafed through a pile of old documents on the table. The light from the glass chandelier above shone down on him. How smooth and thick his hair was! And the parting, so far over to one side, was like a fine white thread.

I wished that Danny knew we belonged to him the way he thought he belonged to us.

Mama went out to do things in the kitchen cupboards and I pulled off my gloves and sat down on the other side of the table to wind up spools of thread that Laura had just spilled out of a round work-basket. Laura was unravelling skeins of embroidery thread from a bundle she now took from another work-basket, a chintz one standing on four crossed legs. Aunt Sheilagh was on her knees before a lovely inlaid escritoire. She was handing

Danny the papers and old letters he was now sorting.

"I'm so glad you've come, darling," Aunt Sheilagh said. "It's such a business sorting out all those cottons and threads. I mustn't leave them behind. They belong to all sorts of half-finished things, some of them Sylvia's. I mightn't be able to match them in Dublin."

This was the only thing Aunt Sheilagh admitted they mightn't be able to do better in Dublin, Meath or Galway.

We all worked and chatted for a long time. Then we stopped in order to accept from Danny the proffered cigarette case.

Danny sat down in a small chintz-covered armchair, one knee crossed over the other, his right shoulder sloping forward and his back a little hunched. His left hand held his cigarette and his right hand did things to his shoe lace.

"How do you come to own shoes so old, Danny?" I said.

"I like old shoes. They're more comfortable. And I can't afford to buy a new pair."

"You do talk nonsense, Danny," said Aunt Sheilagh. "You've at least twelve pairs on the floor upstairs."

458

"If they're not worn through now, they soon will be," said Danny with a grin.

I didn't know whether to take any notice of him or not. Only Laura, standing by the table, her cigarette sending up wreaths of smoke from the ash-tray against which it leaned, her hands still unravelling skeins of thread, looked at him quickly.

"Laura's the money-maker of the family," I said with a laugh. "Better get her to buy some shoes for you."

"I've thought of that," said Danny. "In fact it's a good idea to get Laura to buy everything for me." He looked up and half smiled at her and then, with a faintly creased brow, at the oil-painting over the mantelshelf.

"There's only one way to buy salvation for the Montgomery family," he said quietly. "That's for Laura and me to join forces. I think we ought to get married. Then I'd have someone to buy my shoes for me and keep my bed warm at nights. Laura would have . . ." He broke off, made a queer little unfinished gesture with his right hand, and glanced at Laura. "What would I have to offer Laura?" he asked quite sadly. "Only this dilapidated self and a few hundred even more dilapidated acres of Magillicuddy."

Aunt Sheilagh, who did not smoke, went on searching the shelves of another cupboard for papers and did not appear to notice or take interest in this conversation.

I felt as if the cigarette between my fingers was transfixed for all time. I knew that Danny meant what he was saying. He was proposing to Laura.

I don't know why he did it this way, and I don't suppose I ever shall. All I know is that, for me and Laura at least, these casual remarks of Danny's not only changed the modes of music but they caused the walls of the city to shake.

I dragged my astonished eyes from Danny's face to Laura's.

Her fingers were also halted. They held a little ball of crimson floss silk. Her face went pale for she too knew Danny meant what he said.

Her eyes were very dark but as she looked at Danny's now averted face there was such a look of pain and then of fleeting tenderness, so quickly veiled, that I knew she would never have the strength to reject him.

Australia was defeated, and by no more than three sentences spoken by an Irishman with a golden head, a gentle voice and a manner of such sudden painful shyness that unbidden one's heart ached for him.

The little crimson ball began to move again in Laura's fingers and her eyes removed themselves painfully from Danny's profile and fixed themselves on the ball.

"At least I've got it in me to clean up Magillicuddy," she said. "And I've got nine thousand pounds. That ought to help."

Startled, Danny turned now and looked at her.

"Good God," he said. "Am I to marry a rich woman?"

"Not rich. Just canny," Laura said, and looked up and smiled at him.

"What are you talking about?" Aunt Sheilagh said, turning her head.

"About getting married. They're talking about getting married," I said anxiously, as if by answering for them I was binding them irrevocably.

"That's the first sensible thing anybody's done since William died," Aunt Sheilagh said. "I can't imagine why you didn't arrange all this before. It would have saved an awful lot of bother." She looked at Laura thoughtfully. "Darling, " she said, "you shall have the pearls for your wedding present."

She nodded her head happily. "I had jewels for a wedding present from *my* mother. The pearls are just the very thing. Darling, you shall have the pearls."

Laura's eyes met mine and her hand fingered the pearls round her throat.

"Thank you, Mama," she said. "I always wanted them for keeps."

Then she looked at Danny and smiled. I shook my head helplessly. Would ever anyone do anything about Aunt Sheilagh, or Laura, for that matter?

Mama came in and asked did we think it was time for a cup of tea.

"I'll get it," Laura said, putting down her little crimson ball.

"I'll . . ." began Mama.

"Don't go, Mama," I said urgently. "Stay here. Let Laura get it. Aunt Sheilagh is about to order the Sheraton escritoire to go out to the fire. And that old bentwood chair. Also the tapestry fire-screen. Stay here and salvage them for us."

Laura gave me an inscrutable look and went outside. Aunt Sheilagh said,

"Have you taken leave of your senses, Theodora? I never said a word about . . . ."

"Oh yes you did," I said feverishly.

"Mama, don't let Aunt Sheilagh out of your sight. She's going to burn nearly everything that's small and burnable in the room."

They both looked at me aghast.

Danny stood up, stubbed out his cigarette and said,

"I'll give Laura a hand."

When he'd gone out the door I sank back in my chair exhausted.

"Would you mind telling me what's the matter with you, Theodora?" said Mama severely.

"Danny and Laura," I said weakly. "He's proposed to her. In here, in front of us all, I just wanted you to leave them alone if he followed her outside."

Mama sat down in the chair which Danny had just vacated.

"Well, I never did," she said. "Whatever has possessed them?"

"Well, it's quite a good idea," said Aunt Sheilagh, sharply for her. "At least it will keep the family together. Laura will have Danny to look after her. And now she can have the pearls to keep."

"Oh, the irony of it!" I said, and put my head down on the table and began to laugh. The only thing about that laugh was that somehow the tears got so mixed up in it. I was like Laura, I never could laugh very hard because I always began to cry.

When they came back with the tea-things Laura and Danny said nothing. Laura's face was faintly flushed but Danny looked pale. One lock of his golden hair fell across his forehead and his eyes looked . . . Why! They looked as if they had had tears in them!

The only comment Laura ever made to me about her engagement was,

"And now Robert Doule can come home."

20

WE all took them to the ship that was to carry them away.

It was evening because there'd been a cargo hold-up.

We milled up the gangway, across the deck into the lounge. We flowed through companionways and along decks that led us from cabin to cabin. We examined the lounges, the dining-saloon and the boat-deck. We decided they would be comfortable. We looked in Danny's cabin, then went back to the big two-berth cabin that was to be inhabited for nearly five weeks by Aunt Sheilagh and Laura. Danny was there too, with a bottle of Irish whiskey and a large bunch of roses. He put the flowers in the tooth-glass over the wash-basin and proceeded to uncork the whiskey. We covered all available space with oranges, apples, magazines, and books. We laughed and talked and told anecdotes about ourselves and about other people. Some were true and some were told just because one or other of us had it in her to make a good story out of nothing.

Mama laughed and joked too, but her eyes were misty with unshed tears.

This was not just the end of a chapter. It was the end of a story. They came . . . they did not conquer . . . and only the remnants were left to retreat.

With them gone, we who were left behind would feel as if our right hand had been cut off at the wrist.

We would be alone now. The umbilical cord was about to be severed.

When a whistle sounded to warn all visitors to leave the ship we kissed them all as if we would see them again next week. They kissed us as if they would be seeing us again next day.

We fled up the labyrinths of decks out into the early evening air.

Aunt Sheilagh stood alone at the deck-rail as the family fled tumultuously down the gangway. Danny and Laura were still below.

I hesitated beside her. There was something forlorn in that slender figure, still elegantly dressed, standing there.

"Aunt Sheilagh . . ." I said.

She started. Her thoughts had been somewhere else.

"Do you hear that sound, Theodora?" she said. Her head was bent a little as if listening.

I could hear the creak of the loading cranes and the noise of dumped cases in the hatch. I could hear the hum of cars along the road beyond the warehouses and Customs sheds. I could hear people laughing and talking and calling out to one another.

"What sound?" I said.

She waved her hand out towards the land.

"Out there . . ." she said. "Miles out there. I used to hear it when we lived in Kalgoorlie. It's the east wind rising . . ."

"It's a bit late in the season for the east wind, Aunty."

"It is the east wind. Listen!"

I listened. Incredible though it was for late summer I could hear—oh hundreds of miles away—the faint whisper that gathered in volume till it was the sound of wind. It came out of the north and east, over the desert, across the bush-clad ranges, brushing the coastal plain, and so to the edge of the sea.

It stirred the little eye veil on Aunt Sheilagh's hat.

"It has a scent . . ." she said.

"It smells of the desert, and the bush."

"It has come all the way from the gold-fields. That's where Uncle Tim is, darling. And across there . . . across there where the others are lying. Tim and Joe and William and Sylvia . . . the wind is coming across their graves."

"Don't, Aunt Sheilagh," I said. I put my hand on hers where it rested on the rail.

For a moment she said nothing, but stood with her face in the wind, her nose pointed upwards.

For a long time we stood there in silence, my hand on hers where it gripped the rail. Then she lowered her head. I could hardly hear her as she spoke. Her words were so sad.

"Goodnight, my darlings. Sleep well."

THE END

We hope this Large Print edition gives you the pleasure and enjoyment we ourselves experienced in its publication.

There are now more than 1,400 titles available in this ULVERSCROFT Large Print Series. Ask to see a Selection at your nearest library.

The Publisher will be delighted to send you, free of charge, upon request a complete and up-to-date list of all titles available.

Ulverscroft Large Print Books Ltd.
The Green, Bradgate Road
Anstey
Leicestershire
England